CN00846970

A Dangerous Weakness

Lorna Page

authorHOUSE®

AuthorHouse™ UK Ltd.
500 Avebury Boulevard
Central Milton Keynes, MK9 2BE
www.authorhouse.co.uk
Phone: 08001974150

© 2008 Lorna Page. All rights reserved.

No part of this book may be reproduced, stored in a retrieval system, or transmitted by any means without the written permission of the author.

First published by AuthorHouse   7/7/2008

ISBN: 978-1-4343-7804-0 (sc)
ISBN: 978-1-4343-7805-7 (hc)

Printed in the United States of America
Bloomington, Indiana

This book is printed on acid-free paper.

Chapter One

Sitting in the plane sipping my brandy, I had time to think. Recently I hadn't wanted to think too deeply, to face the problem of Bill and me head on. Now there was nothing to stop the worries crowding in around me. True, their edges were softened, blunted by the brandy which made looking at them bearable, but they still hurt.

During the first five years of our marriage Bill and I had always shared things, been interested in each other's jobs, tried to help and advise one another. Perhaps we'd been too close, too dependent, I thought ruefully.

Then, two years ago Bill had been promoted, and ever since much of his life had to be spent away from home.

Now Bill never discussed his work with me. "It's secret Em, you know I can't." He said. But I knew it was often dangerous, that colleagues on similar missions, were sometimes injured. Even lost their lives.

Bill came and went at irregular intervals, often in response to the briefest telephone call, and he could be away for weeks at a time.

There was no way of knowing when he would be home again. To put it mildly, it made planning our social life together extremely difficult.

I immersed myself in my work and somehow learned to live with the constant anxiety. But the lack of information, of not knowing where or how he was, gnawed away at me so that when he did come home I was often irritable and edgy. Bill, too, was more distant, the closeness we had known and shared was gone. Inevitable, I thought, when so much of our lives was spent apart. But it was sad.

We both still protested our love for each other but I suspected that Bill, like me, was wondering how long our marriage could last.

I asked the stewardess for a second brandy and as I sipped it, looked through the window of the plane down at the feather clouds. But I wasn't really seeing them, instead my mind was visualising scenes, reliving happenings of two weeks ago when Bill and I had been together.

It had been a damp, chill November day when the order came for Bill to uproot and move south to 'somewhere in a London suburb'. It meant that I went too - as part of Bill's goods and chattels.

The new flat was nice and for a blessed few days we were able to explore and sort things out together. It was almost like old times. Only, to me, there was always the threat of our imminent parting - and I supposed Bill felt it too.

We arranged and rearranged our furniture, trying to make belongings which had been planned for a quite different setting, look at ease in these strange surroundings.

We wandered around the streets and ate ploughman's lunches in local pubs, and hand-in-hand chased across nearby heathland; and at night looked down at the distant city with all its winking, coloured lights transforming it into an enormous Christmas decoration.

Then, without warning, came the order for Bill to leave. We had been ex-directory since Bill changed his job, so as soon as the phone rang I knew what it meant, and Bill's few brief queries at this end of the phone confirmed my fears.

'Oh, no!' I thought as I followed him into the bedroom and perched on the end of the bed. "Can I help?" I asked, sure that he would say 'no'.

"No thanks Em," he spoke over his shoulder as he rummaged through a drawer.

Bill always had a case ready packed so that in an emergency there was nothing to delay him. Now he stowed odds and ends tidily away in the corners of his case. His packing was meticulous, "It has to be Em," he once explained to me. "I've got to be able to put my hand on what I need - even in the dark."

I often wished this tidiness would spill over into more helpful places; when he was at home the rooms looked as if a cyclone was permanently rushing through them. Nowadays I thought that a small price to pay for having him home.

He came and sat by me on the bed and put an arm around my shoulders, the rough tweed of his jacket was warm against me. "I'm truly sorry to go Em, I'd hoped to get everything tidy, all set up for you before- - -"

"Yes I know," my voice was muffled by his coat. In spite of everything I couldn't help smiling to myself at the idea of Bill getting things tidy in the flat.

I pushed my fingers through his thick, unruly brown hair, "Must you go? You know I don't want you to - and it's nearly Christmas."

In response he hugged me, so hard it hurt, but his kiss was distracted and I could sense that part of his mind was already away somewhere, engaged on goodness-knows what strange errand.

He carried his case out and halted by the front door, "You'll be all right Em?" his face was anxious. "Get a job, get to know people."

"I'll be O.K." I hoped it sounded convincing.

Another quick embrace and he was gone.

The front door closed behind him and the place was no longer home. It was empty, silent, soulless.

Chapter Two

I hadn't minded leaving my job in the north. It was possible that something more interesting, more rewarding would turn up - after Christmas. But now, with no job, no familiar faces around, I soon discovered how lonely a big city can be.

So it was really a combination of all these things that led me to accept Betsy Harland's unexpected invitation.

It was a Wednesday, six days after Bill had gone, two weeks and a bit before Christmas when the letter arrived.

I'm not likely to forget it because at that moment I dropped my favourite silver teaspoon down the waste-disposal. And it was really because of the letter that it happened, at least I told myself so.

The mechanism was busy chewing up eggshells and crusts when a sharp rap came at the front door and my spoon slid off the breakfast things I was balancing over the sink, and went straight down the plug-hole.

I should have rescued it immediately but messages from Bill came recorded delivery - and the postman just might be bringing a message from him, so I switched it off and rushed to the front door. My life seemed centered around letters from Bill - or rather the lack of them. Instead there was this pink, scented envelope with the foreign stamp.

Back in the kitchen I retrieved the mangled remains of my precious spoon before settling down to read the letter.

Absolutely none of my friends - or acquaintances either, for that matter - use pink note paper, so it was a puzzle right from the start, but when I read the contents, well at first I thought it must have been meant for someone else. Even the signature 'Betsy Harland' at the end, meant nothing to me.

Then I thought back over the years and gradually there formed in my mind this picture of a plump and, as I recalled, plain girl with a high-pitched, whining voice.

I hadn't liked her much when we were at school and since she was on her own a lot, one assumed the other girls felt the same way. In fact she came low in the pecking order, even I had been known to have a few nips and that is saying a lot. Like most children we were unkind little horrors.

'You will be surprised to receive this letter,' Betsy had written. A safe way to start, obvious too.

'There is much I should tell you to cover all the years since we last met, but it would take too long, so I wonder if you would care to come and stay for a few days here, perhaps even for Christmas. I should be so pleased.'

There was more saying how she now lived in Switzerland and that the house was large and comfortable with a view over the mountains, and that she had ample help in the house. So it's not a new maid-companion she needs, I thought. The letter was signed 'your old friend'.

We hadn't been friends, ever, were not even in the same class at school. In those long-ago days I was pretty sure she hadn't liked me any more than I had her, that is when I bothered to think of her at all.

So why after this long delay had she troubled to seek me out, and how in the name of goodness had she managed to find me?

I would like to have asked Bill if he thought I should accept Betsy's invitation; if it was wise to go and stay with someone I'd never known really well and who, out of the blue had contacted me for whatever reason.

But Bill was away and I'd no means of getting in touch with him. I didn't even know if he'd be home for Christmas and to tell the truth, I was fed up, so the more I thought about Betsy the more intriguing the invitation became. And there seemed only one way to solve it.

Which is how and why I was sipping brandy - my particular form of Dutch courage Bill called it - on board the plane, en route, as they say, for Switzerland.

Betsy Harland had said someone would meet me, probably her chauffeur. He would have a card, she said, and I was to keep a good look out as I came from customs.

How many times have I seen people waiting at airports armed with placards of various sizes, all seeking some visitor just descended from the skies. For some reason I've never seen any of them actually connect with their prey but presumably they do.

It had certainly never entered my mind that I would one day be scanning the proffered cards, and I was scared at the prospect. The effects of the brandy were wearing off and I stood just inside the customs area shuffling my bags on the trolley and screwing up my courage to venture outside. I'll give them five minutes to find me, I promised myself, after that I'll take the first plane home again.

But it was too easy. Looking back I realise it should have warned me but at the time my only sensation was one of great relief.

No sooner had I emerged from the doorway and looked enquiringly towards the waiting mêlée, than a tall, uniformed man stepped forward, a card held discretely towards me. "You are Mrs. Hemming," he stated.

Yes, stated, not asked, and even at the time that surprised me.

"That's right, how did you know?"

He took my cases. "It was easy Madam, I was told you were graceful and distinguished, there was no one else like that."

I had to laugh, it was a good start. And it wasn't until a lot later that I wondered how on earth Betsy Harland knew enough about my appearance to give such a description - even supposing it to be true. But it gave me a warm glow. It is difficult to feel unfriendly towards someone who describes you as graceful and distinguished.

The journey to Lucerne was smooth and uneventful, the chauffeur said it would take only around forty-five minutes - which surprised me, in my complete ignorance I'd expected it to be at least two hours away.

But it was long enough for the butterflies to return. In a mild state of panic I wondered if the driver was indeed Betsy's trusty chauffeur. He could be a terrorist, a kidnapper, there might already be a ransom on my head. Stories from the more lurid papers jostled in my mind. Unreasonably I cried to myself "Bill! Why did you let me come?"

"You'll see the mountains soon Madam," the chauffeur's voice cut across my thoughts, and he certainly didn't sound like the fearsome leader of a gang.

Seconds after, we were approaching Lucerne and a panorama of forests and mountains seemed suddenly to spread before us. Scenery so beautiful it almost took my breath away.

"You see Madam?" The chauffeur didn't turn his head.

"Yes, it's majestic!" I just breathed the words.

I had only a vague impression of the town as we passed through, I was still gazing entranced at the snowy peaks, and again it was the voice from the driver's seat which brought me down to earth, "We are almost there Madam," he said quietly.

We were climbing a steep hill, with large houses on either side and a moment later were driving, between wrought iron gates, and slowing gently to a stop outside a studded front door. Almost at once the door opened and a plump woman came down the steps and held out her hand to help me from the car.

"Marion," she said, "how nice of you to come."

And before I knew it she had enveloped me in a warm embrace.

It was as if we had been friends all our lives. And I could hardly believe this was Betsy Harland, whom I hadn't seen for at least 20 years, and whose name I wouldn't even have remembered two short weeks ago.

She stood back and we gazed at each other. I was looking at a woman in her late thirties with, as it seemed to me, no distinguishing feature. Hair fair to mousy, and just 'done', not styled at all. She was wearing a beige cashmere twin set, obviously expensive, though uninspiring, and had flung a nondescript tweed coat over her shoulders.

One could see a cheaper replica of her in almost any town and never notice.

Only the voice meant anything to me. It was still high-pitched but I couldn't call it whining. Perhaps it never had been. Children can be very critical.

Then I noticed her eyes. Incredibly alert, hazel eyes, almost hypnotic, peering though slim gold frames.

"Come in, dear." She led the way, while a maid hovered discreetly in the background. "I should have known you anywhere. The same tall slim figure, how I envy you! But you weren't the sort to put on weight. Now," she said, "Dora will show you your room. I expect you would like to wash. And then we will have tea."

My room was on the first floor and the suitcases were already there. Dora indicated them, "I will hang your things up later, Madam," she said before leaving me alone. I crossed to the window and looked out. There was a superb view over distant snow covered peaks. It was the kind of scenery I had always wanted to see. Exciting. Magnetic. Somehow not cold or hard looking, despite the ice and snow. I thought that surely it had been right to come to Switzerland, if only for the view. The room, too, was all one could wish. I bounced on the bed, and it proved to be as comfortable and welcoming as it looked.

Downstairs Betsy was seated in a wing chair, before a blazing log fire. As soon as I entered she pressed a bell by her side, and almost immediately the maid, Dora, appeared, carrying a tray with our tea. The teapot and milk jug were shining silver. The bread and butter wafer thin. There was a feeling of opulence, understated, rather than laid on with a trowel. Very much in the more privileged style of pre-war England.

Betsy sipped her tea, "You must be wondering why I asked you to come and see me." She peered over the rim of her cup, and again I was struck by the intense look in those hazel eyes.

"You see," she went on, "I find it difficult to make friends. I'm always thinking it's my money people are interested in, not in me. You knew I inherited a fortune."

She flung the question at me. I nodded. Everyone at school knew about Betsy Harland's money. She was to inherit it when she came of age, but with the callousness of youth it had never occurred to me that she was probably an orphan. Perhaps a lonely and unhappy child.

She answered my unspoken question. "My mother died when I was seven. My father when I was twelve. I lived with a guardian during school holidays, then, when I was eighteen, the money was mine."

Her matter-of-fact statement was made entirely without emotion, but I felt certain there must have been plenty at the time. Perhaps years of suffering and unhappiness, which could have hardened her, made her suspicious of people. I suddenly felt guilty for not taking trouble to find out more about her. Even befriending her, when we were at school. Perhaps I could make up for it now.

Betsy continued "Well, one day I tried to think of someone I knew long years ago who was not remotely interested in me or my money."

"And you came up with me!"

"That's right, and then I had to find you."

"Yes," I said, "however did you manage to?"

She settled herself back in her chair and gazed into the curling flames before answering.

"It's a long story. Did you ever meet Jim Bellamy?"

I shook my head.

"He lived in Camberford, not so far from our school."

"I didn't know him really, I met very few people from the town. And during the holidays, of course, I went home. How did you come to know him?" I asked.

She looked down at her hands. "It's a long time ago, and I forget who did introduce me. One of the girls no doubt." And then again that penetrating gaze met mine.

"But it was Jim who found you for me."

I sat forward with a start. "How on earth!"

"I thought that would surprise you. Well, I had to start somewhere, and Jim was on the spot - that is, where you and I had last met and he was at a loose end too."

"But even so!" I was amazed at the enormity of the task. And also at the idea of being tracked down by this unknown man. It was an uncomfortable thought that someone had been prying into my life, and circumstances. And obviously my indignation showed.

"Oh, my dear, I do hope you don't mind." Betsy was all contrition. "I suppose it was rather an awful thing to do, but I did want to find you and …."

She looked so crestfallen that I hadn't the heart to tell her what I really felt. "Well," I said, "I only hope he didn't uncover too many skeletons while he was sleuthing around."

Betsy gave a sigh of relief. "I was afraid I had really upset you. No, I don't think he did, but you will be able to ask him yourself. He's coming tomorrow to join us for Christmas."

It crossed my mind that for someone who did not get on well with people, she managed to have companions around when she really wanted them. At least one of whom was a friend of long standing.

It was dark outside and Betsy suggested we relax and just chat that evening, then the next day she would show me some of the local sights. "I have two places in mind, dear," she told me, "perhaps you would like to choose which we shall visit tomorrow."

"I really don't mind, it is all new and interesting to me."

"You haven't heard my suggestions yet," her peremptory tone and piercing gaze silenced me. Obviously Betsy Harland was not someone to be treated lightly. My mind shot back to our school days. I couldn't remember her being officious then, but of course, I hadn't known her all that well.

"We can go for a trip around the lake and stop for lunch at Altdorf. There is a monument to William Tell there and some of his supposed possessions in the museum. You might find it interesting."

"Oh I'd forgotten his connections with the area." Actually I hadn't known at all, but didn't want to admit that to Betsy.

"It's all supposition," she dismissed Mr. Tell with an airy wave of her hand. "Of course there was oppression at the time, and no doubt his story had an element of truth in it. My other idea was for Davis to take us to Alpnachstad and we would take the railway from there up Mt. Pilatus. That's the big one you can see from here."

"Railway?"

"It's a rack and pinion. It takes roughly 20 minutes and there is a hotel on the top where we can have lunch."

"It sounds marvellous." My mind was already made up. The mountains had won.

At Betsy's suggestion, I went early to bed. "You must be tired, dear," she said. "Sleep well and tomorrow we will have a nice long day together."

I washed and prepared for bed and then pulled back the curtains and looked out at the lights of Lucerne and the mountains glowing in the moonlight. It all looked so beautiful and peaceful and I suddenly wished with all my heart that Bill was here to share it with me.

I wondered if he had received my letters to him, and what he thought about me going to Switzerland.

I wondered where he was, and exactly what he was doing. It was Christmas - a special time for families and loved ones to be together.

I was lost in thought when the sound of footsteps below on the frosty drive brought me back again to reality. Two dark shadowy figures moved towards the house and faintly I heard the sound of the doorbell.

More of Betsy's nonexistent friends, I supposed. Well, it was no business of mine. I yawned and slid between warm sheets - sheer luxury and just as comfortable as I had expected.

Chapter Three

Betsy had ordered the car for ten o'clock the following morning and promptly, on the hour, the chauffeur pulled up at the door - the Mercedes sparkling in the morning sunlight.

I watched him through the window. "He's very efficient," I remarked.

"Oh, Davis? Yes he is. He doesn't talk a lot. I like that." Betsy smoothed brown leather gloves on to her hands, and picked up her handbag.

"Does he live in?" I wasn't really interested to know. It was just a casual question, but the effect on Betsy was odd.

She stopped on her way to the door, "No. Why?" Her tone was sharp.

It was disconcerting, "I wondered if he did odd jobs around the house as well as driving the car," I said lamely. I would like to have asked if he and Dora, the maid, were man and wife, cook and handy man as it were, but Betsy's attitude did not encourage questions.

Oh, well, it didn't matter. Mentally I shrugged it off and gathered my own gloves and handbag, ready to go. And then Betsy answered my unspoken query. "Davis lives just down the road," she said crisply. "Dora is a cousin of his. They have both been with me for two years." Then she turned and walked out to the car.

I blinked at her, and could swear my mouth fell open. It was clear I would need to be careful what I said to Betsy in future if my stay in Switzerland was to be as pleasant as it was physically comfortable.

I thought it was no wonder she found making friends difficult. Her brusque manner could be very off-putting.

Betsy exuded affability as she tucked the car rug around our knees. "I know we don't really need it, dear, but it is cosy and I like it."

I wondered if such quick change of mood was something I would have to get used to during my stay.

We drove around the lake to Alpnachstad. Betsy spoke only monosyllables and gazed ahead of her, apparently uninterested in the scenery.

"I suppose you've seen it all many times," I said "but I do wonder if I would ever get used to it. It is all so beautiful."

"I suppose so, dear." She spoke absent mindedly. "The important thing is that you are enjoying it."

The small red train was waiting on the steeply raked lines in the station, I was surprised how many people were already seated inside. Betsy and I sat opposite each other - she chose the seat facing up the mountain while I perched on the higher one looking downwards. It was an incredible journey, so steep I wondered how the train clung to the mountainside, and marvelled at the engineering as well as the scenery, as we approached the summit one could see over the peaks of lesser mountains around. All the way there was an excited buzz of conversation from the other passengers, but Betsy sat silent as if in a trance, her eyes tightly closed.

She looked pale when we arrived at the top. "Perhaps you will help me dear," she said as we alighted from the train. I held her arm and could feel her shaking. "You're not well," I said anxiously, wondering what on earth one did for someone taken ill on top of a mountain. "I shall be all right dear. It's the height," she said feebly. "I feel giddy - drawn towards the edge."

"You should have told me, Betsy. We would never have come."

"It was what you chose, dear. I wanted to do whatever you wanted."

She leaned heavily on my arm, and somehow we made our way into the hotel and found her a chair away from the stupendous view which was so obviously upsetting her.

I got her a drink and she sat sipping it, the colour gradually returning to her cheeks.

I felt dreadfully responsible. It was kind of Betsy to suffer such torment just to give me pleasure, but I wished she had given me a hint of how she felt about heights - we would never have attempted the trip. Perhaps I should have suspected when she was so quiet on the way to the train - and inside when she kept her eyes closed; but for all I knew that might have been her normal behaviour.

'Oh dear!' I thought, what a way to start my holiday. I would certainly have to make sure I didn't cause her distress in the future.

Betsy insisted that I go outside to see all there was. "I'll just sit here, I won't move," she promised.

It was slippery on the plateau between the two hotels and people moved cautiously on the glistening ice as they gazed around.

Quickly I looked about, absorbing all the scenery, storing it up inside to be revisited time and again in my mind. But I couldn't be easy about Betsy. She was still sitting there, recovered but naturally uneasy with the prospect of the journey down the mountain. She didn't want to eat so it seemed best to get back home as quickly as possible. We caught the next train and I sat beside Betsy, trying to comfort her by my presence and understanding. At least, I thought, Davis would be waiting for us when we reached ground level.

Tea, Betsy had said, would be at four o'clock as usual in the sitting room, by which time Jim should have arrived. "But we won't wait for him, dear, he may be held up anywhere along the way."

"Does he come all the way from England by car?"

"Sometimes, it just depends."

She didn't say just what it depended on and after my previous experience when questioning her, I thought it better not to pursue the subject. But I did want to know how often he came and what relationship there was between them. After all, this man had been probing into my affairs on Betsy's behalf so I suspected their connection must be quite close.

No one was going to all that trouble without good reason, and the more I thought about Betsy's explanation of wanting a new and disinterested friend, the thinner it seemed, but since I had no idea what other motive there might be, the only thing was to sit back and wait. Maybe Jim would be more forthcoming than his friend, at any rate he owed me some sort of explanation.

I looked across at Betsy. She had quite recovered from the morning expedition and with her back to me, was busy searching through a drawer. Whatever she wanted wasn't there and she became quite agitated, opening another drawer in the bureau and turning things over feverishly. I heard her muttering to herself, "Shall have to watch her, she is getting too inquisitive."

I started across the room. "You have lost something," I said. "Can I help you look for it?"

She turned abruptly, "No. You go and read the paper - or a magazine. I will find it myself."

I sighed and went and sat by the window. It was difficult to get near Betsy, she had a sort of mental fence around her, a guard which only broke down occasionally to let some warmth through. A necessary defence perhaps years ago, and one which had become part of her nature now. There seemed nothing I could do except be patient and try to understand.

The light was fading so I sat with my back to the window, the better to read the newspaper Betsy had indicated. It was, of course, in German and taxed my almost forgotten schoolgirl knowledge of the language, still it was gratifying to find I could remember a little.

A headline caught my eye, 'Schmuggelei', that sounded interesting. I attempted the prose which followed, it wasn't easy but I managed to get the general sense.

Not really surprising, in fact an everyday occurrence, I thought. Especially in Switzerland. There were probably hundreds of people trying to smuggle things out of the country; watches, jewellery and such. If one was to believe the media, people were coming and going all the time with watches hung about their persons.

Some got through customs, some didn't, it was the luck of the game.

But it seemed that a sharp look out was kept on people who travelled to and from the country frequently. Take Jim - for example.

The thought hit me - almost physically, it seemed. I gasped right out loud. Thankfully Betsy had gone, foraging about in another room somewhere, I presumed and smiled to myself with relief. Suppose Jim were engaged in any funny business, it was possible that Betsy was too. Had she a package ready to hand over to Jim - only now she couldn't find it? It could account for her anxiety and her annoyance. I sat in the gathering dusk, my heart pounding with what might be.

And then commonsense took over. You see a chance paragraph in a newspaper Marion, and there you are with new-found friends all deeply involved in sinister goings on. Really, what next? Bill always said your imagination was too well developed. He was right, - well, sometimes he was, I corrected myself.

It was at that moment the door opened and Betsy came in followed by a man head and shoulders taller than herself. "Ah, you are still here Marion," she was obviously excited. "You must meet Jim, he has just arrived."

He came towards me, hand outstretched and there was just enough daylight remaining for me to see his features before Betsy pressed the switch and flooded the room with light. And I think my face was in the shadow for the fleeting second it took to recover from my astonishment.

I had seen Jim before. I knew him.

There wasn't a flicker of recognition on Jim's face, he shook my hand warmly. "I've been looking forward to this meeting Mrs. Hemming, and to getting to know you better."

His words almost took my breath away: considering his recent activities - if Betsy was to be believed, the statement was quite colossal cheek.

I looked up into amused blue eyes. 'Well,' I thought, 'If that's the way he wants to play it, I can follow the rules.'

"I'm interested to know you too." I tried to keep my voice even.

Betsy interrupted. "You will have plenty of time to talk later on my dears. Marion you will want to go and prepare for dinner, we will see you in about an hour." It was kindly said but unmistakably my dismissal from the room. Jim walked across to the door and held it open for me and, with his back towards Betsy, he winked as I passed him. Before he closed the door behind me I heard Betsy say, "Did you ask Davis to look after your car?"

"Yes," came Jim's reply, "he took it to the garage as usual."

The door shut on any further conversation and I went upstairs, seething. I was being told where to go and what to do like a simple-minded child and I resented it. I'd already had enough of Betsy and her strange ways - and of Jim too, if it came to that. If she wanted another and perhaps more accommodating friend, she would have to ask Jim to search again. I was going home, even if it was Christmas and I would have to spend it alone.

Still fuming, I undressed. What was it they had said? Davis was looking after the car, well that was reasonable enough goodness knows, but in my present frame of mind even the most innocent remarks seemed to have hidden meanings.

Was Davis in on this racket, if there was one? Was he even now removing packages from secret compartments in Jim's car? And then it struck me that it would be when he was going home that the packets would be secreted. All sorts of gold and platinum trinkets for sale at enormous profits! Unless, of course, he brought things in as well. But what?

I searched my mind but hadn't the foggiest idea. Books on gun-running, or spy thrillers had never been my favourite reading and my life had certainly not prepared me for dealing with real crooks of whatever kind. And then I thought that Bill would know how to cope, and Bill would recognise Jim too. We had been together the first time we met him. In my mind I could hear Bill saying, "He's charming, Em, but too smooth. Always be suspicious of people like that."

The bath was a pleasing shade of cyclamen, I lay in its scented water and wondered wryly if Betsy had known that was my favourite colour and installed a new suite especially for me. The warmth and perfume were relaxing, as I'd known they would be.

Perhaps, I thought, I'll stay for one more day just for a chance to speak to Jim and find out exactly what is going on, or at least what his part in the proceedings is all about. Then I'll go home and let them get on with it by themselves.

It seemed such a silly mystery - if indeed it was one at all, and I wanted some answers.

I took time to dress, after all I had a full hour allocated to the task. This is the night for my new dress, I thought. The assistant in my pet boutique had been flattering when I tried it on: blues and lilacs and pinks in a smudgy design on the soft folds of silk. At the time the price had nearly scared me off but Pat had persuaded me, and she had been right. It was worth every penny.

My confidence, almost restored, I took a critical look in the long mirror - from the pale, shining hair framing my face, down to the shoes which were exactly the right shade of blue.

Not bad, I thought, not bad at all. I don't know what these people want or expect from you Marion, but, my goodness! you'll knock 'em cold tonight! And I needed that confidence as I descended the stairs.

I was surprised to find Betsy in the sitting room with two strangers and no sign of Jim. She seemed agitated and I got the impression that she was not at ease with these new people.

"Ah Marion, let me introduce you to Dr. and Mrs. Hopper, they live in Geneva but have decided to spend Christmas in Lucerne."

From the way she spoke I deduced it to be a decision she had only just learned of and was not too happy about. "Basil is a banker," she added by way of introduction.

He rose, a fat little man, and gave a stiff bow. "You are staying with Mrs. Harland?"

"That's right."

"We were at school together," Betsy qualified. "We have known each other for years." She emphasized this fact as though anxious to reassure him on the point, and I wondered why it should be so important.

Mrs. Hopper appeared to be a lot younger than her husband, she gazed at me languidly but didn't speak, and, after a long moment evidently decided I wasn't worthy of further interest and turned her attention again to her glass of wine.

"If you come over here Marion," Betsy indicated the far end of the room, "I'll pour you a drink."

I followed her and she made great play with bottles and glasses and, without looking at me, whispered: "Jim has gone to bed, I haven't told them he is staying here." Then, in a voice calculated to carry across the room, "You did say you would have Campari, didn't you?" I hadn't said so, in fact I didn't like Campari but before I knew, the glass was in my hand and Betsy had returned to her guests, chatting in a high-pitched and, for her, falsely animated voice.

The plot thickens, I thought, grimacing as I took a sip of the bitter liquid. She doesn't want these people to know that Jim is staying here. How very awkward that they should turn up at this time. I had half a mind to ask Betsy out loud where Jim was and see what effect it had on them all.

Chapter Four

We were an uneasy quartet, three of us making forced, superficial conversation while Mrs. Hopper - Dorothy the others called her - was plainly disinterested and made no effort to contribute.

I sat in one of the comfortable, cretonne covered armchairs with Betsy and Dr. Hopper ranged in chairs on either side, and whenever Basil - as he begged to be called - tossed me what Betsy considered to be a leading or too searching question, she would intercept and fend it off. It was like being the net in a mental game of ping-pong, occasionally I could stop the query before it reached her, and this obviously pleased Dr. Hopper as much as it troubled Betsy.

I wondered what he was trying to find out, and equally what she was trying to prevent him knowing.

I was seeing a new Betsy too, one who needed to be careful what she said. There was no riding roughshod over these people's feelings, she needed to weigh her words carefully. It was as though an hierarchy existed with the Hoppers a stage higher up than herself.

An interesting situation; and if only I had known what role I was supposed to be playing in the scheme, it might have been entertaining as well, but as it was I think we were all relieved when Dora announced that dinner was ready.

From the chicken and almond soup to the orange crème caramel it was a delicious meal and I hoped that Jim, for whom no doubt it had been planned, had been able to enjoy some in his upstairs prison.

Sitting opposite to Dorothy I watched as she gave her full attention to the food, as before, making no effort to join in the general conversation, and I concluded that if, as it seemed, food and drink were her abiding passion, she was fortunate in not having to bother about her diet. Her slim-fitting red dress emphasized a perfect figure and her complexion and blue-black hair would have done justice to any cosmetic advertisement.

I fell to wondering how she would look if the bored and vapid expression were wiped from her face - and, in cowardly fashion - hoped it would not happen when Bill was around!

Yesterday we'd had our after dinner coffee in the sitting-room and I presumed there would be the same arrangement this evening.

"That was a really wonderful meal Betsy," I said pushing my chair back. "And I'm glad we haven't to be too energetic now, it would be an insult to that splendid dinner."

She placed her napkin on the table without looking at me. "Thank you dear, but you will have to walk a little way because Basil has invited us back to his hotel for a while."

I looked across at the little man and he nodded and gave another of his stiff bows.

"It is kind of you to invite me," I objected. "But I expect you would sooner Betsy came on her own, you must have a lot to talk about and I don't in the least mind staying here."

"The invitation includes you Marion." He said it briefly in a tone which brooked no refusal.

More an order than an invitation, I thought, and again felt my annoyance rising. Those few hours this evening would have given me the opportunity I wanted for a talk with Jim, and I wondered if that was why I had to accompany them. But no, it couldn't be, the Hoppers didn't even know Jim was in Lucerne, did they? There seemed to be a number of petty mysteries and I was becoming irritated and impatient with them all.

We shrugged ourselves into warm coats and stepped out into the crisp darkness.

The hotel where the Hoppers were staying was about half a mile down the road, Betsy said, as we walked together in the cold, clear evening air. I wondered why we were not using the car and, following my trend of thought Betsy murmured, "I've given Davis the evening off, it's rather a nuisance really, I hope you don't mind walking."

She didn't say what was a nuisance but I guessed it to be the Hoppers' unexpected arrival. After all, Davis was seeing to Jim's car, wasn't he?

Aloud I said, "Do the Hoppers not have a car?"

"Yes, but he prefers to walk."

"And Dorothy?"

Betsy didn't answer. So Dorothy doesn't matter? I thought. It seemed unlikely, I looked at the two walking ahead of us, Basil with his hand protectively holding Dorothy's arm. An ill-assorted couple they certainly appeared to be, but I suspected he would consider her very carefully when he chose to.

"She is very lovely," I remarked. "Have they been married long?"

"Long enough," said Betsy sharply. "I suppose she is good looking in an immature way, but I wish she would be more cooperative!"

It was the first glimpse I had seen of her true feelings towards these friends and the vehemence in her voice surprised me.

"She doesn't have much to say," I agreed, hoping to get her to enlarge on their relationship.

"Sullen I'd call her," said Betsy and immediately changed the subject.

I had been hoping to lead the conversation around to Jim before we reached the hotel, but there was no chance. Perhaps because Betsy made sure there wouldn't be.

The hotel was warm and comfortable, we sat in deep chairs by a log fire and drank our coffee and brandy. Christmas decorations reflected the flickering light from the fire and there was a general buzz of cheerful conversation while discreetly hovering waiters were kept busy.

It was all very pleasant but I felt there had to be a reason why we were here instead of drinking Betsy's equally good coffee in her sitting room. I was waiting for something to happen, perhaps a meeting with someone or a telephone call. Something which couldn't take place anywhere else and which had necessitated our walk here after dinner.

Again our talk was uninspiring and Dorothy maintained her detached air. Several times I tried to find some topic which might interest her but always she replied in monosyllables and seemed to look right through me, so eventually I became as bored with her as she appeared to be with me.

And then it happened. Basil was called to the telephone and by pure chance at that moment an acquaintance of Betsy's was passing her chair and paused to speak to her.

In that instant, when their attention was diverted, Dorothy turned and spoke to me in a voice so low and intense, I scarcely heard. "Marion," she said, "Do you know Jim Martin?"

"Why yes," I said, "why?"

"I have a message" - she started as Betsy turned to us again, and at once Dorothy's face was blank and disinterested. I was sure Betsy hadn't seen and did my best to hide my own excitement.

How strange, I thought, how very strange. She called him Jim Martin and that was the name he used when Bill and I first met him.

I couldn't be sure how long it was before Basil reappeared, weaving his way towards us between the chairs and groups of chattering people. And of what Betsy spoke during that waiting time I was scarcely aware.

My mind was buzzing with excitement. So there was a mystery! I hadn't just imagined it. Betsy was edgy too, her fingers tapped nervously on the arm of her chair. This phone call was important for her as well, and when she saw Basil across the room she rose as though going to meet him, then turned back, looking at Dorothy before sitting down again. Obviously Dorothy could not be trusted alone with me, even for a few moments.

The effort of staying there waiting for Basil and whatever message he might have, was difficult for her. Betsy's temperament wasn't suited to sitting placidly and talking inanities.

I scanned Basil's face to see if a chance expression would give any clue to the nature of his phone call, but he was as bland as Betsy was taut and enquiring.

He sat down apologising for his absence, "I've ordered more coffee and brandy," he said. "You must have a final warm up before returning home."

So we could safely be dismissed now the telephone call was finished. But what about Betsy, I wondered. Surely there was a message for her, otherwise why had we come?

I took a sip of my brandy and tried to look completely disinterested, to lull them into a false sense of security, yet all the while watching closely for any sign between them which might give me a clue.

But there was nothing. Absolutely nothing, I could swear it. And the fact that Betsy was practically hopping up and down with barely concealed impatience and curiosity convinced me I hadn't missed anything.

We walked out of the room, Betsy leading and Basil behind me, solicitously holding Dorothy's arm. And we left the hotel without them even shaking hands.

And yet as we sat in the taxi, which Basil had insisted we take - "Can't let you walk back alone and unprotected," he had said - I was suddenly sure that Betsy did know what the phone message had been about. Gone was the nervous impatience, now she was calm and authoritative. Any questions I had thought to ask her were stifled, in this mood Betsy would have given them short shrift.

But how did she know, I puzzled, and when? And if it came to that; 'what' as well. It was a complete mystery.

The house had been in darkness when we arrived, no light anywhere to give a hint of where Jim might be - if indeed he was still here. Betsy had gone straight to her room saying how tired she was. I bade her goodnight outside her door and saw it close before walking farther down the passage to my own room.

For a while I paced up and down far too alert to consider going to sleep. I suppose it was about half an hour before I switched off my light and went to the window to draw back the curtains. Sleep seemed impossible but the peaceful, clear night and glow from the snowcapped mountains in the moonlight, brought a certain calmness and sanity. I gazed out for a while wondering, as no doubt countless others have, how so much unease and subterfuge can exist amidst such beauty and grandeur.

It was when I turned to climb into bed that I realised I was not alone.

Standing a few feet away from me, Jim put his hand swiftly across my mouth to silence the gasp which rose instinctively. Very quietly he led me to the bed and we sat on the edge, side by side almost touching so that we could speak in undertones which could not possibly be heard from outside the room.

"It's our only chance to talk," Jim explained. "Tomorrow I leave."

"You were staying for Christmas, is it because the Hoppers have come?"

"Right. Betsy wasn't expecting them." He smiled, the lopsided smile I remembered from previous meetings.

"Who are you?" I asked, "Jim Martin or Jim Bellamy?"

He shrugged, "It all depends."

"Does Betsy know- - -"

He broke in, "She knows me as Bellamy."

"Why did she get you to trace me - and just how long were you digging around into my life?" This still rankled and I let it show in my voice.

"Poor little Marion!" Again the lopsided grin. "It was very interesting, I learned a lot, about Bill as well as you."

"No doubt, but why?" I repeated.

"Betsy was lonely, surely she told you."

Obviously we weren't getting anywhere so I tried a different tack, there was so much I wanted to know it was pointless to waste time on this one query. "The Hoppers," I said. "Why doesn't Betsy want them to know you are here?"

"You ask a lot of questions, Marion," he said calmly. "Now I am going to ask you one. Just exactly where is Bill and why isn't he at home with you for Christmas?"

It was a personal question and I strongly resented it. Probably, I admitted to myself, because it was a sore point with me too. "That is entirely our affair." I said coldly.

We were silent for a few moments then: "How on earth did you manage to get in here so quietly?" I asked. "Betsy must be listening for any sound - from either of us."

"You are too right, she certainly is. But you see I have been here alone for a long while this evening."

I wasn't sure if that meant he had greased the locks on the bedroom doors and checked all the creaking boards, anything seemed possible, so I tried another line. "Well," I said. "I also am leaving tomorrow."

The effect was satisfactory. A pause, then "Does Betsy know?" he asked.

"Not yet." After all I hardly knew myself.

"Perhaps," Jim said slowly as though thinking hard, "I can give you a lift somewhere."

"I very much doubt it." Suddenly I was silent as we both became aware of the slightest of sounds from the landing, it could have been a board creaking as someone crept along.

We held our breath and listened until it hurt but no other noise came and at last Jim whispered close to my ear, "False alarm maybe, but it was a good thing I took the precaution of locking my door - and yours." He took the keys from his pocket and showed me.

"You certainly used your time to some effect this evening."

Jim smiled and reached out a hand to cover mine, "Perhaps I had better go now," he said. "Unless?"

"Oh no" I said quickly, standing up.

He was walking towards the door when I remembered. "Oh," I said, "Dorothy has a message for you Jim Martin."

Instantly he stopped. "In that case," he said briskly. "I shall not leave tomorrow. And neither will you."

I lay in bed and tried to sort things out in my mind. The facts as I knew them - well, as I thought I knew them, were:

1. Betsy is mixed up in some funny business.

2. So is Basil Hopper, and somehow he is Betsy's superior in the set up.

3. Dorothy knows Jim Martin - not the Jim Bellamy whom Betsy knows.

I ticked them off on my fingers:

4. Davis the chauffeur, was he involved? And the maid Dora, how about her?

And by no means least:

5. Jim. In a way he was the biggest problem of all, and he was trying to involve me in whatever was going on.

Suddenly I smiled to myself at the mental picture of the two of us sitting on my bed in the darkened room, Jim in a quilted satin dressing-gown which shone inky blue in the light from the moon, and me in the diaphanous negligee which I had bought with Bill in mind - how long ago?

Bill would not have considered the situation funny and I thought again of his description of Jim: 'charming but too smooth', and knew for certain that he had been right in his suspicions.

Chapter Five

The three of us had breakfast together in the sunlit morning room but it was an uneasy meal - as, under the circumstances it was bound to be. In her predicament Betsy had, no doubt, hoped to have one problem out of the way today, but Jim's decision to stay meant there was the constant anxiety of the Hoppers coming upon him unexpectedly.

I almost felt sorry for her, life had suddenly become extremely difficult and, for all I knew, dangerous as well, and she was not at all sure how to cope.

I wondered how long it would be before she confided her worries to me, she would obviously have to explain some things, even if what she told me wasn't entirely the truth.

There wasn't long to wait, toying with her second piece of toast she suddenly turned to me, "Marion," she said. "Jim has decided to stay on after all. I want him to go. It is very difficult with the Hoppers here." She took a large bite from her toast and marmalade, and peered anxiously at me.

I looked at her with what I hoped was the innocence I was supposed to have about the goings on. "But why shouldn't they meet? I thought the Hoppers seemed very nice, they would probably get on well together."

This last remark was rather piling it on and was rewarded with a discreetly smothered cough from Jim and a very cold stare from Betsy.

"There are reasons," she said, and those piercing eyes seemed to search my mind.

"Oh, I'm sorry," I said with the same innocence. "But you hadn't told me." The answer appeared to satisfy her for the moment.

For a little while she concentrated on her coffee, then: "You try and persuade him to go." It was a mixture between an order and a plea and showed me just how anxious she was. It also helped me to make up my mind.

I looked across at Jim, he was quite unmoved by Betsy's anxiety, in fact he seemed to be quietly enjoying her discomfiture. Mentally I added 'ruthless' to Bill's previous description of him.

"As a matter of fact," I said. "I am thinking of going home myself today, perhaps Jim could give me a lift."

It wasn't a question, I had no intention of going anywhere with Jim, but it was almost funny the effect it had on them both.

Betsy got to her feet, spilling some of the coffee she had been pouring, over the crisp, white cloth. "Oh my dear," she said. "You can't do that."

Jim also rose, like puppets I thought to myself inconsequently, they both dance to their feet when I pull the string. But my amusement faded quickly.

Jim was decisive: "Neither of us is going Betsy" and the coldness in his eyes as he looked at her made me shiver. "You invited us both for Christmas, remember?"

Betsy was speechless as she watched him stride out of the room then, mechanically she picked up her napkin and dabbed at her mouth. "Really," she said. "He can be very difficult at times."

"Downright rude," I broke in. "Seriously Betsy, it would be better if I were to return, you have been very kind having me to stay but now the Hoppers have come- - -"

Betsy raised her hand in an almost imperious gesture, she was fast regaining her composure. "No," she said. "I won't hear of it. Jim is quite right, I did invite you both to spend Christmas here. It is just so awkward with Basil and Dorothy nearby - and not being able to let them meet Jim."

"Couldn't you just tell them you have friends staying, surely they would understand."

She appeared to look through me and it was fright that I saw in her eyes. "It isn't as easy as that, Marion," she said.

We sat in silence while an oak, long-case clock ticked slowly, I couldn't think what to say to her. A peculiar and rather menacing situation seemed to be building up around me and my whole instinct was to turn and run - as far away from it as I could. After all, Betsy couldn't really stop me. And yet- - - .

Then I heard myself saying, "Do you want me to help keep Jim out of their way?" I must be mad, I thought.

She looked at me for a long moment and I imagined she was weighing in her mind which was the lesser of evils, because, of course, she hadn't wanted Jim and me to be alone together, presumably because of things he might tell me. Things which might perhaps incriminate her.

"It isn't what I intended," she sighed at last. "But if you could keep an eye on him some of the time perhaps. He is very strong willed," she added.

That is one way of putting it, I thought.

"Does Basil - I mean, do the Hoppers know Jim?"

"Yes," Betsy said. "At least Basil does, I'm not sure about Dorothy."

"So they would recognise him." A thought occurred to me: "If Jim doesn't want to meet them, it should be fairly easy to keep them apart," I said.

A heavy cloud seemed to lift from Betsy's brow. "Of course," she smiled. "How silly of me not to think of that. No I'm sure he doesn't want to meet them."

We relaxed and Betsy rang for fresh coffee which we drank while trying to plan various excursions and things we could do without running any risk of being discovered by the Hoppers.

But all the while I knew that somehow Betsy would need to see Basil. And somehow Jim was going to see Dorothy. There looked like being an interesting few days ahead.

"Wait a minute," said Betsy as I rose from the table. "I must tell you," she sucked in her lower lip as she hesitated, then repeated slowly, "Yes, I must tell you. If you should have the misfortune to meet Basil while you are with Jim, please remember that he knows Jim as Jim Martin, not Jim Bellamy."

I didn't have to try to look surprised, I collapsed back on to my chair and must have gaped at her. So Betsy did know of Jim's two identities. What it must have cost her to tell me! And why had Jim lied to me about it?

It was just after eleven o'clock when Jim and I set out for our walk. Before, while we drank our midmorning coffee, Betsy had hovered around us like a broody hen, making no effort to hide her agitation. Plainly she had to be rid of us for a while

- or rather, of Jim, and yet at the same time was reluctant to see us go.

We needed the warm coats and boots which muffled us but it was a perfect morning for a walk. Briskly we strode up and away from the town then branched off on to a small side road where the snow hadn't been cleared. It was heavy going and after a few minutes I paused to gather breath, Jim had been a little way ahead but he came back and held my arm while we rested and looked around us. The snow was untrampled and sparkling in the sunshine, I was enchanted but Jim glanced at his watch. "Ten minutes," he said thoughtfully. "Yes, that should have given them time." Then turning to me, "You and I, Marion, are going back now."

This was a facer. "But," I protested, "Betsy said- - -" He held my arm tightly. "I want to know what they get up to when they think we are out of the way." He grinned down at me, "And so do you."

It was true, I did want to know, but I wasn't at all sure that I wanted Jim to know too - and it was certain that Betsy didn't, and if I was loyal to anyone I supposed it should be to her.

"Let's go a little farther," I said. "I would love to see the view from up there."

"Another day." It was said curtly while his grip on my arm increased.

It was quicker going back down the hill but slippery and I was thankful for the steadying grasp which Jim kept on my arm, in a curious way it was comforting too.

We were nearing the entrance to Betsy's drive when the crunch of wheels on a crisp surface broke the silence. Immediately Jim drew me back into the shelter of a gateway and we huddled there while the Mercedes slid out into the road and turned away from us down the hill.

I sighed with relief, "Phew." It would have been awkward if they had come in this direction.

"It wasn't likely – Hey!" Jim shouted as I stepped forward. "There's a rear view mirror in the car."

I crept in behind the gatepost again. "Oh lord! You mean Davis might tell Betsy- - -?"

"What do you think?"

This touched a raw spot. "I don't know what to think," I said with all the feeling I could muster. "Betsy invites me to spend what I imagine will be a quiet and friendly Christmas with her, then the peculiar Hoppers get involved and, not least, you turn up. I only wish I knew what it was all about."

"There there," he said with an infuriating grin. "I'll explain it all to you one day, little Marion. Now we have work to do."

Once again I was propelled down the road, so quickly I had to jog to keep up with him. It was demoralising.

I tugged my arm free, "Look here Jim," I said. "I am not going to cooperate with anything unless you explain- - -"

"Not now, Marion," he pleaded. 'We have so little time. The terrible twins will settle their business as quickly as they can, you can be sure of that. I want you to see Dorothy now and bring her out to me - or at least take a message from her."

"But how?"

"Quite simple, you just go into the hotel and ask for Mrs. Hopper at the reception desk, making sure that Basil and Betsy don't see you."

"Of course," I smiled ironically.

"I will be waiting - um - let me see," he thought a moment. "Yes, outside the back entrance. I will wait for ten minutes, no longer."

We separated before we reached the hotel, Jim to take a circuitous route to the rear while I made for the front entrance which we had used last night.

Presumably Betsy would be talking to Basil Hopper. I hoped fervently they would be in the lounge so that I would have a chance to perform my part in the proceedings in comparative safety.

I turned the corner of the street and the hotel came into view, and something else which I hadn't reckoned on. Drawn up outside the entrance was the Mercedes and Davis was sitting inside, waiting for Betsy.

My first instinct was to turn for home and just tell Jim that it hadn't been possible even to enter the hotel without being recognised. But there flashed through my mind the look in Jim's eyes when something displeased him.

Somehow or other I had to get through the next few days in the company of these strange people and my brief experience of them had taught me that it could be unwise to upset either of them. Besides, I told myself, I really did want to know some of the answers to the riddles which were being presented to me, and it was just possible I might discover a clue today.

However the immediate problem was how to get into the hotel, Davis had had no difficulty in recognising me at Zurich airport, even though, as far as I knew he had never set eyes on me before.

Tall and graceful he had called me, absurd, of course, but it did mean that I would have to be very careful.

I pulled my thick woollen scarf high around my head and was thankful for the dark sunglasses which shielded my eyes. I would just have to take a chance that he wouldn't remember the coat I was wearing. As for the tall and graceful bit, well a slight stoop and ungainly walk would have to serve.

I strolled as casually as I could towards the entrance, resisting the impulse to look directly at the car or Davis to see if he noticed me. It might have called attention - the one thing I wanted to avoid. I seemed to feel his eyes boring into the back of my head and half expected to hear the car door open and feel Davis' hand on my arm. But nothing happened.

The first hurdle safely over, I thought to myself, now for the second. I stood just inside the glass doors which led on to the street and peered through the inner doors to the dimly lit reception area. There were easy chairs dotted around and a lot of people but no sign of Betsy and Basil. That meant they could be in the lounge, as I had hoped. With renewed courage I crossed to the desk. The receptionist seemed scarcely to notice me as she rang through to the Hopper's room. "Mrs. Hopper will see you," she dismissed me. "Room 116, first floor."

I was out of the lift and walking down the long passage when I sensed, rather than heard, someone following me, the heavy tread of footsteps muffled by the soft pile of the red carpet. I glanced behind me, back in the shadows of the corridor was the unmistakable form of Basil Hopper, and he was coming my way.

Chapter Six

The window at the far end of the passage was flanked by doors on either side. No way of escape there, and I couldn't turn back.

I had a moment of pure panic. Suddenly there was no doubt in my mind that these people were sinister in the extreme and if Basil caught me up here with the obvious intention of going to see Dorothy I would end up as a crumpled heap packed in a trunk, or toppled off a mountain. "So sad," I could imagine Basil saying. "We warned her it was foolish to climb up so far when the weather was uncertain." And he would shake his head and cluck over the foolishness of this poor woman - who was me.

Chambermaids were busy farther along the landing and as I neared No. 116, a door nearly opposite opened and two girls came out laden with soiled linen. Instantly I slid past them into the room praying no one else was in there. I shut the door and leaned against it, my heart pounding.

A moment later there was a sharp rap on the door. Dear God, I thought, it's Basil, he did see me.

The bathroom door was ajar and I slipped into the darkened room as another knock sounded. It was no use trying to pretend the room was empty so I called out, "Who is there?"

A girl's voice replied and the sound of a key turning in the lock, then the bathroom light flicked on and one of the chambermaids came in carrying clean towels.

She peered curiously at me, as well she might. I must have looked as scared as I felt.

I gripped the side of the washbasin, "I'm sorry," I said. "I felt ill." My voice trailed as she looked at me blankly.

I breathed in deeply trying to collect my scattered wits. Of course, she wouldn't understand, she probably only spoke German.

Searching the recesses of my mind I dredged up some halting phrases and was rewarded with a look of concern from the girl. "You are ill Madam?" she queried. "Can I help? Can I get a doctor?"

"No no, I will rest. Have you finished in here?" I almost pushed her out of the room. It was lucky she apparently didn't realise I had no business to be there at all, but at any moment the rightful inhabitant could appear.

I strained my ears for the sound of Basil's voice or the click of his door opening or closing. I daren't stay here long but the risk of leaving the room at that moment seemed even greater.

I couldn't have told anyone what the room looked like, I was far too overwrought to notice, and it seemed an eternity passed before the sound of a door opening and Basil's voice reached me, though really it could have been only a matter of minutes.

Quite distinctly I heard Basil say: "I shall be about half an hour, you rest here."

Then the door closed and a creaking board told me he was on his way down the corridor again.

I forced myself to count slowly to twenty, giving him time to reach the lift. All the while in my mind the fear that the rightful occupants would come and discover me in their room.

Cautiously I opened the door and peered out, there was no one about.

I crossed the passageway and a moment later was looking into startled, dark eyes. "Marion!" Dorothy exclaimed. "Why are you here? Does Basil know?"

"No." There wasn't time for long and complicated explanations. "No," I said again. "Jim Martin wants to see you, he is waiting outside the back door."

For a few seconds she gazed at me as if trying to decide if I could be trusted.

"Oh come!" I was impatient. "You have only half an hour, I heard Basil say so. I can take a message to Jim if you prefer."

"I'll come." She was already shrugging into a warm coat and wrapping a muffler round her neck. Seconds later she looked up from pulling on pale suede boots. "The back door?" she asked.

"Yes," I hesitated. "I'm not sure how we will find the way."

She interrupted me, "I know. I always make a point of finding my way around. Sometimes one needs a different exit."

She was about to open the door when abruptly she turned and looked directly into my eyes. "I trust you Marion," she said. "You won't tell the others about this, this meeting?"

"Indeed no. I haven't an idea what it is all about, but no, I'll not say anything."

Dorothy smiled, a happy, excited smile which lit up her face like the sun breaking through on a particularly dull and gloomy day. It was difficult to believe this was the same girl who seemed to have no interest in or animation for anything.

She peered cautiously out on to the landing just as I had done a few short minutes ago, and again it was deserted.

Quickly and unerringly she went downstairs and along passages which were like a maze to me. There was no opportunity to talk and I just followed her. Like a lamb, I thought, or rather a mother sheep trying to keep pace with its wayward offspring.

We were nearing the back of the hotel, the business quarters, before we met anyone, then suddenly there was noise and hubbub and people everywhere. Dorothy appeared unconcerned and merely smiled as we passed by, but I felt awkward and out of my depth.

Then we were opening the back door and glancing across the road to where a figure emerged from the shadows and ran to greet us. Well, not exactly us, because all at once Dorothy and Jim were in each other's arms, while I stood by in amazement.

I don't know what I had expected; a brisk interchange of plans? A handshake and passing of a secret package? Instead it was a lovers' meeting.

I had never felt quite so alone as I stood on the pavement and watched them. It was absurd, of course, but in a funny way, and in spite of my misgivings, I had been drawn to Jim, he was the most likable of my new acquaintances, and he had been attentive to me - I grimaced, perhaps too attentive, all things considered.

Thinking it over afterwards I supposed I should have expected something of this sort last evening when Dorothy made her surprising remark.

After all, this beautiful young girl was apparently not a conscious member of the strange set up which I had unwittingly stumbled into, and Jim was an extremely attractive man. More than could be said about Basil.

But how and when they knew each other- - - well, perhaps I would find out in due course.

Jim took us to a small cafe nearby, it was owl-dim inside except where pink-shaded candles made flickering pools of light on the check tablecloths.

There were only two other people in the cafe and they did not even bother to look up as we entered. I sat a few tables away from Dorothy and Jim, obviously they had a lot to say to one another, the sort of things better said without an audience.

Slowly I stirred thick cream into my coffee and watched the pattern it made swirl and change until it merged completely with the dark liquid. Rather like my emotions, I thought, very muddled.

I glanced across at the other table, Dorothy and Jim were leaning towards each other, talking in low voices, their hands tightly clasped as if they could not bear the prospect of being parted again.

By now I'd had time to think and my chief sensation was of annoyance. Why couldn't Jim have given me a hint of how he felt about Dorothy? All right, there hadn't been much time but it only needed a second or two to warn me.

Yes, 'warn' was probably the right word, it had a sinister ring about it which would certainly be justified if either Basil or Betsy suspected what was going on at this moment.

For the second time that day I felt quite sick with fright. In spite of myself I was involved with these people and now it seemed I was running with the hares - whoever they might be - and hunting with the hounds as well. And I didn't want to do either.

It seemed only a few moments passed before Jim signalled me to join them again. "We both thank you for being so understanding," he said.

I smiled grimly at that. "Hardly the appropriate term," I reminded him. "I don't really understand anything that is going on."

Dorothy laid her hand on my arm, "Well thank you just the same, please help us to meet again soon." She pleaded. "Basil doesn't know Jim is here so he may just let me see you alone sometimes."

Jim stood up, "Dearest you must leave now or we shall all be in trouble."

"Shall you go in through the back way?" I queried.

"No, the front entrance. I'll just say I needed fresh air and went for a quick walk."

For the moment my annoyance was forgotten as we sat and watched her go. My heart ached for them both, whatever the problems were and whoever was to blame, it was hard to see these two, so obviously in love yet forced to be apart.

But however sorry I was for them, here, for the first time was an opportunity to question Jim and I didn't intend to waste it.

"I want an explanation- - -" I started.

He smiled bleakly, "I'm quite sure you do." He paused, then, "It's a long story Marion." His eyebrow quirked in the familiar way but I was proof against it.

I had no means of making him tell me what was going on, as far as I could see there was absolutely no reason why he should, unless in some way he wanted my help or cooperation. But I had to push him, to try and force some information from him, there was so much I wanted - perhaps needed to know.

I settled in my chair. "I'm waiting," I said.

Jim spoke slowly. "Well, it started about five years ago," he spread his hands, palm up on the check cloth and examined the lines on them, exaggerated as they were by the light from the candles. "I met Dorothy and it was love at first sight for us both." He looked up but it wasn't me he was seeing, "We were together for two, nearly three years then Basil Hopper suddenly turned up and threatened to blackmail me."

I watched his face closely but it was expressionless, as if he was still looking into the past. "Whatever for?" I asked.

He frowned, "That's another story, but it was serious - so serious I couldn't ignore it."

"Then Hopper met Dorothy and said he would forget the charge in exchange for her."

"But that's preposterous!"

Jim ignored me. "Of course I was horrified and prepared for anything rather than that, but Dorothy wasn't. She insisted that if she went with him we would at least be able to meet sometimes and one day be together again. So," said Jim. "Without telling me they married two years ago and I hadn't seen her since then until today."

He looked at me with cold, hard eyes, the signs of strain etched on his face.

It was a bald story, just a statement of a few relevant facts and it was obvious that he hadn't wanted to tell me any of it. Even so I couldn't help wondering if what he said was the truth or just something to satisfy me, keep me quiet. It had the feel of truth about it, or half-truth because clearly there was a lot of filling in needed.

Jim was speaking again. "I was in a bad state when Davis found me and suggested a way of getting even with Hopper."

I sucked in my breath quickly. So Davis <u>was</u> involved in the funny business!

And then I remembered.

"Davis!" I broke in. "Oh my goodness, I forgot. He's waiting outside the front entrance, he will have seen Dorothy. Does it matter?"

In his mind Jim was obviously reliving that time two years ago and it took a long moment for him to climb back into the present. "No," his voice was flat and mechanical. "No it doesn't matter."

Our walk home was silent and grim, I was appalled at the change in Jim, he was so dejected, his overcoat hung on rounded shoulders while his arms flopped loosely at his sides. Several times I tried to interest him in passing incidents, but he didn't even bother to look up let alone answer. His depression seemed real enough and I was prepared to believe that some, at least, of his story was true.

Davis was driving the Mercedes out of the gates as we turned into the drive and I saw him glance sharply at Jim as we passed, but there was no sign of recognition, even from Jim.

Dora opened the front door to us and immediately Betsy was there, still wearing her brown hat and loose tweed coat. She didn't waste any time, "Where have you been?" Her voice was rasping and strained and she glared at me, those penetrating eyes searching my face as if our guilty secret was printed on it.

It was not possible that she could know, that those eyes really looked into my mind, and yet something had seriously upset her - and goodness knows we had given her cause to be angry. If indeed she did know.

"We have been out for our walk, you knew we were going." I couldn't think what else to say.

She put a hand up to her forehead and stamped her foot with rage. "Yes, but where?"

And then Jim elbowed his way rudely past her into the drawing-room. "I need a drink," he muttered and a moment later came the sound of a bottle opening followed by the hiss of a syphon.

It broke the spell and gave Betsy a chance to recover some composure.

"I'm sorry dear," she said collapsing suddenly into a carved oak chair. "I'm so worried I hardly know what I'm doing." She gripped the arms of the chair, her knuckles showing white against the dark wood. "You see," she went on. "I went to call on Basil while you were out and we were standing in the foyer saying good-bye when Dorothy came in."

"Oh yes," I said and hoped the words sounded better to her than they did to me.

"Yes dear, and Basil was furious - not with her, you understand, but with me." She closed her eyes and I imagined she was picturing again the scene in the hotel foyer. If I hadn't been so anxious I'd have felt like laughing at such a ridiculous situation. But to Betsy it was anything but funny. She looked up at me with scared eyes. "He seemed to think that I had arranged for you to meet her somewhere, to talk to her. He said I had brought you over here to try and take her away from him. It isn't true, of course."

"Of course it isn't," I repeated. The whole thing no longer seemed amusing - even though it was still absurd.

"You will have to try and convince Basil," said Betsy, looking at me with pin-point hazel eyes. "You see when Basil is angry he can be very dangerous."

Chapter Seven

The chairs were covered in orchid pink silk which exactly matched some of the painted flowers on the curtains and bedcover, the deep pile carpet was the colour of hare bells. I sat by the window appreciating it all.

If someone had given me unlimited money and insisted that I furnish a bedroom for myself in exactly the right spot with a view I could enjoy for a lifetime, this is what I would have chosen. I thought, how strange that Betsy, whom I hardly knew, should have such a room to offer me.

It was just one odd thing among so many strange happenings. This time a pleasant one in immediate contrast to the many unpleasant and sometimes frightening things connected with my visit to Switzerland.

I gazed out at the stupendous view and tried to draw from the impassive mountains some reserves of calm and strength that I sorely needed. It had worked before but now wasn't so easy and my mind refused to be stilled. If only Bill was here. The longing for him was almost unbearable; for his strength and reliability, his sensible advice and, perhaps most of all, for the safe shield he would provide from the dangers around me.

But Bill wasn't here, and I was alone.

Yet again I relived some of the events of that morning and it seemed to me that even if only a part of what Jim had told me was true, he and Basil certainly should not meet while they were in Lucerne. Betsy knew that, but I doubted that she knew Basil's wife and Jim had been lovers. If I was to believe her, Betsy wasn't sure they had never even met.

Then, for some reason, I was necessary to both Jim and Betsy, otherwise why had I been invited here? And yet neither of them was willing to explain to me exactly what was going on.

And now Basil wanted to see me because he suspected I was trying to lure Dorothy away from him. It was a ludicrous situation but one which obviously scared Betsy.

It was Friday and tomorrow would be Christmas Eve, I sat there in the peaceful room and wondered just what sort of Christmas we would have been spending if the Hoppers had not turned up so unexpectedly.

And that led me to wondering just why they had come. Was it possible that somehow Basil knew Jim was here? But under the circumstances, if he had known surely he wouldn't have come at all - especially with Dorothy.

There must be another, and sufficiently important reason for his visit. One which involved Betsy but certainly didn't appear to please her.

Again I pondered just what her relationship with Basil was. She disapproved of Dorothy so was it possible that she had herself hoped to marry him, but had been superseded by Dorothy?

Or were they merely friends, or business acquaintances? There seemed more to it than that since Basil obviously had some sort of hold over her.

I stood up. Well, I had some sort of hold over her too; she wanted my help. I looked at my watch, there was a quarter of an hour to go before lunch. A whole lot of questions to be answered in so short a time but at least I could make a start.

I found Betsy in the drawing-room, she was sitting at her bureau, looking out of the window from where the winter sun slanted across the papers which she had been studying. She didn't hear me come in and for a fleeting moment I considered creeping up and looking to see what she had been reading.

But before I could move she sensed my presence, "Ah, Marion," she said. "I'm glad you've come down early, there is something I want to tell you."

"There are a lot of things I want to know." I sat down near her with my back to the window so that I could watch her face with the sun shining directly on it. There just might be expressions which could tell me when - or if - she was telling me the truth.

She came directly to the point.

"I'm sorry I was so cross, dear, when you came home from your walk. You must excuse me - I had a difficult morning with Basil."

She paused and looked at me as if trying to gauge my reaction. It would have been easy to murmur words of sympathy, to tell her not to worry, that I understood. And that, no doubt, was what she hoped I would do.

But I didn't want to put her at ease, if she was going to tell me anything useful it was better that she was anxious and felt she had to explain things.

So I sat and waited for her to continue, all the while watching her closely and at the same time trying to keep my own expression as impassive as possible.

For what seemed a long moment Betsy was silent, her nervous fingers shuffling the papers on her desk, composure slipping away from her. As she moved the pages about the perfume from her pink note paper wafted towards me. Involuntarily I asked; "It's Chanel, isn't it?"

"What? Oh the note paper. Yes, it's my one small luxury, I do like it."

In spite of myself I smiled, the pink, scented note paper was her 'one small luxury' in a home which, if not luxurious, at least had all the comforts which money could provide.

But she was serious and I thought that, just for a moment I had seen the real Betsy, pleased and happy with something small and apparently unconscious of, or just accepting as normal, the elegance which surrounded her.

There was another pause then she spoke softly, almost as though she expected me to have been following her thoughts.

"I was so worried about my meeting with Basil this morning and then when Dorothy came in and he accused me of trying to seduce her," her voice rose shrilly, and fleetingly I smiled at the mental picture of Betsy seducing Dorothy.

She was quiet for a moment then, still fiddling with the papers on her desk, and continued in a calmer tone, "Well, not seduced, dear, but you know what I mean. And then he tried to involve you as well."

"Me?" I said. "Why should he do that?"

"I think he is suspicious of you being here with me."

"I can't think why," I persisted. "Surely you can have friends to stay without his approval."

She nodded vaguely. "Of course, dear, but he is a very difficult man."

"You said he could be dangerous," I reminded her.

She glanced at me quickly. "Did I dear? Well I don't think he is always honest. I mean I've seen him with some very strange people."

"What do you mean - strange people or in strange circumstances?"

She thought for a moment and in the strong sunlight I could see conflicting emotions flickering across her face.

"Well, perhaps both, dear," she said at last. "I know it sounds silly but since he has known Dorothy he hasn't been the same."

"You have known him a long time?"

"Oh yes, since I first came to Lucerne, he was my local bank manager in those days. He was very helpful," her face softened and eyes held a reminiscent look. "We became good friends, it was a pleasant association," she looked across, willing me to believe her. "Nothing silly you know, just a valuable friendship. And then," the voice became hard and cold, "he came home one day with his new, young wife and soon after, moved to Geneva. It was a step up for him, of course, but he has been very trying since then, not at all the same."

"How long ago was that?" I asked, already knowing the answer.

"Two years."

I nodded to myself, yes it tallied. So both Betsy and Jim were telling me the truth over that, at least.

"Basil has gone a long way since then," her face wore a puzzled look, as if she was trying to understand this strange fact, and again those penetrating eyes met mine. "He is a very important man in some circles, you know."

"And dangerous too," I brought her back again to the point at issue, and a sudden coldness came over me, a sort of premonition of just how dangerous Basil could be if he was in a tight corner.

Mentally I shook myself free of it. "That reminds me," I said. "When do you want me to see Basil and exactly what do you want me to say to him?"

"Well dear, I thought if you took a small gift for Dorothy - just from you, you understand, nothing to do with me. Basil might be - mollified, I think that is the word I want."

I smiled, "He just might be. What do you suggest I get for her?"

"I've already got something, dear," she poked about under an untidy pile of papers and brought out a small cardboard box and handed it to me. Inside, carefully wrapped in tissue paper, was a porcelain robin. Anxiously Betsy watched me as I took it from the box and cradled it in my hand. "I thought a robin would be best as it is Christmas," she said defensively.

I looked at the little figurine, it was perfect, every feather etched - one almost expected it to stretch its wings or sing. "It's exquisite," I said, "but it must have cost a small fortune, far too much for me to be giving to someone I scarcely know."

"Oh I don't think so dear, I forget how much it did cost but not a great deal. You think she would like it?"

"I'm quite sure she would, but I still think it too expensive."

"Nonsense dear," she broke in. "Now I will tell you what I want you to do for me."

It was the old familiar Betsy again, dismissing any dissenting voice as irrelevant. She had bought the bird for me to give to Dorothy, and that was settled. I sat there uneasily holding the delicate little figure in my hands and wondering what I had let myself in for.

Basil wouldn't be fooled for a moment, he would realise it was not the sort of gift I would be giving to his wife - whom I hardly knew. Far from allaying his suspicions, it would confirm them.

I had heard of people with 'no money sense' but never before met one. I thought; what a time to choose.

Betsy was businesslike and decisive. "It would be better for you not to mention my visit this morning," she said, turning in her chair to look directly at me. "Unless, of course, Basil does, but if you tell him how much you enjoyed your walk this morning and describe some of the scenery, he will realise how silly his suspicions were."

I nodded, an innocent approach did seem to be the most sensible.

"Exactly where did you go?" Suddenly Betsy shot the question at me, the penetrating eyes searching my face.

"Why, up the hill," I could feel the guilt flooding through me and hunted quickly for a handkerchief to cover an imaginary sneeze. A moment later, recovering myself I added, "We turned off to the right, it was hard going in the deep snow but worth it."

Thankfully this appeared to satisfy her. "Yes, the view from there is very lovely. What did you talk about?"

I had been expecting this, naturally she would be anxious to know if Jim had told me - well, anything which could possibly involve her and which might arouse suspicions in my mind. Suspicions which she had never intended me to have.

"Not much," I said frankly, looking right into her eyes. "I had been hoping he would, but no."

She was unable to conceal a smile of pure relief, which made me more than ever determined to discover exactly what she was taking so much trouble to hide from me.

It was then that Dora knocked and announced that our lunch was ready. Betsy stood up: "Just before we go into the dining room there is something else I must say- - that I want you to do for me Marion."

"If I can," I said cautiously.

"When you see Basil tell him how tired and ill you think I look and that you are trying to persuade me to go back to England with you for a holiday."

I gaped at her in amazement. "But," I protested. "I don't think you are ill at all."

She raised a hand imperiously. "No, but I want you to make quite sure that Basil does."

"And will you really come back to London with me?"

"Oh yes," she said. "I shall accept your kind invitation."

I followed her into the dining room wondering; had she always been such a complex character? I raked my mind but our schooldays were a long time ago, and in any case I hadn't known her well then. I smiled grimly to myself, it looked as if that, at any rate, was going to be remedied.

We sat opposite each other, there was no sign of Jim.

"Did you tell him lunch was ready?" Betsy asked as Dora brought in the soup.

"Yes Madam, I knocked on his door."

"And did he reply?"

"Yes Madam," she looked uncertainly at Betsy. "At least I heard him say something so I knew he was there."

"I'd better go and see," Betsy pushed back her chair.

"Don't bother," I said. "I'll go." Suddenly I was anxious about him, he had been very disturbed this morning and now I felt guilty for not having thought about him since we returned. Perhaps a quick word on our way downstairs might help.

The voice which answered my tap on the door didn't sound like Jim's. "All right," it said impatiently. "You've already called me once."

I opened the door and peered in, Jim was stretched out on the bed, his hair tousled and his face red and glowing, there was a smell in the room which, for a moment I couldn't place. Then I saw the glass and half empty bottle on the side table.

"Oh no," I said. "Not that."

After what he'd told me this morning I suppose I should have expected something like this, but it had just never entered my head.

Jim smiled cheerfully, "I was fed up," he explained. "But I feel better now."

"You will feel even better when you've had some lunch," I hoped my voice carried a conviction I certainly didn't feel.

I went over to the bed, "Come on," I said "I'll help you, Betsy is waiting in the dining room."

He made a sudden grab at my arm and pulled hard. "Damn Betsy, you come here," he shouted - at least it would have been a shout if the sound hadn't been muffled as I lost my balance and fell on top of him.

It happened so quickly and I was completely unprepared. We struggled but Jim seemed possessed of maniacal strength, he rolled on top of me and his weight on my body was more than I could move, while the grip on my arm as we twisted and turned was excruciating.

"Jim!" I screamed. "My arm, you're breaking it."

I don't know if he heard me but suddenly my arm was released and he made a grab for my hair, forcing my head back. I felt his breath on my neck and face and the strong smell of the spirit was smothering. His free hand was pulling at my dress.

Then suddenly he stopped, his grip slackened and his body lost its urgency, I didn't wait to see why. Using all my strength I shoved him away, at the same time pushing myself off the edge of the bed.

I fell with a thud and lay there - it can only have been for seconds though it seemed much longer. Inconsequentially I noticed that the carpet was a soft green, the same shade as the crumpled bedspread which must have followed me on to the floor.

And then I saw the shoes and wondered idly why Jim had a pair of Betsy's sensible brogues in his room.

Jim! The panic flooded back. I pushed the bedspread aside and struggled to my feet - only now there were hands helping me and Betsy's voice was calling in my ear.

"Marion! What is going on? Why don't you answer me?"

"Oh Betsy!" I'd never expected to be so pleased to see her.

"There, there dear," she patted my shoulder as one would soothe a child. "But Marion what - - -"

A low groan sounded from the bed, I looked across at Jim, he was lying face down, head propped on his arms, an abject figure, I thought, and shivered, remembering the latent strength he had shown a few moments before.

"Let us go outside," I pulled Betsy towards the door, then I saw the half empty bottle; better to remove that. I reached across to the bedside table, Jim raised his head to watch but made no effort to prevent me.

"I don't understand," Betsy took the bottle from me, hands shaking in her anxiety. "Jim doesn't drink, I know he hasn't for several years."

Two years. I just stopped myself from correcting her. I leaned against the door, suddenly unutterably weary. "Well he has now," my voice seemed to be coming from far away. "It needs a man's strength to cope with him, who - - -" And then I remembered, Davis, of course. It was Davis who had helped Jim before.

"Where is Davis, Betsy?"

"Davis? Oh I don't think so dear."

"There isn't anyone else," I said slowly, trying to be patient. Why couldn't she understand without me having to persuade her, that he was the obvious person. "No one else knows Jim is here - and we can't ask Basil."

That decided her, "Very well, dear, yes you are right. I think Davis is downstairs having lunch with Dora, I'll go and see him. "And you Marion," she took control again. "Just go and tidy yourself up, dear, you can't let Davis see you like that. Then come down and have a good stiff brandy."

I passed Davis on my way downstairs, he stood aside and the dark grey of his uniform merged with the shadows against the wall. I was uneasily conscious of his gaze and for a moment I hesitated. Should I tell him what had happened? He was going to try to sort Jim out so perhaps he ought to know. I had no idea what Betsy had said to him but was pretty sure she would not have told him about my part in it, she hadn't really wanted him to know at all.

I held on to the banister rail still feeling somewhat shaken.

"Are you all right Madam?"

I glanced up, Davis was looking anxiously at me, his dark eyes reflecting the light from the well of the hall. He had a thick mop of black hair which fell over his brow, I had only seen him with his chauffeur's cap on and now, without it, he seemed suddenly to be a person in his own right.

I looked away again, "Yes, yes thank you - - I just felt a little faint."

"Oh no!" I added quickly as he put his hand on my arm to steady me, it was the arm Jim had twisted so badly and the slight pressure made me wince. I took a deep breath and tried a smile.

"Thank you Davis, I'm perfectly all right." Slowly I went on down and could feel him watching until the door of the dining room closed behind me.

The brandy was very welcome, it slid down warm and comforting and I began to see things in better perspective.

"What did you tell Davis?" I asked Betsy.

"Oh, I just said Jim had taken something that disagreed with him." She dismissed the matter airily, obviously there were more immediate things on her mind. "I expect Davis will stay with Jim for a while," she went on. "So I hope you will not mind walking down to see Dorothy this afternoon."

It was an order not an enquiry and it brought me back to the present with a jolt, in the turmoil I'd forgotten about the Hoppers and my proposed Christmas gift to Dorothy. I sighed, even the brandy didn't make the visit seem attractive.

"It is necessary," said Betsy firmly. "I've wrapped up the little gift and there is just the card for you to sign." She handed them to me and the Christmassy paper looked pretty and festive - and so much in contrast with the happenings around me.

Chapter Eight

I held the package in my hand wondering just what to do. Obviously I could not give Dorothy the gift which Betsy had chosen without arousing suspicions in Basil's mind, suspicions which might be dangerous for me as well as Betsy.

I searched in my dressing table drawers. I had a scarf somewhere, a new one which could be just the thing. Yes, that was it! A small paisley design in soft, muted shades. It was synthetic too, not real silk which would have been as awkward a gift as the little bird.

Carefully I unwrapped the package and took out the porcelain figure then I tucked the scarf into the box and tied the paper on again. I thought, even if she didn't like the scarf at least it wasn't a dangerous present and it was one I might have chosen to give Dorothy in any case without Betsy's prompting.

Basil was in the foyer and almost before I saw him, his squat figure was out of the deep red chair and striding towards me. He held out a hand in greeting: "Marion, I was waiting for you."

"You knew I was coming?" I was surprised to see him - and at his welcome. Betsy hadn't said they would be expecting me.

"Of course," he led me into the lounge. There was no sign of Dorothy.

I wanted to ask how he knew - after all I hadn't known myself until a short while ago and I'd got the impression that Betsy had been too scared this morning to make any arrangements with him. I paused, that would be it, of course. Basil knew he had frightened her and he knew her sufficiently well to realise she would either come herself or else, as soon as possible, send me to allay any suspicions.

Basil motioned me to a chair, "You will have tea or coffee?" he asked.

"No thank you, we only finished our lunch a short while ago, I came to see Dorothy." I watched him carefully to see what effect - if any - the remark would have.

His mouth set in a hard line and the expression in his eyes was suddenly cold. For what seemed a long moment he looked at me without speaking, then: "Dorothy is resting," he said briefly. "I will give her your message."

"Please don't bother," I tried to speak calmly. "I'm not in a hurry, I'll wait for her." Then before he had a chance to reply I added, "You look very forbidding! It is Christmas, you know and I have a small gift for your wife."

For a moment he was obviously nonplussed, his fingers drummed on the arms of his chair, then he stood and gave one of his formal little bows. "That is kind of you Marion, I will ask someone to call her." There was no warmth in his voice and he signalled to a waiter nearby and spoke to him quickly in German.

What he said was of no significance, just a request that Dorothy be told to come downstairs, but I gave no hint that I had understood. A sixth sense seemed to warn me that my knowledge of the language might be useful in the future - providing Basil did not know that I understood it.

After a moment he sat down again, "You enjoyed your walk this morning?"

"Very much."

"Did you go alone?"

I hesitated, this was a question I had not anticipated. He knew, of course, that Betsy had not accompanied me, so did he, after all, suspect that Jim was staying here? Perhaps I was being hyper sensitive and it was just a polite, innocuous remark, but I didn't think so.

He was watching me through half-closed eyes, a bland expression on his face but I could feel the tension emanating from him: like a cat watching a rat hole, still and yet ready to spring.

Attack, I thought, the best form of defence.

"What a strange question for you to ask," I tried to keep my voice both disapproving and at the same time puzzled. After all I must not annoy him too much for Betsy's sake - and maybe for my own as well.

"Why Marion?" His voice was dangerously calm.

"Well, you knew Betsy was here, who else could I go out with? But in any case I really cannot see that- - -"

"It is any concern of mine," he finished for me and laughed, quite genuinely it seemed.

"I'm glad you said that," I smiled with relief. "But if you are really interested to know, it was a most enjoyable walk and the view from the top of the hill was worth coming here to see."

"You haven't seen it before?"

"This is my first visit to Switzerland; I've always wanted to come so I was very pleased to have this opportunity to stay with Betsy." It was nice to speak frankly and without fear that an innocent remark might be misconstrued.

He seemed to relax and was quite cheerful when Dorothy appeared. She looked pale and drawn and the green dress she was wearing reflected on to her face, emphasising the pallor. Languidly she reclined in one of the deep chairs, the mask of disinterest firmly over her face. She was the Dorothy of last night, no look or gesture indicated that we had come to know each other more intimately this morning.

I took my cue from her.

"I'm sorry to disturb your rest," I said.

She looked across at me but didn't reply.

I felt in my handbag for the little package in its Christmassy paper. "I wanted to wish you a happy Christmas," I said. "In case we don't meet again before Sunday."

I leaned towards her but before Dorothy could take the box, Basil reached out his hand for it. He held the package up to his nose and sniffed, peering at me over the top of his spectacles. "I see Betsy had a hand in this."

"Oh, her perfume, yes it is distinctive isn't it? I had to ask her for the wrapping."

He looked at me quizzically but appeared to be satisfied and handed the package to Dorothy. She laid it in her lap making no effort to see what was inside. I wondered if she thought there might be some word from Jim in there and so was waiting until she was alone to unwrap it.

"See what it is then, dear." Basil was impatient.

Slowly Dorothy undid the wrapping, resisting Basil's offer of help; he was sitting on the edge of his chair watching her closely and I couldn't help smiling to myself, he was so anxious not to miss anything.

Dorothy took out the scarf and read the accompanying card before handing them to Basil.

"Thank you, it was very kind of you." She said completely without emotion, either of gratitude or disappointment. Basil too seemed deflated, and, with relief I knew I had chosen the right gift. Betsy's little robin would surely have confirmed his worst fears about me.

We were silent for a moment, I was very aware of Basil's presence, like an evil spirit hovering over us, I wanted to get away out into the fresh air. Through the window I could see the low afternoon sun reflecting on the roofs of the buildings, and the Christmas lights and decorations in the street.

I got to my feet, and then remembered the strange message Betsy had insisted I tell Basil.

I looked across at Dorothy, "I have a little shopping to do, would you care to come with me?"

I didn't expect that she would and was not surprised when she glanced at Basil, referring my query to him. He frowned but before he could answer I qualified my invitation: "I want to get something small for Betsy, perhaps some flowers. She is resting," I pressed on quickly. "As a matter of fact she doesn't look at all well and I am wondering if she will come back with me when I go home - the change might cheer her up."

I paused, had I overdone it? Did it sound like a rehearsed speech?

Basil continued to frown but otherwise his face was expression-less. Suddenly he stood up. "Very well Marion," he said crisply. "We will all go and buy some flowers for Betsy and take them back to her."

I opened mouth to protest but he didn't bother to listen. "Wait here Marion," he said. "We will be five minutes."

For the third time that day cold fright seemed a tangible thing that slid down the back of my neck. There was no chance to warn Betsy that we were coming, it would take at least five minutes for the receptionist to get the number, and in any case if Basil caught me telephoning he would surely guess why.

And yet, if she was not forewarned Betsy would probably tell them what she had been doing during the afternoon - and it certainly would not have been resting. Even worse, Jim might be downstairs - and perhaps still rather drunk.

It was exactly five minutes later when Basil and Dorothy returned and we walked out of the hotel to a nearby flower shop. I bought two bunches of anemones and Basil got some expensive, out-of-season yellow roses.

We crossed the busy street and I glanced back at the crowds of cheerful, smiling people. It almost seemed that we were the only ones weighed down with problems and grim suspicions.

As I looked, a blue Mercedes emerged from a side turning farther down the road, it was indicating to come our way but suddenly changed direction and disappeared as quickly as the crowds would allow. It was not near enough for me to read the number plates or see who was in it. I thought, if it was Betsy, she probably wouldn't be at home at all when we got there. That might be the lesser of two evils, but at the same time a very awkward anticlimax.

Basil and Dorothy were a few paces ahead of me and, as last night, he was holding her arm tightly. Only now, to me it was not a sign of his affection for her, more an exercise of authority.

Dora looked surprised when she let us in. Yes, she said, Mrs. Harland was at home, upstairs resting. Should she call her down?

For a moment there was silence in the hall, I glanced quickly at Basil, he had obviously expected to catch me out - and Betsy too, for that matter. For a split second his square figure sagged, and the roses hung from a limp hand. I saw a flicker of interest cross Dorothy's face.

As for me, like a drowning person thoughts flashed across my mind. Was there really such a thing as thought transference? Did Betsy practice a sort of mental sleight-of-hand and had she been tuned in to me a short time ago when I'd told Basil she was resting? I'd never believed in such things but perhaps I was wrong, perhaps Betsy was psychic.

Quickly I collected my wits together, don't try to analyse it now Marion, I told myself. Just be thankful that, whatever the reason, Betsy really is resting, "Oh no, Dora," I said. "It would be a pity to disturb her."

But Basil interrupted me, "Yes, I should like to see Mrs. Harland." He took off his overcoat and hung it over the arm of one of Betsy's carved oak chairs, then he stood, obviously watching to see what I would do.

I took a deep breath forcing back the irritation I felt. Turning again to Dora I tried to speak evenly. "In that case I will tell Mrs. Harland, Dora, I have to go up anyway."

I walked towards the stairs but Basil followed me and again intervened. "No Marion," he said, and his hand grasped my arm

- the arm Jim had wrenched so badly a few hours ago. Involuntarily I winced as the pain swept upwards.

I turned and looked into his face and his cold eyes stared back, challenging me. Betsy's words flashed into my mind; 'when Basil is angry he can be dangerous'.

But I was angry too and for the moment it overcame any fear I had of this unpleasant little man. I was furious not only with him, but at being forced into a situation where I was expected to tolerate his rudeness.

"I am going upstairs Mr. Hopper," I said, and even to me my voice sounded firm and cold. "Will you kindly let go of my arm."

For a moment he hesitated and glanced towards Dora, I saw that she was watching him, her dark eyes wide and alert. Then he turned and strutted down the hall into the drawing-room.

"Phew" I breathed. Dora smiled sympathetically and shrugged her shoulders.

Slowly I climbed up the stairs holding on to the banister rail. It had been a ridiculous and frightening episode. Of course I realised Basil would not want me to see Betsy and possibly warn her of his arrival, but that he would attempt physically to prevent me was something I hadn't reckoned on.

I knocked on Betsy's door, immediately it opened and I was beckoned inside. Betsy was wearing a warm blue dressing-gown, her hair was dishevelled as though she had been tossing sleeplessly on the bed and her eyes without the gold-rimmed glasses, peered anxiously at me from a white, strained face.

"What did you say to Basil? Did you tell him- - -"

"I told him that you were resting, that you weren't well," I looked at her critically, she really did look ill. "Are you all right Betsy?"

"Yes dear, no! no!" She corrected herself abstractedly, holding on to her dressing table for support.

"Good." It sounded callous, but if Betsy really wasn't well it might allay Basil's suspicions. "Just tidy your hair and then go down as you are - perhaps Basil will believe me after all."

"What do you mean dear? Didn't he - wasn't he- - -" her voice trailed.

"He was extremely rude." I didn't attempt to soften the blow. As I saw it, the more anxious Betsy became the more ill she appeared to be and, at the moment that could only be to the benefit of us both.

"But the little present," she almost whimpered, twisting her fingers together. "Weren't they pleased with it?"

I shrugged, "It was difficult to know, Dorothy did say thank you," I added.

We needed to hurry downstairs and I was going out of the door when it occurred to me that Betsy would have to know about the gift and there was no time to explain tactfully as I had intended to. I faced her, "I didn't give Dorothy the little robin after all."

"Why Marion?" For a brief moment the imperious Betsy took charge again.

"I'll tell you later," I said as I closed the door behind me.

I sat on the edge of my bed trying to get the events of the day into perspective.

I thought back over it all, from Betsy's astonishing admission this morning that she knew Jim as both Martin and Bellamy, on to my discovery that Dorothy and Jim were lovers, and now my recent - and unpleasant - encounter with Basil.

Somehow or other all these things were connected, in some way these people were involved in a mysterious and it seemed, sinister affair.

Again I thought, if only Bill was here it would be an adventure to share instead of a series of sometimes frightening happenings that part of me wanted to be far away from. And yet there was the other side of me that needed to know what it was all about - even at the risk of sometimes being scared out of my wits.

I was itching to know why Betsy had been resting this afternoon, I didn't believe she really was ill, so had she known the three of us were coming? And if so how? And also there was the nagging worry about Jim, I certainly didn't want to be around if he suddenly appeared in the drawing-room while Basil and Dorothy were there.

The urgent thing was to get rid of the Hoppers as soon as possible, and surely with Betsy looking so obviously unwell, Basil would not persist in staying or causing more trouble.

For a few more precious minutes I stayed in the peace of my room then I stood and smoothed the pretty, flowered bedspread. Time to face the music again Marion, I told myself.

Basil stood as I entered the drawing-room, unsmiling he gave one of his formal little bows. Dorothy looked up casually and then away again, apparently completely without interest in her surroundings.

Betsy was sitting on the edge of a deep armchair, her face flushed from the fire, the yellow roses on her lap were already wilting.

I handed her the anemones which had lain forgotten on the hall table since our arrival.

"Oh thank you dear, you are kind, I am being spoiled." Betsy smiled feebly up at me.

"It is too hot for them here," I said. "Shall I ask Dora to put them in water for you?"

"Yes please," she lay back in the chair but her fingers gripped tightly on to the cretonne cover. "Oh, and ask her to bring in tea, will you dear."

I paused on my way to the door, so they were staying for tea. Somehow they had to be persuaded to go - quickly. I looked anxiously at Betsy, "I'm sure you should go back to bed, I think you have flu or something. If Mr. and Mrs. Hopper are staying," I emphasised the 'if', "I will have tea with them."

Betsy passed a hand across her brow, "I really don't feel well," she said in a small voice.

It was convincing, Basil bounced out of his chair. "Marion is right," he said briskly. "Come along Dorothy, we will enquire how you are tomorrow Betsy."

I hadn't expected him to give in so easily, relief flooded through me and I turned my head away in case it showed. I was looking towards the end of the room where Betsy kept her well stocked cupboard of wines and spirits. Involuntarily I held my breath, the door of the cupboard was open and on the top of it lay Jim's gloves - just where he had flung them this morning.

Thoughts chased each other in my mind; had Basil seen them, and if so would a pair of man's gloves in Betsy's drawing-room make him more suspicious? It seemed very likely.

One thing was certain, I mustn't for a second let Basil know that I was disturbed or anxious about anything.

"I'll see you out," I said turning towards them again, but Dorothy was ahead of me. With surprise I saw that she was holding Basil's arm and leading him - almost pulling him I thought - from the room. During my short acquaintance with them Basil had often held Dorothy's arm, as though he was keeping a tight hold on her.

Now, for a moment their roles appeared to be reversed with Dorothy playing the lead and Basil meekly obeying.

Wonderingly I followed them out of the room, as impressed by Dorothy's behaviour as I was mystified by Basil's submissive acceptance.

In silence Dorothy helped him on with his overcoat and gloves, her face, when the hall light shone on it, wore its usual mask of indifference, her movements were unhurried but firm and purposeful. I wondered if this was a new side to Dorothy's character, new that is, to Basil, and if so what he thought of it. From all appearances he was going along with her quite willingly.

I opened the front door and they stepped outside, then suddenly Basil turned to me, shaking off Dorothy's restraining hand. His cold, stony eyes gazed directly into mine, "I won't say goodbye Marion," he said. "Because I shall be back again quite soon."

It was a threat - and a promise - I had no doubt of it.

Chapter Nine

Betsy was standing by her chair when I returned, her face still glowing from the fire. She held out the gloves to me, "Did Basil see them?" she asked, her eyes bright with anxiety.

"He may have," I no longer felt any need to protect her from worrying, after all she had been the cause of some anxious moments for me during my short stay with her. She may as well know the brutal truth.

"In fact," I went on, watching her closely. "I suspect he did. He told me - no, perhaps 'threatened' would be more accurate - that he would be back again soon."

Betsy hesitated. "Are you sure dear? I mean, he did say tomorrow."

"That was probably before he saw the gloves."

She sat down, it looked as if her legs would no longer hold her and her face seemed to crumple, after a moment she peered at me pathetically. "What am I going to do Marion?" she whispered.

I forced back the sympathy for her which part of me still felt. As I saw it the only way to help her - and myself - was to be severe.

Perhaps then she might be persuaded to tell me exactly what the trouble was. Obviously it was serious and somehow or other had to be faced up to squarely.

"Supposing you tell me why you are so frightened of Basil."

Betsy looked out of the window. Down the hill the lights of the town glowed in the early dusk, but I didn't think she was seeing them, her eyes were blank as if she was looking inwards, seeing again things which had happened in the past. Things which had led to the situation she was now facing.

At last she turned to me. "I can't do that Marion," she said and her voice was quiet and so full of sadness that I wanted to put my arms around her, to comfort her.

But it was exasperating too, and frustrating. "I can't help you Betsy," I said, "if I don't know what's wrong."

"No dear." The voice was expressionless.

For a while we sat there on either side of the fire in Betsy's deep arm chairs. The flames licked and played with the coal and logs and the lights from them danced on the ceiling. It was warm and comfortable and in a few minutes Dora would be bringing in the tea.

And yet the room was full of trouble and foreboding. I reminded myself that it was Christmas Eve, surely the strangest one I had ever spent.

We were sipping our first cups of tea and over the rim I had been watching Betsy, her hands were shaking and her eyes, behind the spectacles, were blurred with tears. She looked near to breaking point.

I racked my mind for something I could say which might ease the strain a little, even if it was only a temporary escape from one small worry. And then it occurred to me, and it was obvious - the way simple solutions often are.

"Betsy" I said. "Basil can't be sure those gloves are Jim's, for all he knows they might belong to any friend of yours who has called. Someone he has never met and can have no interest in."

Betsy sat straight in her chair, "That is true," she said quickly. "Oh, what a relief. Thank you dear."

"We should have thought of it before, but I suppose we were too worried."

She nodded, swallowing hard and dabbing at her eyes.

"Don't be confident, though," I warned. "Just put the gloves out in the hall as though you are waiting for someone to call and collect them."

"I'll tell Dora," Betsy was taking an interest in things again.

I smiled across at her. "Of course, it won't stop Basil being suspicious and don't forget there is still Jim to contend with," I reminded her.

"Where is he?"

"Upstairs I believe, Davis is looking after him."

She was silent for a moment while she finished her tea, then, "It is very good of him - I mean it is not really in his duties but he said he would be responsible and I was not to worry."

She sounded puzzled that Davis should behave in this manner, but for me another small piece of this strange and sinister jigsaw had slipped into place. Now I was sure that Betsy didn't know that Davis had done the same thing for Jim at least once before.

The atmosphere had relaxed a little and we lay back in our chairs watching the pictures in the fire as we ate our buttered toast. My thoughts were with Bill. If only I knew where he was, our separation at this time would have been easier to bear. I was used to him being away - used, even, to not knowing where he was all the time. But Christmas was different and because I was worried I was also angry with him.

Somehow he could have let me know he was all right, perhaps even sent me a card to wish me a happy Christmas.

Betsy's voice broke into my reverie, she was speaking softly, almost as if talking to herself. "If only Basil hadn't married Dorothy, there was no trouble until then."

I wondered if another piece of the puzzle was about to be revealed to me. "Do you think Dorothy is happy?" I asked quietly.

"Why shouldn't she be?"

The peaceful moment had gone. Betsy's voice was harsh, obviously it had never occurred to her that Dorothy might not be content in her marriage.

"She doesn't appear to be," I persisted.

"Huh." It was almost a grunt. "Basil gives her everything she wants."

Not quite everything, I thought. Silently I pondered Betsy's belligerent attitude whenever she spoke of Dorothy and this train of thought inevitably brought another question to my mind. One which I doubted I would have the courage to ask her.

But it was Betsy herself who precipitated the query in that strange, almost psychic way of hers. In one of her quick changes of mood the question was suddenly shot at me and I was aware of her penetrating eyes on my face. "Where is your husband at the moment?" she said.

"Bill?" I said. "He is away on business."

"You haven't told me anything about him," she continued. "What does he do?"

It wasn't so much the questions, after all it was reasonable that she should be interested, it was her whole manner and the tone of voice she used, autocratic and dictatorial.

"You haven't mentioned Mr. Harland to me." I countered.

The effect was startling.

"What do you mean Marion?" Betsy stood up and glared at me, her voice rising until I was sure Dora must hear it in the kitchen. "How dare you, a guest in my own house be so inquisitive and rude."

It was then that the door opened, Betsy and I turned instinctively to see who was there, and I imagine she was even more fearful than I, that it might be Basil returning.

But it was Jim who stepped into the room and looked casually across at us.

"Tut, tut," he said and smiled in a way which I believe the romantic novelists call sardonic. It wasn't a nice smile.

"Raised voices," he said turning to Betsy. "You really must be more controlled unless you want the staff to hear your private conversations."

Betsy's face was already flushed and angry, she didn't look to be in a mood to suffer unpleasant remarks from Jim.

"What are you doing here?" her voice was still angry but quieter now. "Did Davis say you could come down?"

Unblinking Jim glared at her from steely blue eyes. Obviously he had no intention of apologising to her, of expressing any penitence for his behaviour this morning.

"Davis was with me a while ago, now I feel quite fit." He spoke with no outward sign of emotion. Almost he seemed to be taunting her.

I was still sitting in my chair and so far the conversation had passed me by, but it had been interesting to watch these two, to see their expressions and how they fenced with each other.

Of course, these were not normal circumstances. Nothing here seemed to be normal, I thought ruefully. It appeared that Betsy was intimidated by Jim - not in the way that Basil frightened her, on the other hand Jim was not deferring to her. Perhaps he was almost too determined not to.

From my point of view it was an interesting relationship, and from theirs I suspected one of mutual convenience rather than affection or respect.

I thought, how strange that they should choose to spend Christmas - of all times - together. But then, I also had been invited so presumably my part in their scheme was vital. I sat there for several minutes digesting this new angle. These two people needed me for some reason, I had no idea what, but the fact that I was necessary to them gave me a certain sense of power. If my thinking was right, it followed that they wouldn't wish to offend me in any way. Or let anyone else.

And yet, when I considered it further, the events of this day alone contradicted that theory. Betsy was involving me uncomfortably with Basil - whom she admitted was dangerous, and Jim certainly hadn't shown a lot of consideration.

I gazed into the fire, the fleeting sense of power evaporating as quickly as it had come.

Jim's voice broke into my thoughts. "You are a long way off, Marion." He spoke gently and I saw he was sitting in Betsy's chair, I looked round but she had gone from the room.

"She's upstairs," Jim said, following my gaze. "Gone to change, I imagine. She'll be down."

He reached out a hand to me. "I owe you an apology Marion, afraid I behaved badly this morning."

An apology to me, I noted, but not to Betsy. Aloud I said: "Yes you did."

"I'm sorry, I don't know why it happened."

I looked across at him steadily. "I do," I said. "Perhaps you had cause after this morning but it certainly hasn't helped either Betsy or me."

"How do you mean Marion?"

"Basil, I think he suspects you are here."

He sat up straight in his chair. "How?" he almost barked at me. I looked towards the drinks cupboard, "You left your gloves over there."

"Oh hell" he slumped back in his chair.

"You will have to keep out of the way - and sober." I rubbed in my temporary advantage. "Basil has threatened to come back at any time to check and I don't need to tell you how dangerous that could be for us all - Dorothy included."

For a long moment he sat there, shoulders hunched, staring into the fire and once again, despite my misgivings, I felt sorry for him - just as I had for Betsy a short time ago. Whatever their problems were and whatever they had done to cause them, it was impossible not to be concerned. And not only for them, I also was involved. At last Jim raised his head wearily and looked across at me, for the time being all the bravado and assurance had gone.

"What a Christmas!" he said.

He echoed my sentiments.

Chapter Ten

It seemed ages that we sat there, both sunk in gloom and I suppose a fair helping of self-pity too. It was the sound of a car pulling up outside the house that roused us from our respective reveries.

I glanced quickly at Jim and was in time to see the alarm on his face before the mask of indifference closed over it again.

"You had better disappear quickly," I said. "It may be Basil - or someone else you shouldn't see."

"There isn't anyone else to worry about," he said shortly. "Marion, be a love and peep out of the window, it may only be Davis."

So Basil is the only problem here, I thought as I crept in behind the heavy velvet curtains. They completely shut out the room lights and it took me a moment to get accustomed to the dark outside.

Then the shape of a vehicle formed; a van, and a man was emerging from the open rear doors, he was carrying a large bunch of flowers. A Christmas present for Betsy I thought, she was doing quite well for flowers today: yellow roses from Basil, anemones from me, and now these.

I stayed hidden and watched while Dora received the bouquet, then I saw the man get back into the van and drive away, the rear lights edged towards the gate and turned off into the road.

I hadn't been able to see the man at all clearly but his build and the way he moved reminded me of my Bill. Suddenly all the pent up yearning for him swept over me and I wanted to rush after the van - just to make certain it wasn't him. Stupid, of course, but I found myself brushing away tears of mortification from my eyes.

Jim's plaintive voice sounded muffled through the curtains. "Is it safe Marion, or ought I to hide under the sofa?"

I couldn't help laughing, what a strange mixture this man was; arrogant one minute, boyish the next. Sometimes thoughtful - even kind - but also beyond the law and, for all I knew, a dangerous criminal. I peered around the curtain. "You are all right for the moment," I said, blinking in the light.

Jim was standing with his back to the fire, smiling and at ease, it was difficult to reconcile him with the dejected man of a few moments ago. And still more with the drunken scene of this morning.

"What was the bother Marion?" Jim was still standing in front of the fire and his voice showed no sign of the urgency which I sensed underlined the question.

Back in my comfortable chair I looked up at him, deliberately misunderstanding his question. "What bother?" I asked.

"You can do better than that Marion," he said crisply. "When I came in Betsy was annoyed about something. What was it?"

"Well, I asked her something and she didn't seem to approve."

"What?"

"I asked her where Mr. Harland was." I watched him closely to see if the question had any effect on him. I was in for a rough time if he also became excited.

But he didn't, for a moment his face drained of colour, then a wry smile curved his lips. "I'm not surprised she was upset." He said quietly.

"But why?" It was my turn to pose the questions. "It seemed a reasonable thing to ask. I know nothing of him, or if she ever <u>had</u> a husband."

Jim was looking at me curiously. "You really don't know, do you little Marion."

His tone was guaranteed to infuriate me. "Perhaps <u>you</u> do," I said coldly, "in which case you can tell me."

"Oh no, Marion, you ask her again sometime - only make sure I'm present when you do it." There was a look of quite malicious pleasure on his face, as if relishing my discomfiture - and even more the prospect of Betsy's.

We both jumped at the soft tap on the door.

"I'll go," I said, stifling my first impulse to say 'come in'. Dora was outside and in her arms a quite enormous bunch of flowers. "These are for you Madam," she said.

Never in my life have I held such a huge bouquet, I wondered who on earth they could be from, I didn't know anyone here - other than Basil and Jim and it was very unlikely either of them would send me flowers.

I was closing the door again when a thought occurred to me. "Oh Dora," I called. "Could you please give us some warning if Mr. Hopper comes again."

Dora walked back down the hall to me, "Yes Madam, but Mrs. Harland has already asked me to do that. She said to be sure to let her know before allowing Mr. Hopper in, particularly if Mr. Bellamy is about." She smiled at me almost as if we were fellow conspirators. "I'll fetch you some vases Madam," she said.

Jim gave a low whistle when he saw the flowers, "Are you there Marion?" he said. "A large bouquet has just walked into the room- - -"

I peered round the flowers at him. "Aren't they lovely! I can't imagine who can have sent them."

"There's a card here," he unravelled it for me. "From one of your many admirers no doubt."

I could feel his eyes watching me as I slid the little card from its envelope and there was a waiting stillness in the room, as though it mattered to Jim almost as much as to me, who the bouquet was from.

I looked at the card then buried my face in amongst the blooms. Perfume from roses and freesias enveloped me and, most important of all, separately wrapped, a small posy of lilies-of-the-valley.

Lilies-of-the-valley were our flowers, Bill's and mine. The very first time we met he had bought me some, and since then celebrations, 'thank you's' and even apologies have been accompanied by the small, white, sweetly scented flowers.

I could feel the tears slipping down my cheeks. Dear Bill, where was he now? I wanted so badly to be with him, not here with these strange people, not at Christmas, not at anytime.

I blinked away the tears and looked again at the card but there was no clue, the flowers had been sent Interflora, even the writing on the card wasn't Bill's.

"Do I need to ask where they come from?"

With a jolt, the coldness in Jim's voice brought me back to reality, reminded me that I couldn't afford to be on bad terms with this man - any more than I could with Basil.

Silently I handed the card to Jim and was surprised when he read the message aloud. The tone of his voice as he spoke the words made then seem trivial and inane; 'For you Em, with all my love.'

Shaken, I stared at him as he flung the card back at me and it fluttered to the floor. Then he strode over to Betsy's cupboard and helped himself generously to her brandy.

"Oh no!" I said.

He turned towards me and I could see the strain on his face. Of course, the pain from this morning was still there and my message from Bill must have reminded him forcibly of it.

"I'm sorry- - -" I hesitated.

"Are you?" his voice was scathing.

"I was thinking of what you told me this morning."

He tipped the glass to drain it before replying. "So was I," he said bitterly.

Betsy hadn't come downstairs yet and Jim was sitting, staring moodily into the fire. To my great relief he hadn't attempted to refill his glass, but had watched my every movement as I sorted the flowers into their various containers.

"Glad you aren't torturing them into extraordinary shapes," he commented.

"Some arrangements are gorgeous, afraid I just 'put' them."

"Better that way." His tone was curt but at least he was taking an interest.

There were flowers on Betsy's bookshelves, on tables and every available space and the perfume from them filled the room. The lilies I put in a small Waterford vase and intended taking them up to my room to be enjoyed at leisure.

"Now I'd like a drink," I said. Maybe if we had one together, socially, it might prevent Jim just swigging in order to forget.

"That's my girl," he smiled as he got to his feet.

We were comfortably ensconced when Betsy came in, she had changed already for dinner and the dark brown velvet of her dress seemed to add colour to her hair. Even those hypnotic hazel eyes were softer and velvety.

"You look charming," I shuffled my chair to make room for her and was delighted to note that Jim, without prompting, rose when she entered and poured her usual dry sherry for her. I almost fooled myself that it was cosy and friendly as we sat there in the firelight sipping our aperitifs.

But it was too good to last.

"Now," said Betsy turning her all-seeing gaze upon me. "Tell me about these flowers, Dora says they were delivered to you."

"They are from Bill, I seem to have used most of your vases but they do look lovely, don't they?"

"Beautiful," she looked around, apparently considering them carefully before turning again to me. "How did he know you were here?" she asked abruptly.

"Well, of course, I left him a note so that he would know where to find me." If I had blinked at that moment I would have missed the quick glance that passed between Betsy and Jim. It was almost as if, like dogs, they had pricked up their ears.

What had I said to be of such immediate interest to them? Surely they didn't think I would go away without leaving Bill an address where he could contact me. I crushed down the knowledge that Bill often did just that to me.

"Marion, it is time you went to change," the glass of Betsy's watch glinted in the light from the flames and her eyes behind the gold-edged spectacles were no longer soft and relaxed.

I looked across at Jim, he wore an air of studied indifference. I sensed tension in the atmosphere. There were things they needed to discuss so they wanted me out of the room, and it was because I had said Bill would know where to find me.

For the second time in two days I had been dismissed from the room, told, like a grubby child to go upstairs and wash my face so that they could talk freely. I found it as annoying now as I had the first time.

I picked up the little vase full of lilies. "I'm taking these upstairs," I said, but I don't think either of them heard me.

I placed the flowers on my bedside table just under the lamp and the rosy glow from the shade spread over them, changing them to the palest pink, while the crystal sparked rainbows in its deep-cut facets.

I sat for a while on the bed drinking in the fragrance from the lilies, memories of Bill crowding across my mind. Mostly they were happy but a few, the more recent ones, hurt.

When I thought about them objectively I knew the unpleasant ones were due to Bill's disappearances, sometimes, as now for weeks on end. It was a tremendous strain and anxiety.

Sitting here in the physical comfort of Betsy's home it was easy to see the logic of this. Not so simple to cope with in reality. I loved Bill so much and was sure he felt the same way about me, though, goodness knows, I must have been difficult to live with sometimes. I switched off the light and went to the window, drawing back the curtains just enough to look out at the town and sleeping mountains beyond.

It all looked so peaceful, and yet downstairs Betsy and Jim were probably hatching some plot which involved me but would certainly not be intended to benefit me. And a short distance away Dorothy, young and beautiful, was caught in a net - partly of her own weaving - coping with a husband who watched her every action, and whom she knew would not hesitate to punish severely any deviation from his will.

How petty my own problems were in comparison: Perhaps it was worth this journey to Switzerland, with its consequent troubles, just to discover that.

I'm not sure how long I stayed there looking out of the window, my thoughts turned inwards, longing to be home again, to be more understanding, more sympathetic to Bill, rather than to myself.

I was just about to draw the curtains again when my eye was caught by a movement. At first I thought it was a branch or bush blowing in the slight breeze, or a cat prowling in the night air. But then a shadow fell across the driveway, followed by a dark figure, muffled against the cold, and shapeless.

It moved with elaborate stealth and flattened itself against the wall of the house. Basil? It wasn't possible to tell, but certainly no legitimate caller would behave in such a way.

As quickly as I could feel my way in the dark I hurried out of my room and downstairs.

"Betsy" I cried, flinging open the drawing-room door. "There is someone prowling around outside."

Her white, startled face looked up at me. "Basil." There was no doubting the sheer panic in her voice.

"Jim!" Betsy waved her arms at him. "You go upstairs now and don't come down again until I say so. Marion, ring for Dora."

"I already have." In spite of the scare I could hardly repress a smile, Betsy's sergeant major act was pure melodrama.

Jim was still sitting in his chair while Betsy stamped with frustration. "Move!" she shouted running over and attempting to pull him up.

Angrily he flung her away, "I don't care to be shouted at," he said coldly. "And I shall go upstairs when I want to."

"But Basil- - -" Betsy was almost weeping in her agitation.

"If Basil is out there I will go and deal with him." He strode to the door, obviously angry enough to attempt just that.

For all our sakes he had to be prevented, with my back against the door I stood in his way. "Please Jim," I said quietly. "If you do confront Basil it won't help Dorothy."

He hesitated and I could see the look of hopelessness cloud his eyes before he pushed me roughly away. "I won't be told what to do." His voice was ice cold.

Anxiously I watched as he reached for his coat, it looked as if he really did mean to deal with the intruder, whoever it was.

Then the front door opened and Davis came in. He looked stern and dependable - and so very welcome.

He spoke directly to Jim, seeming to take in the situation at a glance. "It was a youngster from the town I think. He ran off down the road but if you'd care to come out with me, two would be better than one and we could make quite sure."

I sighed with relief and turned back into the drawing-room. With one of her quick changes of mood, Betsy was sitting passively in her chair. Only the flushed face and gimlet eyes betrayed the scene of a few moments ago.

"Marion," she spoke quietly. "What did you mean when you told Jim 'it won't help Dorothy'?"

I had to think quickly, obviously it was useless to deny having said it, or to make up some impossible yarn. Betsy was no fool.

"I had to try and prevent him going out there," I said, searching feverishly in my mind for a plausible reason that would satisfy Betsy.

"Yes, but you haven't answered my question," her gaze was unswerving.

I gripped the back of a nearby chair and tried again.

"You didn't want Jim and the Hoppers to meet so it was obvious to me that they must know and would recognise each other."

"But why Dorothy?" Her voice was still quiet but it held a menacing quality. She was a Betsy I had not seen or heard before.

"Dorothy is young and beautiful, it seemed reasonable that if Basil is angry she might suffer. You told me yourself he can be dangerous when he is annoyed."

"What makes you think that would worry Jim?" Betsy was still staring, her eyes unblinking behind the gold-framed spectacles. I felt as if she was looking right through me.

I sat down on the arm of a chair and forced myself to look around the room. My flowers, so lovely in the soft glow from the lamplight, restored a feeling of sanity to the situation, reminded me that there was a life beyond this house and the strange and sinister people connected with it.

I turned back to Betsy. I'd had enough of her mysteries and she might as well know it.

"Have you quite finished interrogating me?" I asked angrily. "I don't know what the Hoppers and Jim are about - or you either if it comes to that - and I'm fed up with you all. Now, if you will excuse me," I walked towards the door. "I will go and pack and spend the rest of Christmas in a hotel. At least that should be more restful."

Instantly she was contrite. "Oh no dear, I couldn't let you. I'm so worried I hardly know what I'm saying."

"I find that difficult to believe." It was my turn for the stony gaze.

"Please," she was standing now and holding out her arms to me, her expression pleading, in direct contrast to the accusing stare of a few moments ago.

But I'd no intention of being won over so easily. I was fed up with the situation here. In comparison the peace of being alone in a hotel would seem a rest cure.

"Betsy," I kept my voice low and even. "I came here to spend a holiday with you, it has turned into a sort of nightmare involving me with people I don't like and who are dangerous. I can't go home until after the holiday but I can - and shall - spend the remaining days quietly, and away from you."

"No, dear, I can't let you go!" she was weeping in her agitation, but I'd seen it all before and watched unmoved, as if she was a character in a bad play.

"Do I understand you are thinking of leaving us?" Jim's voice came from the doorway. I glanced quickly round, he looked more relaxed, though his eyes were still cold and hard.

"Yes, yes," Betsy turned to him for support.

He came into the room and placed a hand casually, yet firmly on my arm.

"You are not going, you know little Marion. You are staying here with us until after Christmas, just as we arranged."

I looked from one to the other. As 'we' arranged he had said. Of course it wouldn't have been just Betsy who invited me to Switzerland, they both wanted me here.

"I wonder how you intend stopping me?" I was surprised how calm I felt. No doubt the reckoning would come later.

"We will think of a way," the corners of Jim's mouth curved but it wasn't a pleasant smile.

Betsy suddenly bustled into activity. "That's all right then dear. Now it's all settled perhaps you'd better go and change or we shall be late for dinner." She was all friendliness and affability as though nothing untoward had happened.

I stared at her, these quick changes of mood left me speechless, but in any case there was no time to demur.

Jim's grip was firm on my arm, "I'll come with you," he said, leading me through the open door and upstairs. "See you in twenty minutes."

I didn't bother to reply.

Chapter Eleven

Dinner was a delicious meal, as always Dora's cooking left nothing to be desired but the three of us hardly did justice to it, we were too preoccupied with our personal problems.

Uppermost in my mind was finding a chance to get away from this house. Jim had collected me from my room before dinner so it looked as if I was going to be closely shadowed from now on.

If only there was someone to help! But the only ones possible were Davis or Dora, and on reflection, I thought it hardly likely that either of them would be willing to assist Betsy's guest to escape from her house.

In any case what possible reason could I give them for wanting to go? 'Your mistress is making my stay unpleasant' or ' I don't care for my fellow guest.' Both feeble enough excuses.

Davis and Dora had been working here for two years, I reminded myself. Their sympathies and loyalties would be with Betsy - and Jim too, if it came to that. Davis particularly knew Jim quite well, it was unlikely that he would accept my complaint, leave alone actually help me to get away.

Surreptitiously I watched the other two, if, as seemed likely, I was going to be stuck with them for the next two days, I might as well spend my time usefully, trying to find out just what they were up to.

Suddenly a surge of excitement filled me; the thrill of the chase, I thought, and for the very first time had an inkling of the way Bill must feel as he patiently followed trails and clues. Sometimes spending weeks and months - even years - working to track down undesirable citizens in various parts of the world.

Of course I'd have to be careful not to give either Betsy or Jim any hint of my changed role. From passive annoyance at their behaviour, to actually doing some private detective work on my own account.

I thought, dear Bill, he was in for a shock when next we met, not only would his wife be sympathetic about his absences, she would be understanding too!

Quickly my napkin concealed the smile which I couldn't prevent. I glanced across the table, the conspirators were still absorbed with their own problems.

Concentrate Marion, I told myself, you might as well start work right now.

I knew that Betsy was anxious about Basil finding Jim here but there were other, deeper worries about which I could only guess. No doubt they were concentrating her mind now, she appeared to be eating automatically, not really tasting the food. It could well have been gruel or bread and water for all the pleasure she seemed to be deriving from it.

Jim was easier to understand. His main concern, I was certain, was how to get Dorothy safely away from Basil - and as quickly as possible. But, I thought, even if she does escape, Basil will undoubtedly follow her so the situation will be the same as before: Jim threatened by Basil. And probably Dorothy in danger too.

There was only one way out of it that I could see and that was to dispose of Basil.

Would Jim be prepared to do that? Smooth, ruthless - I thought him all these. But murder, that was quite different!

Studying his face as he spooned in his raspberry sorbet, I could see determination etched in every line. He would certainly do whatever he considered necessary.

I pushed the thought to the back of my mind - it was going too far. But the coldness inside me was not entirely due to Dora's exquisite dessert.

We hadn't finished our coffee when Jim pushed back his chair impatiently, "I'm going out," he said heading for the door. "I can't stay here any longer doing nothing, waiting to see if Basil appears." He almost spat out the name.

"No, of course not dear," Betsy didn't attempt to dissuade him. "But I do think we must be sensible - for all our sakes."

"Meaning?" Jim paused by the door.

"Well, if Basil is out there," Betsy waved an arm in the general direction of the garden, "it would be unwise for you to meet him, so Marion had better go out first - as a sort of scout, and then if it is safe she will return for you."

"And if it isn't safe?" I really wanted to know. Was I being sent because I was the only person readily expendable?

"Well dear, if you do see him you will give an arranged signal, I suggest you sneeze and use a white handkerchief. We who are watching will know to take care."

"What am I to do with Basil if I find him?"

"You bring him in, of course, dear." She sounded surprised that I should ask such a stupid question. "You see we will be ready for him, Jim will be upstairs."

I supposed it had been a silly question but in my mind lurked Betsy's statement of this morning; 'Basil can be dangerous when he is annoyed.'

Now he was not only annoyed, he was suspicious as well.

The front door closed behind me and immediately the cold nipped my face and stung my eyes. I huddled into my coat and pulled my wooly hat well down over my ears. I took in deep breaths of the icy air as my eyes gradually became accustomed to the dark; it was necessary to look as if I was enjoying this evening prowl, as though it was something I meant to do and not merely a reconnaissance.

I used the flashlight which Betsy had pressed into my hand and shone it around as I walked along the drive in front of the house. Basil might be anywhere out here, hiding behind a shrub perhaps. I don't know what I expected him to do if I came upon him, but it was a horribly uncomfortable feeling and the knowledge that two pairs of eyes were watching from inside the house, did very little to help.

But there didn't seem to be anyone about, I strode to and fro across the driveway for several minutes, my footsteps crunching on the frosty ground; better go out in the road and have a look, I thought. A little way up and a short distance down then, if the coast was clear, I'd go back and collect Jim.

My confidence was returning, it would be good to have a brisk walk - perhaps along the road where Jim and I had started this morning. Centuries ago it seemed, so much had happened since.

I walked up the road for a few minutes then turned and walked back, there was no one about but the lights and Christmas decorations which glowed in the houses, showed that people were there, and the festive spirit strong around us.

The contrast with Betsy's house was most noticeable; very little light showed from the windows and the wreath of holly on the front door was the only apparent concession to Christmas.

Poor Betsy. Despite her schemes for me - whatever they were, or had been - I was sure she had planned a cheerful and happy holiday, spoiled for each of us by the Hoppers.

I was a few yards down the road when, with a sickening feeling, I saw Basil coming towards me, his plump figure unmistakable under the street lamps. He seemed to bound up the hill and again I was reminded of a remark Betsy had made: 'He likes to walk' she had said. He certainly liked to keep fit too, energy emanated from him.

I stopped and with an effort forced myself to wait for him, after all, in one way it was a good thing we had met, at least now we would know where he was for a while and could act accordingly.

"I was just going back," I said as he approached. "Betsy will be pleased to see you." Like hell, I thought.

"That is not strictly truthful, Marion," he said calmly. "And anyway it was you I wanted to see so I will accompany you on your walk. We will go down to the hotel."

He had immediately taken charge and that was definitely not part of the plan. I was out of sight from the house so my handkerchief signal would flutter unseen, hidden behind the hedge which bordered the road.

"I must go and tell Betsy," I turned up the road again. "I said I'd only be a few minutes and she will worry if I am longer."

"Oh no," he barred my way. "There is no need, I will explain. In any case she is in bed, isn't she?"

"She came down to sit by the fire, I don't want her to be worried, especially as she's not feeling well."

I was trying to think quickly, this man was an absolute pest and my natural instinct was to point blank refuse his company. To tell him to go home - or to go and see Betsy. It was of no consequence to me which he chose to do.

But, and it was a big 'but', come what may I was stuck here until Monday when transport resumed after the holiday, and it would be easier if I was on reasonable terms with all these odd people. Even if the terms were theirs.

Also there was my newly acquired task of super detective. A talk with Basil might, if I was careful, prove useful to me - but not to him. It was, as they say, 'a challenge'.

"Very well," I said. "But I suppose you will allow me to sneeze first?" I think he noticed the irony in my voice.

Acting was never my strong point but I reckoned my performance of the sneeze and accompanying flourish with a white handkerchief, would have won an Oscar anywhere. All to no avail, of course, unless Betsy or Jim were peering around the gatepost, which, with Basil's eagle eyes watching, was very unlikely.

I pulled away from Basil's grip on my arm as we walked down the hill. "Thank you," I said. "But I have no intention of trying to escape."

He didn't reply, in fact he hardly spoke until we reached the hotel.

It was not the walk I had planned to take with Jim, under the clear, starry skies, but all the same I was glowing with warmth when we entered the foyer.

"You will have coffee Marion?" he asked.

I nodded, "Please."

"I will ask them to send it up to my room," he turned to a waiter nearby.

Oh no you won't, I thought. We are staying downstairs where there are people about. Where I can call for help if necessary.

Quickly I intervened, "We will have it in the lounge," I said sharply, addressing myself to the waiter.

For an instant Basil appeared nonplussed while the man looked to him for confirmation. Then, with a brief bow to me, he agreed. "Yes," he said. "In the lounge."

Round number one to you Marion, I thought and wondered how Basil would counter. He wasn't the person to allow me many points, not if he could prevent it.

"Is Dorothy going to join us?" I asked when we had settled ourselves in the red velvet chairs.

"Perhaps, there are some questions I wish to ask you first." He was unsmiling in a room full of cheerful faces.

"Marion," he was sitting on the edge of his chair, his grey eyes coldly calculating, stared into mine. "I want to know just exactly why you are here with Betsy."

"I thought we had settled that, I told you this afternoon she invited me to spend Christmas with her. For a holiday," I added.

He raised a hand impatiently brushing away my words. "There is more to it than that."

"If there is I certainly haven't been told." I was trying to keep my temper, losing it now would mean leaving without uncovering a single clue - an awful waste of the two days allocated to me for sleuthing!

He was quiet for a few moments but his eyes still focussed on my face. "You see, he said at last. "I am finding it difficult to believe you are as innocent as you appear to be."

In spite of my resolution I was beginning to boil over. "Well," I said, "I find you extremely offensive. In fact if you were not Betsy's friend I would not acknowledge you at all."

A slight smile hovered around his lips but didn't reach his eyes. "Surely even your innocence allows you to realise we are not <u>friends</u>?"

That shook me, even Basil must have seen my surprise was genuine. "Then why did you come to see her - at Christmas too?"

"Because Marion, she is double-crossing me and I have reason to believe that you also are involved."

I caught my breath and sank back in the chair. I had been looking for clues but this was a bombshell. I shook my head and looked at him, my mouth agape. "I don't believe it."

He watched me closely for several minutes then, "I really think you are telling the truth Marion, in that case you can help me."

"How?"

"You will tell me," he said slowly, "of any other visitors Betsy has while you are there. Anyone who calls and, of course, people who come to stay."

"I'm only here until after the holiday." I protested.

'When do you leave?"

"On Monday I expect." Immediately I wondered if it was wise to have told him. Would Betsy want him to know? Would Jim?

"You expect?" He picked up my hesitation.

"It's a holiday - I - Betsy - we have no special plans."

His cold gaze was still searching my face. "When did you arrive Marion?"

"On Wednesday, why?"

He appeared to be performing some mental calculations and the answer didn't look encouraging to me, his mouth set in a grim line. "I don't like being double-crossed Marion," he said. "I don't like it at all."

"And I don't like being grilled in this manner," I said briskly, pulling myself up out of the chair. Better to go before I got myself even more deeply involved. Until now I'd only been running with the hare as well as hunting with the hounds, goodness alone knew what I'd be doing with Basil also wanting my services.

Well, perhaps 'wanting' was hardly the word, demanding might be more accurate. Demanding with menaces.

I glanced across the lounge towards the foyer, a man was just going through the doorway. I could only see his back but he looked familiar; his height and thatch of unruly dark brown hair.

I tried to will him to turn around so that I could see his face.

You are imagining things again Marion, I told myself severely. It's not surprising, but take a grip on yourself. You thought you saw Bill delivering your flowers, now you see him in this hotel.

"You recognise someone?" Abruptly Basil brought me back to reality. He was standing beside his chair, following my gaze.

Wearily I turned and looked at him, I felt horribly deflated and homesick. Wanting so much the man to be Bill, to rush into his arms and feel safe, with no need to stay longer in Betsy's home. To forget all the problems and dangers of the past few days.

"I thought I recognised someone," I said. "But I was wrong."

"You haven't had your coffee Marion," Basil's voice was surprisingly gentle.

"I'd like a brandy too," I said. It had been quite an evening and the reaction was setting in; my legs felt wobbly and my hand shook as I held my cup.

Basil signalled to the waiter. "There is one more question," he said as I sipped the golden liquid. "Where do you live when you are at home?"

I felt the warmth of the brandy trickling down inside me, it was comforting and, as usual, it bolstered my courage. I thought; if I lived with these people for long I would become an alcoholic from sheer self-protection.

I gave it a moment more to work before replying, then: "Basil" I said, "where I live has absolutely nothing to do with you."

"It makes no difference," his manner was offhand. "I shall find out."

I didn't feel like walking back up the hill yet, the brandy taken on top of all the strain and excitement of the day, was making me feel drowsy. I lay back in the chair and looked at Basil over the rim of my glass.

Does he ever relax, I wondered idly, it was difficult to imagine him doing so. His dark suit was immaculate and the tie, subdued stripes of navy and grey. Smart and businesslike but hardly Christmassy or friendly.

Casually I glanced around the room, a lot of the men were wearing dinner suits and those who weren't sported pullovers in cheerful colours.

It was Basil's pent up energy which impressed me most. I felt it was an effort for him to keep still. Now he was perched on the edge of his chair, his fingers drumming on the arms, looking about him with cold, observant eyes.

When Betsy had told me he'd 'got on' she had sounded surprised about it. I wasn't surprised, I could picture him being almost too efficient, and with enough mental strength to hold down more than one important job.

Abruptly he bounced up from his chair. "Wait here Marion," he said. "I will ring for Dorothy to come down."

"I must be getting back," I made an attempt to rise from the chair. "Betsy will- - -"

He interrupted me, speaking over his shoulder as he went from the room. "Betsy will be calling for you shortly," he said.

I frowned, did he mean he was going to phone and let her know I was here? I tried to shake my addled mind into some sort of cohesion, I wouldn't make much of a detective if I went to sleep on the job.

He was away from the room for less than a minute and immediately took up his theme as if there hadn't been a pause: "You see Marion," he said. "I don't believe she _is_ ill."

I looked at him helplessly, no wonder Betsy was scared of this man. He would be like a weasel chasing a rabbit, quite relentless when once he had the scent.

But what could he mean by Betsy double-crossing him. And why on earth would she need to do so - leave alone want my, or anyone else's help in the process. And yet undoubtedly she was frightened, and Basil had been right when he'd said they were not friends. I could see that now, quite plainly.

As for Jim, he'd already been in Basil's clutches once and I'd formed the opinion he wouldn't readily risk it again. Even for Dorothy.

And then, like a flash of light, it dawned on me.

For some reason Basil had been sure that Betsy had a guest staying with her, someone whom he believed was an accomplice, helping her to do whatever it was he objected to. That was why he had come to Lucerne, presumably hoping to catch them red-handed.

He had found me there and, lacking evidence of anyone else around, not unnaturally thought I filled the bill.

I put my glass carefully on the round walnut table at my elbow. Is this what it's like being a detective, I wondered. You fret and puzzle and then suddenly a whole lot of jigsaw pieces fall into place. In my case the pieces fitted well enough but they weren't very comfortable. They put me high on the list of Basil's suspects and I had to admit that, from his point of view, it was a very reasonable deduction.

I took a deep breath, the plot had thickened with a vengeance.

It seemed much longer, but can have been only a few minutes, that we sat there, Basil and me, unspeaking, wary as cats waiting for the adversary to make the first move. He just watched and I had the uncomfortable feeling that, like Betsy, he was able to read my mind.

Well, he'd have a job working it out now I thought. I had come down here hoping to beat Basil at his own game, to discover his intentions without letting him know of my own suspicions.

You are just a beginner Marion, I told myself. He is the professional and he has won this round hands down. True, now you know he believes Betsy is double-crossing him and that you are helping her, but that doesn't really get you anywhere. You've no idea what he suspects you of doing, or how to set about finding out.

I glanced towards the door, Dorothy was just entering the room. I watched as Basil stirred in his chair, his chin jutting forward and a look of possessive pride on his face. Not affection, I noted, just satisfaction at owning something beautiful. I thought he would probably look in the same way at a bar of gold or a perfect jewel.

Heads turned to watch as Dorothy appeared to glide across the room towards us, her white dress clinging, Grecian style, and shimmering as she moved. Her dark hair was now free and hung, loosely curled around her shoulders, and she smiled at people as she passed them by.

It was in complete contrast to her usual, almost sullen indifference when she was with Basil. Not, I reminded myself, when she was with Jim.

"She is very lovely," involuntarily I echoed the words I had used to Betsy on that first evening.

Basil didn't reply, he was standing now and looking at her through narrowed eyes, his brows drawn together in a frown. "What delayed you?" His voice was quiet and sinister and suspicious all at the same time.

Dorothy put a hand on the back of his chair and her smile included him and me. "Have I been long?" she said, there was no hint of an apology.

"Yes."

"Oh well," she shrugged. "I've been making myself beautiful." She pirouetted before him. "It's Christmas," she said. "And I've decided to enjoy myself."

I watched Basil's face, poor Basil, he was suspicious of everyone, even his own wife, and now she was not being his docile, inanimate shadow, she was alert and starry-eyed.

I had seen her look like that this morning and I reckoned he had cause for his suspicions.

"I would like to dance," Dorothy was still standing, her feet tapping to a rhythm coming from within her head. "Let's go to the ballroom, you will come too Marion?" She was anxious to be moving, as though she had a secret fountain of energy bubbling inside, making it impossible for her to sit quietly and talk.

It was an interesting situation and I wondered how Basil would cope. Obviously he would not want to go and leave me - and possibly Betsy as well, since he seemed to be expecting her. And yet Dorothy had to be humoured.

In the event he compromised, "Have a drink and then we will go and dance," he said.

"Not for me," I said quickly. My mind was just beginning to clear and if Betsy did arrive in a moment I wanted all my wits to be in full working order. "But I'll stay a minute or two while you have yours," I added.

"You won't dance?" Dorothy's dark blue eyes appealed to me.

"I'd really love to but," I grimaced down at my warm clothes and sensible walking shoes, "I'm just not dressed for it."

Basil intervened, "Marion is going back to care of Betsy, you remember darling, she is not well."

"I'd forgotten," for a moment the mask came down over her face, the look of complete indifference which had seemed so much a part of her, and then it cleared again - as if she had remembered something especially nice.

"Perhaps tomorrow," she said and held out her hands in a welcoming gesture. "You will come tomorrow evening Marion, and Betsy too if she is better, and we will dance and be happy."

Her smile was difficult to resist, I didn't want to anyway. After the grim problems which had surrounded me recently, the prospect of music and laughter was like a magnet drawing me. One which even the presence of Basil and Betsy would not spoil.

I looked around me, the room was crowded and noisy with cheerful voices, but they merged and it was impossible to distinguish one from another.

I wondered; could he have come back into the room again, that man with Bill's unruly brown hair? Shaded lamps made it difficult to see into the alcoves, but I was certain I would have known if Bill had been there, a charge would have sparked between us, making an actual meeting unnecessary - however desirable.

"Are you still looking for your friend?" Basil's tone was cynical and I could almost see the quotes around the word 'friend'. I thought, he doesn't miss even a glance. If, just if, Bill was here, it would be disastrous for Basil to know.

Disastrous for me as suspect number one and even worse for Bill since there must be a very good reason for his presence, and it followed that he would not want other people to know.

Especially people like Basil.

I turned to him with what I hoped was a puzzled expression. "I'm sorry," I said. "What friend do you mean?"

"Never mind Marion," his smile was unpleasant and frankly disbelieving. I had a horrid feeling he would be searching for 'Bill' as soon as I had gone.

It wouldn't matter, of course, if he was a complete stranger, in fact it would be funny, the first red herring I had managed to put in Basil's way.

But if by chance it was my Bill I could see no way to warn him, to prepare him for Basil and his scheming. And then my second flash of insight came and it was as illuminating as the first had been.

If indeed Bill was in Lucerne, in this hotel, the chances were that he knew of my problems already. Probably better than I did.

I sat there digesting this thought and the conflicting emotions it aroused. The first - and paramount one - was of tremendous comfort, mingled with the excitement at the knowledge of Bill being near at hand.

There would be someone I could turn to, someone whose word really meant what it said. He would be able to advise me how to cope. More; he could take over and remove me altogether from the problems.

I felt almost lightheaded, and then reason took over. If, and once again it was a big 'if', Bill was nearby, he had certainly done his best to keep out of my way. Therefore it would be unreasonable to expect him suddenly to emerge and whisk me away. From years of experience I knew that his current job was vital. It had to be to keep him away from home at Christmas.

No, it was the mixture as before: trying to fathom these strange people and deal with them by myself, and hope that by doing so I might also be helping Bill.

"You look pensive Marion."

I jerked back to reality. 'Oh dear,' I thought. Have there been expressions on my face, emotions which I must not reveal? Dorothy's voice had been gentle but it would be stupid to be lulled into false security, her first loyalty would be to Jim and after that, I supposed, to Basil, neither of whom were friends of mine.

I really would have to take myself in hand, no more drifting off into daydreams, just feet firmly planted on the ground and mind fully alert all the time.

I yawned and stretched, "As a matter of fact I'm so tired I was almost asleep. You must forgive me, I'll go back to Betsy now - and an early night."

Basil stood up, "I'll see you home," he said.

"Oh no, I'm perfectly capable of walking back alone - since Betsy hasn't come for me." I couldn't resist this dig at Basil, and his discomfiture was very satisfying.

They both came to the foyer to see me off, Basil shook my hand formally. "Don't forget Marion," he said quietly. "I shall expect some information when I see you tomorrow."

There was no point in replying.

I turned to wave before opening the outer doors and was relieved to see that Dorothy was pulling Basil towards the ballroom.

Thank goodness I thought. With any luck he would be kept busy for the rest of the evening and I would know he was not following me up the hill. Or watching the house.

I took deep breaths of the chill air. Relief at being outside on my own, away from innuendo and subterfuge, for the moment blotted out any other feelings.

Stars were bright in a cloudless sky and a full moon seemed to hang, resting momentarily against a distant mountain. It was breathtakingly lovely and a perfect evening for a walk.

I thought, I'll go back and collect Jim and we will take that walk after all, a lot later than we had intended, but at least for a while there shouldn't be any need to worry about Basil.

I had turned to go up the hill when someone tapped me on my arm.

"Mrs. Hemming," the man spoke quietly.

I peered at him, strangely not scared, but trying to focus in the light from a street lamp.

Then I realised, of course, it was Davis. Davis unfamiliar without his uniform.

"I'm sorry to startle you Madam. I have the car here - and Mr. Bellamy is in the back."

I looked across to where he indicated, the Mercedes was parked in a turning off the main road. It seemed to be lurking in the shadows, ready for a quick getaway. Or a rescue mission.

I looked curiously up at Davis. "How- - -" I started.

He interrupted me. "I happened to be out and saw Mr. Hopper taking you down the hill. I knew Mrs. Harland would be worried."

"And Mr. Bellamy?"

Davis hesitated as if considering what he should tell me.

"Is he all right?" I persisted. "I mean, he isn't- - -"

"He is quite sober Madam. At the moment."

There was a pause and I had the feeling that he was wondering if he should talk to me like this. Even perhaps, how much I ought to know. Then he went on, and his tone was flat, as if he was relating a number of facts, not telling me things about people I knew.

"Mr. Bellamy came down to the hotel shortly after you. He was there while you and Mr. Hopper were talking in the lounge, and he came out when Mrs. Hopper joined you."

I don't think I whistled under my breath, though I couldn't be too sure. Jim had been taking a chance - and Dorothy too - and certainly his visit accounted for the glow which surrounded her when she came into the lounge.

As for Davis, it seemed I wasn't the only one doing detective work, but his had been far more useful than mine. I tried to see his face but he had turned away from me towards the Mercedes, so it might have been as devoid of expression as his voice had been.

"Shall I take you back Madam?"

His manner was unassuming as usual. Perhaps I'm imagining things, I thought. Getting to be as suspicious of everyone as Basil is.

After all Davis did know that Betsy was anxious about Basil, and so did Dora, so it wasn't surprising that he had followed to make sure all was well. It was good of him though.

"Yes please Davis," I said. "And thank you for keeping a watchful eye on me, I'm really most grateful."

Jim's lop-sided smile was turned on me as I sat beside him in the back of the Mercedes. In my mind the smile had become synonymous with a feeling of well-being, however transitory. Jim's well-being, not mine.

"You had a pleasant evening, little Marion?" There was a sneer in his voice.

"No," I replied evenly. "Did you?"

"Very satisfactory," he said slowly. "Not exactly what we had planned, of course, but- - -"

I broke in, "How did you know where I was - that it was safe for you to go to the hotel? I suppose that is where you have been," I added hastily. Better not to implicate Davis, there were enough problems and cross-purposes without adding him to the list.

"You were a long time doing your scouting act Marion, so I went out to see for myself, and there you were disappearing down the road with our mutual friend."

"Did Betsy know where you'd gone?"

"No. I imagine she's in quite a state by now." There was malicious pleasure in his tone.

I thought, Jim is no friend of hers any more than Basil is. But she can hardly be double-crossing him as well. And then I answered myself.

Of course she wasn't, but Jim was helping her to double-cross Basil. Why hadn't I thought of that before, it was so obvious.

Sitting beside Jim in the Mercedes I wondered how on earth Betsy had come to know such a motley collection of people, most of the time they didn't even bother to be polite to her. But undoubtedly each of them had some hold over her. She was scared of them.

Betsy hadn't ever been short of money so personal gain couldn't be the reason. In my mind that left only her husband. Had the unmentionable Mr. Harland been mixed up in some shady business in which she - perhaps unwittingly - had become involved?

More: Was he still?

I glanced at Jim; he knew. He had already said that if I wanted to know more I was to ask Betsy again, when he was present, so that he could take sadistic pleasure in her distress.

Some friend.

Lights from either side of the street slid across the interior of the car as we drove up the hill, making patterns first one way then the other. By my side Jim was as restless as the shadows and his hands clasped and unclasped.

It occurred to me that he may want to talk of his meeting with Dorothy this evening, perhaps even discuss any plans they might have made. I could learn something worthwhile from him - ever the optimist, Marion, I thought. But it was worth a try especially considering I was the only person to whom he could speak of Dorothy.

I swallowed my annoyance at his unpleasant manner and just plain rudeness.

"Do you still feel like going for a walk?" I asked. "After being shut indoors with Basil I could do with some fresh air."

He was silent for a moment, then: "Yes, all right Marion." He sounded pleased at the prospect.

"But we will tell Betsy first," I said firmly.

He put a hand over mine and laughed. I thought it was probably the lop-sided one.

Betsy was surprisingly willing for us to go out again, she smiled up at us from the armchair, her face pink from the warmth of the fire.

"It will do you good, dears, after the difficult time you have had. It is such a relief to know that Basil won't be troubling us any more this evening."

"Don't be too confident," I warned.

Betsy sighed, "I don't think one can ever be quite sure of Basil," she said.

As we walked away from the house and up the hill, I wondered why Betsy had been so happy for us to go out now, she hadn't been at all anxious as I had feared she would be.

Just relief perhaps? But sometimes she became distraught with far less cause. And what could she have meant when she said 'after the difficult time you've had'? True I had, but she'd been addressing both Jim and me, and he most certainly had not.

What did she believe he had been doing while I was with Basil, and why didn't she want to know immediately how we had both got on? She was not usually willing to postpone such reckoning.

Oh well, I thought, one problem at a time Marion, at the moment you should be concentrating on Jim and Dorothy.

Neither of us spoke until we turned off into the crisp snow on the track where we had started our walk that morning. I'd forgotten how deep the snow was and cursed my stupidity in not staying to put on my long boots before setting out. I'd been afraid Jim might change his mind if I kept him waiting. Silly, of course, he probably needed to talk to me, more even, than I wanted to listen.

I sighed, "It's been quite a day," I said.

Jim looked down at me, "This is where we paused this morning," he said. "Shall you be cold if we stop now for a few minutes? There are some things I want to tell you."

I caught my breath, was my ploy going to work? "I'm all right for a moment or two," I said calmly, it wouldn't do to appear too eager.

He was silent for what seemed an age and my toes in the sensible shoes began to turn into cubes of ice. I stood there with the snow coming up over my ankles, freezing to the spot but determined not to break the spell.

At last he spoke: "I'm wondering where to start."

"Almost anywhere would do." I tried not to let my teeth chatter too audibly.

He laughed and put an arm around my shoulders. It was comforting. "Poor little Marion" his voice was caressing. Then abruptly: "I've seen Dorothy this evening."

I nodded, "I thought you had, she was so excited when she came into the lounge."

"Do you think Basil was suspicious?" There was a sharp note of enquiry in his voice.

"Yes, but then he's suspicious of everyone - including me." I could have kicked myself for adding that.

"That is true," Jim spoke slowly. "I suppose he believes you are helping Betsy to defraud him."

"No," I said. "To double-cross him."

Jim whistled. "He does, does he?" There was another laugh, not such a pleasant one this time. "Betsy will be interested," he said.

It occurred to me that so far I had given him information but he had told me nothing I hadn't already known. I thought; if I'm going to get pneumonia something useful must come from it.

"Jim," I said plaintively. "You were going to tell me something. If I stand here much longer I shall freeze to death, so please get on with it."

"How thoughtless of me," he wrapped his other arm around me, holding me in a close embrace. I could feel the roughness of his coat on my face, and the strength of his arms, but not the warmth he was meaning to share.

"You see Marion," he said, "we can't manage without each other any longer so we are going away together."

"What about Basil?" My voice was muffled by his overcoat.

"Basil is a menace, he has to be dealt with."

"What do you mean 'dealt with'?" A coldness was coming from inside me now as well as outside.

"That is what I want to tell you. We need your help Marion."

"Oh no, not you and Dorothy as well." I was shivering and my mind felt as if it was encased in a thin layer of ice.

Jim seemed not to have heard which wasn't surprising, it had been a whispered moan, stifled as soon as it emerged.

"We go on Monday morning while you and Basil- - -" he stopped as if suddenly aware of me. "You're shivering!" he sounded surprised, then, freeing one hand he tipped my face up to his and kissed me lightly on my forehead. "Bill should take more care of you," I heard him say, the words scarcely audible through the layers of wool and my numbed mind.

"Come on." The words were clear and loud now. 'We are going back, I'll tell you the rest later. Can't have you laid up with a chill, the whole thing hinges on you."

Chapter Twelve

I sat up in bed, warm from my bath and replete from the 'light supper' Betsy had insisted I ate upstairs.

Unlike the other occasions when she'd as good as ordered me to my room, this time I had been thankful. "A warm bath and a good night's sleep" she had prescribed, taking in the situation at a glance. "We can't have you being ill dear." And the hazel eyes behind their gold-framed spectacles had looked genuinely anxious.

About my well-being? Wearily I supposed it was because, like the others she needed my help. If I was ill her schemes would be frustrated.

Well at least I was being taken good care of and that was enough for the moment. It had been an exhausting day and I was too weary even to think about it now.

I was nearly asleep when Dora came to fetch the tray. "Good night Madam," she spoke quietly. "Oh, and I have a message for you from Mr. Davis."

I turned between the pale lilac sheets and looked up at her. Dora's brown hair curled softly around her face and the hands that held my tray were capable. Betsy was lucky, I thought sleepily, not only could this girl cook superbly, she looked a really nice, reliable person too.

"Yes Dora." I said, not really wanting to know, filled only with an overwhelming desire to sleep. To forget all my problems for a while.

"Mr. Davis said it would be advisable to lock your door tonight."

I was halfway out of bed when I remembered Jim still had the key. Oh well, why worry, I thought as I snuggled down again, both Betsy and Jim needed my help - Basil too if it came to that. None of them was going to harm me. Not for a day or two anyway- - -.

I opened my eyes; the soft glow from the moon touched the bedspread and glistened on my bedside table. But there was no movement anywhere, and yet I had an uneasy feeling that there had been.

I closed my eyes again but the prickly feeling was still there and creeping through my sleepy mind came Davis' warning: The door, I hadn't locked it.

Suddenly I was wide awake. What had Davis suspected? What had he been warning me about?

I reached out my hand for the light switch and a quiet voice nearby said, "It's all right Marion."

"Jim. What on earth are you doing here?"

"I'm sorry, I didn't mean to scare you but I had to talk to you and this seemed the only chance."

The bedside light was softly shaded but for a moment it glowed like a beacon.

"I brought this," Jim grinned as he held up a newly opened bottle of Cognac. "Davis saw me take it upstairs - I don't think he approved."

So that was the reason for the warning. Relief flowed through me; Davis knew what happened this morning and through his previous experience with Jim, he knew what might happen again.

"We'll have one to start with, shall we?" Jim was already pouring a liberal measure into tooth glasses.

I sat up in bed and pulled a wrap around my shoulders. Jim's visits in the middle of the night were becoming a habit, I would have to make a point of getting back the key to my room. 'No key, no help for Jim and Dorothy' I thought firmly and it gave me a certain confidence.

But the situation was funny too and I had to grin. "I don't usually drink brandy in my room with strange men at - - - what is the time?"

"About two, and keep your voice down Woman, we don't want the whole household joining us."

We were silent for a few moments while the liquid, warm and friendly, slid down.

"Now," said Jim. "We've some serious talking to do."

I lay back against the pillows, at the moment serious talking was the last thing I wanted to do. I was tired and my mind, already fuddled with sleep, was now coping with the brandy as well. I squinted at my watch, Jim was right, it was a little after two o'clock.

I thought, what a time to be discussing life and death matters.

"Yes," I said, trying to collect my wits, and perhaps even to look intelligent. Jim seemed so very wide awake.

"Here," he said, refilling my glass. "You look half asleep, toss that down, it'll wake you up."

I wasn't so sure but, under the circumstances it might make being awake more bearable.

As it happened I felt almost lightheaded afterwards. When I looked at Jim he appeared to be hovering - not just sitting on the edge of my bed. He was talking earnestly too, but what he was saying was more than I could be bothered with.

I thought, if only it was Bill there, I needed him so badly. But it was Jim and he longed for Dorothy. It was a crazy world and we were all wasting so much precious time.

I wished Jim would keep still, I tried to focus on his face, to make some sense of what he was saying. Only now he wasn't talking, he was looking down at me and the look in his eyes reminded me of my Bill.

I felt the tears come to my eyes as I reached out my arms to him and, quite plainly, close to my ear I heard Jim say: "Bill really should take more care of you."

When next I looked at my watch it was nine o'clock and light outside. I wondered if I should go downstairs in my dressing-gown so as not to keep Betsy waiting any longer for breakfast. But, on second thought, after last evening she was probably expecting me to sleep on for a while.

I stretched luxuriously and closed my eyes again, postponing for a few more precious moments the problems and worries which surrounded me. They were still there, tucked away, my mind shut fast against them for as long as possible.

But it was no use, they had to be faced. I sighed and swung my legs over the side of the bed. As I sat there a memory stirred faintly. A hazy, disembodied Jim sitting on my bed, just as I was now.

I frowned, trying to recall the scene. We were both drinking Cognac. I was wishing Bill had been there, not Jim. I ran a hand through my rumpled hair and shook my head. "Wake up Marion, you've been dreaming." But the longing for Bill was real enough.

I padded across to the bathroom and watched as the bowl filled with swirling, warm water. Then I reached for my tooth glass, and the unmistakable aroma of brandy wafted up to me.

Sitting on the edge of the bath I tried to think clearly. Last night Davis had warned me to lock my bedroom door - but then I couldn't when Jim had the key.

Dora had taken my tray and I'd gone to sleep quickly, from sheer exhaustion. And that, as far as I could remember, was all. Apart from the dream.

But it couldn't have been a dream; I looked again at the glass. Dear Lord! What had I done?

Of course, Jim might have put the brandy in it just to scare me, to give him a hold over me, a power to insist that I help him and Dorothy - whether I agreed to or not.

But with a sickening feeling I knew that was grasping at shadows. Jim had been in my room last night and goodness knows what had happened. I certainly couldn't remember. But I could visualise his unpleasant grin when he made quite plain to me the alternative to cooperation.

"You make a rotten detective," I told myself bitterly. "You drink too much and now it seems you may have fraternised too closely with a chief suspect."

Mechanically I washed and dressed, the accumulated worries of last evening now seemed almost trivial.

Oh Bill, I thought. What an unholy mess.

And it was Christmas day.

Betsy was in the drawing-room standing beside a large Christmas tree which was sparkling with tinsel and coloured lights. Underneath the branches brightly wrapped parcels were stacked.

It was completely unexpected. "Oh Betsy!" I said involuntarily. "It really looks like Christmas."

"I'm so glad you like it dear," she smiled self-consciously. "I decorated it last evening. In a way I was pleased when you went straight to bed instead of coming in here - it made the tree more of a surprise for you this morning. Though, of course, dear," she added hastily, "I didn't wish you to be unwell. How do you feel today?"

Her concern appeared to be genuine and, as so often before, my annoyance and distrust of her seemed ungracious and out of place.

"I asked Dora to bring your breakfast in here on a tray," Betsy indicated a chair ready for me beside the fire. "I thought it would be more friendly and Christmassy than having it alone in your room."

"You are very kind," I wished that I could mean it more sincerely, that it wasn't necessary for my emotions regarding her to be constantly changing directions. She was kind, but there was always the ulterior motive - whatever it was - which meant I had to be on the defensive.

"Is Jim in his room?" I tried to make the query sound casual.

"Yes, we had breakfast together then he went upstairs to collect his presents, he will be down again in a few minutes. But we shall have to be cautious about Basil, dear, even if it is Christmas day." She didn't seem to be at all suspicious - not in the way she certainly would have been if an inkling of last night's performance had reached her.

I relaxed a few notches. Now for Jim, I thought, and there wasn't long to wait.

He was carrying a small tower of packages all wrapped in Christmassy paper, over the top of them he grinned across at me. "Ah Marion, did you sleep well and are you feeling better this morning?"

I took a mouthful of toast and marmalade and chewed it carefully, after all he didn't really expect an answer.

Jim added his parcels to those already under the tree while Betsy cooed excitedly like a child, I half expected her to clap her hands and jump up and down, then he put an arm around her waist and gave her a quick peck under the mistletoe ball. "A very happy Christmas," he said - and sounded as if he meant it.

Yet another view of their relationship, I thought. Or was it just a truce, called for Christmas day?

There weren't many packages to bring down from my room; Betsy's I had brought with me when I came to Switzerland, but, of course, I hadn't known who else to prepare for. In my few free moments I had foraged in the shops for small presents for Dora and Davis; warm gloves and a woolly scarf respectively.

Jim had been more of a problem but, I'd finally decided on something traditional and Swiss; a small cuckoo clock.

I looked now at the parcel in its shiny red wrapping and thought why on earth should I give it to him? I felt more like throwing it at him - or throwing it out of the window.

But Betsy would think it odd if I hadn't anything for Jim and I supposed the pretence would have to be kept up for a day or two longer.

I had to pause at the top of the stairs for Jim to pass, instead he stopped and reached for my small pile of gifts. "I'll carry those for you," he said. "But first I want to ask your opinion about this for Betsy."

His voice was louder than necessary under the circumstances and I peered over the banisters into the stairwell. Down below in the hall Dora was busy, I could see her shadowy figure moving around. Obviously Jim's remarks were intended for her ears.

He paused at my bedroom door before opening it. "May I?" he asked with the familiar quirk of eyebrow.

"How kind of you to ask," I put a lot of irony into my voice.

He closed the door behind us and plonked my parcels down on the bed.

"I think," he said slowly, "we need to get one or two facts clear between us."

I didn't reply, I just watched him, determined that nothing, not even an expression on my face should make the situation easy for him.

He seemed nonplussed and I guessed he had been expecting some sort of scene, a protest, anything other than silence. Instead I sat impassively on my bed and waited for him to continue, interested to see how he would cope.

After a moment he sat down beside me and put a hand over mine. "Thank you for last night," he said simply.

I hadn't expected that and it cut the ground from under my feet. Touché, I thought when I'd recovered a little.

"I don't remember," I hesitated. "I was very tired."

"And sozzled," his smile was disarming.

It was impossible to deny, all the same I made an effort at firmness, "I will have the key to my room please."

He put his hand in a pocket, "Of course, Marion. Afraid I've rather taken advantage of you." He dropped the key into the palm of my hand. "But you see," he continued. "I didn't know if you would be prepared to cooperate."

In spite of everything I couldn't restrain a wry smile. "Very appropriate," I said.

He grinned again, "I meant- - -"

"I think I know what you mean," I interposed. "At least I know some of the ways I am to cooperate, but I suspect I've a larger part in the proceedings than anyone has bothered to tell me about."

He didn't attempt to deny it, to make fatuous remarks about how wrong I was. Instead he sat, obviously deep in thought.

At last: "I can't tell you Marion, too much depends on it, but I promise I'll do my best to see you are not hurt."

"Thank you," the irony was there again.

He looked at me seriously. "You see Marion, to begin with you were just a means to an end, I didn't allow for actually liking you. For being fond of you."

His words had the feel of truth and they quite took the wind out of my sails. I had just made a discovery. I had discovered that it is impossible to feel hostile towards someone who admits to being fond of you. Especially when he is attractive and someone with whom you have had 'close relations' - even if you don't actually remember them.

And, perhaps more important, even if he is at the same time involving you in unknown, dangerous happenings.

Chapter Thirteen

Brightly coloured papers littered the floor by the time we had finished unwrapping our parcels.

Betsy's excitement was infectious and I sensed that, for her, this was the happy day she had meant it to be. Perhaps the sort of day she had longed for when she was a girl, and now was determined that nothing should spoil.

For today her problems and anxieties were pushed aside; I took my cue from her and shelved my own worries, there seemed no point in doing otherwise.

Davis and Dora joined in the festivities and Jim distributed charm equally, there was certainly no hint of a 'special relationship' with me - for which I was devoutly thankful. Indeed, a casual observer would have found no hint of subservience or suspicion between either of us.

All during the day we were alert for any sign of the Hoppers but it seemed that they too, were keeping a Christmas truce.

With mixed feelings Betsy and I prepared to join Dorothy and Basil in the evening, we were full of Christmas cheer as well as turkey and plum pudding and it seemed a pity to spoil a happy day by spending time in Basil's company.

"I think we had better, though dear," the anxious look returned to Betsy's hazel eyes as Jim held her dark mink coat for her. "We don't want to upset him too much do we?"

"No, but we are going to," I thought glancing up at Jim. His expression was enigmatic, tomorrow morning he and Dorothy were going away together and, whatever their plans, one thing was quite certain: Basil was going to be very upset indeed.

As we were leaving Betsy turned and put out her hands to Jim. "I shall always remember today," she said quietly. "Thank you for making it so happy."

For a moment he was still, then he took her hands in his own and his voice was gruff as he replied: "I shall remember it too."

They were genuine emotions, I thought as I watched them, and again I wondered how their curious relationship had come about. In the normal way Jim showed no sign of affection for Betsy - rather the reverse, and Betsy seemed to tolerate Jim because in some way he was useful - even necessary, to her.

And yet today had been so pleasant with no sign of ill feeling, surely it was not entirely an act? The spirit of Christmas personified for one day only.

Betsy hesitated again by the door as if she really was loath to go. "I don't like leaving you like this," she said to Jim. "On Christmas evening too."

In reply he opened the front door and gave her a little push towards it.

"Don't fuss Woman! I have things to do."

I intercepted the look that passed between them, it was a smile of understanding. Betsy knew - or thought she knew - just what Jim was going to be busy doing while we were away.

All the same she was uneasy as we sat warmly in the back of the Mercedes. Several times she opened and closed her small, black handbag and wiped her nose on a perfumed square of lace. "I don't like leaving him alone, dear," she murmured. "It doesn't seem friendly to be alone today."

"It is a pity," my mind was busy trying to sort out the various reasons for Betsy's reluctance to go out this evening.

Understandably she would sooner be at home sharing the rest of Christmas with Jim rather than coping with Basil. But was that uppermost in her mind now? Could she perhaps be worried that Jim might not do, to her entire satisfaction, whatever he was supposed to be doing?

Or was she afraid that, left to himself, he might 'take to the bottle' again. Three possible reasons for her anxiety, I thought, and probably all of them were true.

As we approached the hotel all my misgivings returned; Betsy had said it had been a happy day. Surprisingly happy, I thought. A small island of a day, isolated in a sea of suspicion and intrigue, with always the underlying current of fear.

Now, to complete the metaphor, we were back in the open sea, and personally I felt as if I was sitting in a small punt, exposed and without any sure means of direction.

Basil and Dorothy were waiting in the foyer, Basil shook hands formally but Dorothy hugged us in turn. "I'm so glad you could come," she said. And to Betsy, "Are you sure you are feeling better?"

"Well, not completely," Betsy was flushed and her fingers shook as she adjusted the gold frames of her spectacles. I supposed she had never seen Dorothy look anything other then morose and disinterested and was quite unprepared for this transformation and show of affection.

On that first evening when the Hoppers had arrived in Lucerne, Betsy had described Dorothy to me as 'sullen and immature', now she would have to revise her opinion.

It <u>was</u> difficult to reconcile the two Dorothys. This dynamic one with the shoulder length hair and sparkling silver gown, looked as if she had just flown down from the top of a Christmas tree, and was the complete antithesis of the dour, disinterested girl of previous occasions.

Betsy's hazel eyes wore a puzzled, almost unbelieving expression as she followed every movement Dorothy made.

I watched Basil, trying to fathom his reactions, obviously possessive pride was uppermost as he saw the envious glances from people around our little group. But he was wary too and I was sure must be suspicious of what had caused this change in her behaviour. Last evening Dorothy had said casually that it was Christmas and she was going to enjoy herself, but I wondered, did Basil suspect there might be another reason as well.

The orchestra was playing an old-fashioned waltz and I became aware that Basil was standing in front of me. He gave one of his little bows, "Shall we dance?" he said.

In silence we circled the room, Basil's dancing left a lot to be desired. He held me at arm's length and moved to a rhythm entirely his own, while his eyes kept a sharp look out on the other dancing couples as well as those seated at the various tables.

Suddenly he spoke and I felt the full bore of his gaze on my face. "I had a word with your friend," he said.

"My friend?" I was genuinely puzzled.

"Last evening," he reminded me, "you saw a man whom you thought familiar. I spoke with him."

There was no beating about the bush, just a bald statement and I knew he had felt the jerk of surprise - alarm even - which his words had caused.

He would, of course, put the most sinister meaning into my reaction and I knew I must immediately try to allay any suspicion.

"I'm sorry, I really don't remember. That woman," I grimaced, "just kicked my ankle."

"We must be more careful Marion," his tone showed that he didn't believe the kick, and his half smile was not friendly. "I was interested," he said.

"Perhaps you would care to tell me about it - and point out this man." I'd had a few seconds to collect my wits.

"Perhaps," he said. "But I don't see him at the moment."

I thought, Bill, if indeed it was Bill, was well able to take care of himself, he might even welcome an opportunity to speak to Basil Hopper.

It was me I was thinking about now. With a shock I realised I didn't want to meet Bill. Not yet. Not until I'd had time to sort myself out, to quieten my conscience after what had happened last night.

Betsy and Dorothy made an incongruous pair, over Basil's shoulder I watched them as we drew level with our table.

Obviously Betsy had not yet come to terms with Dorothy's vivacious manner and bright, enquiring eyes. She sat as though hypnotised, scarcely saying a word. Somehow she must be rescued or it would be a wretched evening for her.

"Shall we sit for a moment?" I suggested as we passed them. "I'm sure Dorothy would like to dance," I added, hoping to prise him from my side for a while.

"She will have no difficulty in finding someone to dance with." His tone was bland, there was no hint as to whether or not he approved. Another puzzle, I thought. I had expected his possessiveness to extend - no, to begin with Dorothy but it seemed that, to some extent he was prepared to share her this evening.

Another Christmas truce? Knowing Basil there had to be an ulterior motive.

As we came near to our table again I saw that Dorothy was introducing Betsy to some people seated a short distance away. A comfortable, middle-aged couple and younger man whom I assumed to be their son. He, of course, immediately whirled Dorothy off into the throng, leaving Betsy to talk with the older folk.

Very neatly done, and Basil didn't seem to mind, in fact he was smiling slightly as though in approval. As though Dorothy had followed instructions to his exact satisfaction.

I wondered if we also would join the group but instead Basil motioned me to our table.

So this is the plan, I thought. He wants to devote his time to me without the distractions of dancing and small talk. As far as he was concerned Christmas was over - if indeed it had ever begun.

As usual he didn't waste time coming to the point. "You have some information for me?" The tone was brisk and businesslike.

I answered him in the same manner. "No. It has been a pleasant day with no ill-feeling, no interruptions. It was what I came here for, to spend Christmas with Betsy. As I say, it was a happy day and Davis and Dora enjoyed it with us."

"Davis and Dora?" His brows rose above gimlet, grey eyes.

"Betsy's maid and chauffeur, you must have seen them."

"I hadn't noticed them," his voice was thoughtful.

I relaxed a little, for a moment I'd succeeded in concentrating his attention away from myself. And in a safe direction too.

"How long have they worked for her?"

I hesitated before replying, there would have been no harm in telling him 'two years' but some inner voice stopped me. After all it was entirely their business - and Betsy's - absolutely nothing to do with me. Or Basil either.

"With respect," I said coldly. "You had better ask Betsy, she employs them."

He gave a satisfied smirk and sat forward on the edge of his chair, bringing his uncompromising gaze closer. "I get nearer the truth when you are annoyed," he said. "Davis and Dora," he repeated the names slowly, mulling them reflectively around his tongue. "English names, wouldn't you think?"

"Possibly," I looked at him with distaste. The conversation was getting nowhere but if he chose to devote his energies to proving Betsy's employees guilty of wrongdoing, at least he might not be such a nuisance to me. And I didn't see how it could harm them, anyone could see at a glance they weren't the sort to be involved in gunrunning or whatever it was.

I changed the subject. "You were going to tell me about this man you spoke with," I hoped my tone sounded disinterested.

"Oh yes, your friend."

I didn't rise to this bait and after a moment he went on: "He is spending Christmas here, all by himself. I think that is strange, don't you?"

He was watching me closely as he spoke, hoping, I supposed, for a telltale exclamation or expression. I looked straight at him. "I can think of worse things than being by oneself."

He bounced back in his chair and beamed at me. "Splendid Marion! I'm beginning to like you."

His reaction was unexpected. I wondered; did he really thrive on discourteous behaviour or was this yet another Christmas exception to the rule.

"What a pity," I said, "that it cannot be mutual."

His hands gripped the arms of his chair as he sat quietly appraising me. I thought: I've gone too far, and once again the chill of fear crept down my spine. This man was already suspicious of me and after tomorrow, when he discovered that Dorothy had gone away with Jim, I would be in the direct firing line. He would blame me for not telling him that Jim was in Lucerne. For not warning him of what might happen.

A small eternity passed as we sat there with the noise and jollity, the paper hats and dancing feet around us. It seemed, like the rest of Christmas, to be going on for ever, I could scarcely believe that four days ago the only one of these strange people I had known was Betsy, and she only a dim, shadowy figure from my past. That was, of course, discounting Jim.

Now, like spectres, they were all hovering around me, threatening, and each for apparently different reasons. I felt small and alone and vulnerable.

"You know," said Basil, and the sound of his voice made me jump. "You should be on my side, we would work famously together."

I looked at him wearily. "I'm not on anyone's side, Basil," I said. "Other than my own."

138

The rest of the evening was far from being the cheerful, dancing time I had hoped for, instead it was a travesty of Christmas. Basil and I joined Betsy and her new acquaintances who appeared to be kindly, unexceptional people, but Betsy was ill at ease and Basil brusque and uncommunicative. Dorothy came several times to the table and once tried to persuade Basil to dance but he waved her away, seemingly uninterested in such frivolities though apparently content that she should participate.

Maybe, I thought, he feels she will soon be safely under control again, back in Zurich. Certainly he didn't appear to suspect danger from her direction. Only from Betsy's - and consequently from mine as well- - -. It just shows, I comforted myself, how even the Basils of this world can be fooled.

It was half past eleven when next I looked at my watch. Too soon, I wondered, to leave this disagreeable gathering? I glanced across the table, no doubt those people would be pleased to see us go, we were hardly cheerful company.

In normal circumstances I would have felt horribly embarrassed by the situation but now there were too many other serious problems on my mind to trouble about the effect we were having on two people whom I, at any rate, would never meet again.

"Betsy," I said. "It's been a long day, do you think we should go home now?"

She hesitated, looking at Basil as if for permission to leave and her eyes behind the spectacles were anxious and red, as if she had been crying.

She's thoroughly demoralised, I thought, and once again anger threatened to drive away discretion. How dare this pompous little man hold such sway over people. Over Betsy.

Basil stood up and held out his hand to her: "I had forgotten you were not well," his voice was sarcastic and his expression frankly disbelieving. "Yes, you had better go, will your chauffeur be waiting?" He turned to me. "Davis you said was his name?"

I didn't reply and he turned again to Betsy obviously pleased at the effect his behaviour was having on her. "You know," he said. "I hadn't really noticed Davis - and Dora. That must now be remedied."

Dorothy came with Basil to wave good-bye to us from the foyer, she still looked enchanting and as if she hadn't a care to bother her, in direct contrast to Basil who gave off an almost visible aura of distrust and menace.

I supposed she was living for tomorrow, 'over the moon' seemed an apt way to describe her. I hoped sincerely that she would not be back firmly on earth before another day had gone.

Jim! During the evening I'd hardly spared him a thought but now memory flooded back and in the dim interior of the car I felt my cheeks flush and a surge of excitement flow through me.

'Bill really should take more care of you.' It was as if I had just heard the words, softly spoken, close to my ear. He was right, I thought. It wasn't good for either Bill or me to be apart so much. It could well be the way even good marriages broke down.

"What do you mean by discussing Davis and Dora with that man?" Betsy's voice broke harshly across my thoughts, and she was obviously intent on venting her pent up anger and frustration on me.

I couldn't blame her, she had spent a miserable evening and Basil had done his best to goad and humiliate her in front of strangers. Somehow she had to cleanse her system - to explode the wretchedness out of herself. And I was handy.

Betsy was almost beside herself with anger. "I won't have you talking about my - my friends with that man," she raised her arm and for an instant I thought she was going to strike me, instead she banged her fist down on to the handbag in her lap and I heard the muffled tinkle of breaking glass.

Betsy didn't seem to notice. "You ask questions, you interfere, you tell lies to 'that man'. I wish you had never come!"

That struck a sympathetic chord. "Betsy," I tried hard to keep a hold on my own temper, knowing and understanding how she must be feeling.

"Betsy," I repeated as she was silent for a moment. "I only told him that we had a happy day and that Davis and Dora were with us, surely that- - -"

"You had no business to tell him anything!" She was obviously beyond reasoning with. "Well," she glared at me, waggling a forefinger in my face. "You will go home tomorrow and I will go with you. And, I'm not sorry," she added, her voice was shrill. For a brief moment a chilling stab numbed my senses before it descended and settled, like a small iceberg, deep inside me. I thought, am I at last to know the true reason for my invitation to Lucerne.

"You are not sorry for what Betsy?" My voice sounded like a croak but I tried to keep it steady.

She passed a hand across her brow and peered at me in the gloom. "I don't know, what did I say dear?" It was another of her quick changes of mood. I could have screamed and shaken her if it would have done any good, but I already knew her well enough to realise the moment was over, she wouldn't tell me any more now.

I thought bitterly; Basil said it earlier this evening: 'I get nearer the truth when you are annoyed.'

"You go in dear," said Betsy as she stepped out on to the drive. "I want to arrange with Davis about tomorrow."

Davis had his back towards the house so his face was in shadow as he held open the car door for us. I wondered what he thought about Betsy's recent scene in the Mercedes. She was his employer - seemingly a good one too - so no doubt he would consider I had been grossly at fault. That, as a guest in Betsy's house my behaviour must have been insupportable to cause her so much distress.

The snow had been swept from the steps and Dora was waiting at the door to welcome us into the warmth. I handed her my wrap and walked towards the drawing-room.

Oh well! Mentally I shrugged, what did it matter what Davis thought - or Dora either if it came to that. I was going home tomorrow and even if Betsy was going with me, we would be on my home ground and she would find the rules were different there.

And yet I was unhappy that Davis should think ill of me - that anyone should - when really the faults had been on the other side.

True, my own behaviour recently could hardly be considered blameless but, I told myself there were mitigating circumstances. I'd been plunged, willy-nilly into a series of situations. Dangerous as well as unpleasant ones, for which I had been totally unprepared. I thought wryly: That'll teach you not to accept invitations from people you hardly know, Marion.

Jim was reclining in a deep armchair by the fire, his feet propped on the tiled surround.

"You look comfortable," I was thinking of the difference between his evening and ours. "Have you been toasting there all the time?"

"No, I went out for a while," he got up and came close to me speaking quietly. "Is Betsy coming?"

"She will be a moment or two, she is talking to Davis about tomorrow - you are not the only one leaving in the morning."

"I know."

"You know?" Then it was not just an on the spot decision because Betsy was upset.

"No. Now do stop chattering Woman, I must tell you before Betsy comes. First thing tomorrow you will go and keep Basil talking - ten minutes will be long enough for us to get away. You understand?" he added as I remained silent.

"I'm not chattering."

He spared a half-smile. "At first, after you've gone, Basil will think Dorothy is out for a walk and by the time he is really suspicious, you and Betsy will have left Lucerne."

"Betsy will wonder why I've gone down to see Basil." A suspicion suddenly shot through my mind. "Surely she doesn't know about you and Dorothy?"

"No on both points. Betsy will want you to go and see him, she will pick you up from the hotel, or nearby, but don't let her know I've told you."

He moved away, back to the fireside as we heard the front door close. "Come and sit by the fire," he said in a voice loud enough to be heard from the hall.

I ignored the invitation. "Supposing I don't go and talk to Basil?" I asked slowly.

He looked at me steadily for a long moment while the firelight reflected in his eyes so that they appeared to flicker with little flames. Like dragon's eyes, I thought absent-mindedly. But no, of course, it was their noses that breathed smoke and flames, not their eyes.

Jim's voice was cold and firm when he replied. "You will go," he said. My retort had to be stifled as Betsy came into the room.

"I wonder what made me think of dragons," I mused as we sipped our bedtime hot chocolate.

Jim looked up lazily, "Dangerous creatures, dragons," he observed. "But mainly all bluff and bluster."

"It's the fire dear - the flames I mean, and your imagination, of course." Betsy put her cup down on the table and looked wistfully at the blazing logs. "I haven't thought about dragons for years." She sounded sad as if not thinking about dragons really mattered.

"You've met a few." Jim got up and stretched. "I'm going to bed," he said. "We've an early start, remember?"

The anxiety returned to Betsy's eyes. "Did you - have you- - -?" she queried.

"Yes." The reply was curt and to the point; no explanation, no feeling in his voice. Just a job done, a task completed. And it concerns me, I thought.

As soon as the door had closed behind Jim, I turned to Betsy. "You really mean we are going tomorrow?" I asked.

"Yes dear," she had assumed her air of authority. There was no Jim - or Basil - present to deflate her ego; for the moment she was in charge. I thought wryly: you are of no consequence Marion, that is, as far as tormenting Betsy goes. And I couldn't feel any regret about it, despite the significance of my position in their schemes.

"But what about my ticket? I'm booked to fly home on Wednesday as we arranged. You remember you invited me to stay for a week at least."

"Yes, but I didn't know then that the Hoppers would be in Lucerne." I nodded, that made sense.

"I must get away from them dear - and there is also- - -She stopped and her hazel eyes behind the gold frames stared at me.

"Also?" I prompted.

"Oh, it doesn't matter," she waved a hand vaguely in the air.

"I think it does matter Betsy." I tried to sound as authoritative as she was, willing her to tell me more. "I seem to have a part in this plan of yours and I'd like to know just what it is, after all you were very rude and unpleasant to me in the car." I thought, why should she get away with it? She had been horribly rude and even though one understood why, it still hurt and rankled.

"Oh dear," her face seemed to crumple. "I'm really sorry Marion. That man -- - and Dorothy! I couldn't believe it was the same girl. No wonder he's changed if she behaves like that very often."

Useless to say I thought the new Dorothy was a great improvement on the sullen, couldn't-care-less one. Betsy wouldn't agree and it would only complicate matters needlessly. I brought her back again to the point at issue.

"I still don't understand about my ticket Betsy, and will you be able to find a space on the plane tomorrow - they are sure to be fully booked after the holiday."

"No, well dear, as a matter of fact," she looked at me almost apologetically. "We are booked into a hotel for a couple of days - the Hoppers shouldn't find us there. And then we will go to England together on Wednesday - as arranged."

'As arranged' she'd said. I gaped at her. "Then you've already booked - you must have before I came." As soon as you knew my flight number, I thought.

So her coming home with me was all part of the plan, the Hoppers had just hurried it up a bit. They and something else connected with me.

Betsy pulled herself up out of the deep armchair and smoothed down her dress. The rings on her fingers glinted, contrasting with the sheen of black velvet.

She picked up her handbag and again I heard the clink of broken glass, but she ignored the sounds, perhaps didn't even hear. The officious mood was uppermost and her attention concentrated on me.

I tried again. "But why Betsy? You didn't even know you were going to like me - that you would want to go home with me."

It was, of course, the crux of the whole business and I didn't expect an explanation from her. Not a true one anyway.

She had the grace to look ashamed. "Well dear," she took off her spectacles and wiped her eyes with the little lace handkerchief. "When I'd found you again after all those years, I knew I'd want to go back with you - so as to be sure not to lose touch, you understand?"

It wasn't a good explanation and I didn't for an instant believe her, so I sat and watched, waiting for her to make another effort, just as I had done this morning, only it had been Jim then not Betsy.

She moved uncomfortably in her chair. "I didn't mean to tell you like this," she hesitated then continued in a firmer voice. "And it wouldn't have been necessary if the Hoppers hadn't come!"

Our conversation seemed to be going round in circles and with every turn I was battering myself against a metaphorical brick wall. I knew now that Betsy and Jim's carefully made plans had included her coming home with me, but for what reason I couldn't for the life of me fathom.

I sighed, right out loud, it didn't matter if she heard. She must know how fed-up I was with all the mystery and unpleasantness. "I don't have anyone to cook and care for me at home." I made a last-ditch attempt to dissuade her from accompanying me, knowing that it wouldn't succeed. "You will miss Dora."

"Oh that's all right dear," she smiled comfortably. "We will take her with us."

Wearily I shook my head. Useless, I thought to explain that our small flat just couldn't accommodate Betsy and Dora, that the kitchen was cluttered when I was alone in it. Or how Dora would manage after all the space and things she was used to.

I looked around the room, my flowers were still as I'd arranged them, casually in the vases. The only lovely, unspoiled things in the room, I thought, purposefully ignoring all Betsy's furniture and treasures.

"I shan't want to leave my flowers," I said. "They are still fresh and so beautiful."

Betsy raised her head and looked slowly at the blooms and her mouth became a hard, thin line. "Yes," she said and there was venom in her voice.

Because of my flowers? They were innocent enough, a Christmas present from my husband. Could it be because they were a present from Bill that she objected to them. Was Bill in some way connected with their schemes?

"You have to pack your things so we will go up to bed now," Betsy said, moving towards the door. "We must leave Lucerne at nine o'clock tomorrow morning but before that I want you to take a note down to Basil for me. I will meet you just round the corner - at the back of the hotel - promptly at nine."

She held the door open for me, it was my dismissal. I'd had my orders and could now retire.

My hackles were beginning to rise, I'd been told what to do and when to do it too many times since I arrived in Lucerne. Jim had said that Betsy would want me to go and see Basil in the morning but I had expected to be asked, not ordered to do so.

I walked over to the door, close to her so that it was not necessary to raise my voice.

"You expect me to cooperate with you Betsy?" I asked.

The hazel eyes opened wide in surprise, "Of course."

I shook my head, "There is no 'of course' about it."

She blinked at me, obviously unaccustomed to people querying her orders. "I don't understand what you mean Marion."

I said slowly: "I came here to stay with you for a week, if there has to be a change of plan I prefer to be consulted, not just informed." The worm has turned at last, I thought.

She put a hand on the doorpost as if to steady herself, the aggressive manner suddenly gone. "I'm sorry dear, I'm afraid I took it for granted that you would- - - would- - -"

I could see she was searching for the right word and wondered if she had rejected 'cooperate'.

"Want to help me get away from the Hoppers," she said at last, and it had the effect she no doubt wanted.

"I don't want to stay near the Hoppers either." The worm gave a final little wriggle before submitting. "But if I'm to take a message to Basil I'd like to know what it is about. Don't forget I shall be with him when he reads it."

"Yes, I understand dear," once again she was anxious to please me. "Well it is just to let him know we are going away for a while, so that he will have no excuse for staying on in Lucerne - or being unpleasant."

"But it doesn't matter if he does stay on since we won't be here," I pointed out.

"I suppose not dear, but you know what I mean. He would be angry if we just went without letting him know."

He will be angry in any case, I thought as I went upstairs, and there was something else worrying me, something of which Betsy was unaware.

I wasn't just going to hand Basil her note and then leave; I had to keep him talking while Jim and Dorothy got away. Ten minutes would be enough Jim had said, not long when one is in congenial company but a very long time to be closeted with Basil, trying not to arouse his suspicions, either about Dorothy or about Betsy's household - which at the moment included me.

So much hinged on the way that meeting went and if Betsy's note was not very diplomatically worded - I shut my mind to the probabilities, they didn't bear thinking about.

Chapter Fourteen

Jim had already gone when I came down to breakfast. "He asked me to say good-bye to you," Betsy said between mouthfuls of toast and marmalade.

I didn't know whether to be glad or sorry not to be seeing him, Betsy's related message didn't help much. 'Good bye' sounded very final, 'farewell' might have been better.

But the parting probably was final, the chances of Jim and me ever meeting again were very slight. And a good thing too, I told myself resolutely as I sipped my coffee, but all the same a sense of loss and emptiness pervaded the house, as if the whole reason for me being here had suddenly gone.

I was glad when the time came for me to be out and walking down the road towards the hotel. But I didn't feel any better out of doors, all the problems were piling in on top of me, and even walking down the road needed a superhuman effort. Part of my mind felt numb and unable to cope, almost as if I was in a state of shock.

Why don't I just go off on my own, I thought. Why submit meekly to Betsy's plans - or Jim's either. What did it matter if I couldn't get a flight home until Wednesday, there was nothing to stop me going away on my own until then.

Except, of course, that all my possessions were now packed in the Mercedes and, as it was a holiday, it wouldn't be possible to replace them. In any case, where to go? In my present state of mind I couldn't even think clearly.

"If only Jim was here it would help," I moaned to myself and then stopped in my tracks, appalled that it had been Jim I'd wanted in this time of stress, not Bill. I stood for a moment on the icy pavement. Dear God, I thought, what a holiday this has turned out to be. A few days which perhaps have wrecked my whole life.

I suppose it was willpower which persuaded me to continue on my way down to the hotel, but it seemed more as if I was an automaton. A robot programmed to toddle down the hill to see Basil. I felt no anxiety about the meeting, there was just no feeling at all.

I stood in the foyer waiting for Basil to appear in answer to the receptionist's call. Vaguely I knew I should have had a speech prepared - and several alternatives as well. My mind ought to have been clear and alert, instead the awful coldness and lethargy persisted.

Basil was a dangerous man. So what, I thought, and couldn't find it in me to bother about what he might do to Betsy. After all, but for her I wouldn't be here. Jim and Dorothy would be safely away, free from his clutches for the time being anyway.

There were a lot of people milling about and chattering, I was aware of them but entirely without interest. Someone jostled me and I didn't even bother to look round. Then I realised that something had been pressed into my hand, I glanced around quickly then, but there was no one I recognised.

A mistake, I thought, unfolding the screw of paper, but the words on it made me blink: 'Don't worry Em. We are with you.' A hasty, cryptic note scrawled unmistakably by Bill.

My first reaction was one of shocked certainty that Bill was here, that it really had been him I'd glimpsed the other evening - and with whom Basil had spoken. And then the actual written message penetrated through to my sluggish brain: 'Don't worry Em. We are with you.' Not just Bill alone but 'we'.

Who else? I looked around the foyer in case a familiar face detached itself from the crowd.

It did, and it was Basil.

"You have a note for me?" he said looking at the paper in my hand.

"No, at least- - -" I hesitated, my mind trying to deal with this new situation. There were people depending on me, Bill and others, it was obvious I had to do my bit, play my part somehow to help them. I made a determined effort to pull myself together.

"Basil," I said. "I really don't feel well, could you please get me a cup of coffee?"

"Of course," he signalled to a waiter then led me to a chair in the lounge. Gratefully I sank into it and stuffed the scrap of paper into my handbag. I smiled feebly at Basil, "I'm always writing notes to myself.

"You don't look well," he said and sat opposite watching my every expression.

The coffee was hot and black and revived me no end. As I sipped it thoughts chased through my mind and the barest outline of a plan to deal with the next ten minutes formed. There was no time to consider it carefully, to ponder the ifs and buts. It had to be acted on now and what was more, it had to be convincing.

Basil wasn't easy to fool but perhaps the mere chance of me looking - not to mention feeling - ill, might prove a godsend. Any hesitation and groping or tactless remarks could be passed off, but it was necessary that I should continue to be 'unwell' while at the same time keeping my mind acutely aware.

And all under the watchful eyes of Basil.

Well, here goes, I thought, taking a deep breath.

"Is Dorothy in?" I asked. "I should like to thank her, and you, of course, for entertaining us last evening."

It was a gamble, I was banking on him conforming to pattern; wanting to interrogate me and only calling for her later on, by which time she and Jim would be safely away.

"Did you come here just to say that Marion?" His eyes were like dark granite chips.

I put my hand up to my brow and closed my eyes for a moment, of course I knew it wasn't going to be easy but this man seemed to lack the common humanities. Most people would have been pleased and murmured 'how kind' or words to that effect. Basil looked only for the ulterior motive. Perhaps for him there always was one.

"I felt all right when I left," I murmured and even to me my voice sounded weak and strained.

Basil stood up, "I'll take you back," he said briskly, turning towards the door.

"No, not yet," I called. "I have to tell you - I mean I have a note for you from Betsy."

154

He came back and stood over me: "Is she saying 'thank you' too?" There was sardonic amusement on his face.

"You really are unpleasant, aren't you?" Almost without realising it I voiced my thoughts.

"That's better Marion", he was smiling broadly now as he sat down again. "You are improving rapidly."

"If disliking you helps I should be quite fit soon." This wasn't part of my plan, but then I always seemed to get sidetracked. Lack of concentration, Bill called it.

Oh Bill! I thought. And the others. What am I doing venting my feelings on Basil when I should be skillfully managing him, calming him, making the escape easier for Jim and Dorothy.

I looked at Basil again, he was laughing now, perhaps I wasn't doing so badly after all, perhaps if I continued to hate him enough, he would be in such a good mood he would agree to anything.

"You have a note for me." It wasn't a question and Basil was no longer laughing, his eyes were hard and seemed to bore right through me.

I fumbled in my handbag at the same time peering at my watch. Five minutes gone. Five more still to go.

Betsy had written quite a short note and it was impossible to tell from Basil's expression how he felt about it. After he had read it he sat for a moment watching me.

"So," he said eventually. "You are going this morning, you and Betsy."

"Yes."

"You are going alone?"

"Apart from Davis, yes."

"Ah, Davis. He will be driving you I suppose."

He didn't expect an answer and I didn't offer one.

After a moment: "Why are you going?" he asked.

The question surprised me. "Didn't Betsy tell you?" I indicated the note still in his hand.

"I'm asking <u>you</u>," he said.

It would have helped if I'd known what she had written in the note, I didn't want to contradict anything she had told him, to make life more difficult for her than it already was, but I had to say something to this man, and something which sounded reasonably convincing.

"We are going to stay in a hotel, I'm not sure where but Geneva was mentioned. It is to be a surprise for me, you see."

"I asked you 'why'." The tone was cold and stilted.

I frowned. "Can we not just go away without having to answer questions from you?" I knew it was a mistake as soon as I'd said it. Another of my lapses. Thank goodness M.I.5. doesn't have to depend on me, I thought.

The colour seemed to drain from Basil's face. "You are playing a dangerous game Marion." He said quietly.

Again I looked at my watch; nine o'clock, ten minutes had gone, I'd done my job. Jim and Dorothy would be away by now and Betsy would be outside in the Mercedes waiting for me.

I felt exhausted, drained of emotion. I never wanted to see Basil or Betsy again. I probably never would see Jim. I wanted to go away from them all, even from Bill - and just die quietly by myself.

But it wasn't as easy as that.

I pressed my palms on the arms of the chair, my fingers white against the soft, red plush, and forced myself upright. My legs felt unsteady and my hands were shaking.

"Basil," I said. "I'm going now, perhaps you will give Dorothy my message."

"Oh no," he smiled blandly. "You will give it to her yourself. I will ask her to come down."

I gripped the back of my chair and watched him summon a page, he spoke in fluent German, obviously unaware that I could understand, and the message he gave scared me into instant action. It was not Dorothy he asked to see but that a room be prepared for 'this lady who has been taken ill'.

The page scurried off and Basil turned to me, "She will be down in a moment," he said.

I looked around me quickly but couldn't see Bill. 'We are with you' his note had said but there didn't seem to be anyone remotely interested in me in the hotel lounge.

There was no time to lose, I had to get away before Basil discovered that Dorothy had gone. It's now or never I told myself, and the never had a horribly ominous sound.

I looked at Basil now, standing by me as if on guard. I thought, there is only one place where I can go without him.

I forced my legs into action. "I'm going to the ladies room while we are waiting," I said. "I shall be several minutes."

He looked angry and frustrated and for a few seconds I feared he was going to forcibly restrain me but there were too many people around. "I'll take your arm," he compromised.

He's afraid I shall slip away, I thought. And I was afraid that I wouldn't.

I shook off his restraining hand. "I can manage," somehow I had to.

The toilets were at the far end of the foyer, towards the back of the building. 'Please let there be a window large enough for me to climb through,' I breathed a silent prayer.

Before opening the door I glanced around, there was still no sign of Bill, but Basil had followed me and I knew that if I wasn't out again in a very few minutes he would send someone in to find me. To bring out 'the woman who has been taken ill'.

There was no one else in the room, the rows of cubicles were empty, their doors wide open - and there were no windows.

I turned quickly, my heels digging into the pink carpet, panic making me feel sick. Then I saw the door at the other end of the room, it was painted pink to match the walls and I'd missed it in my first hasty look.

Perhaps the assistant sat in there when she was on duty, perhaps- - - but there was no time to speculate.

I ran to it and turned the handle, the door opened and I shot through it and locked it behind me.

I paused then, breathing deeply. It was a little room with a pink upholstered chair and a small table with a mirror and tissues on it. And, praise be! There was a window.

I tried to peer through but the frosted glass made it impossible, there was an inner window too and I wasted precious seconds seeing how that could be removed.

After that came the outer window, feverishly I tried to open it but it was screwed firmly into place. Fixed to keep intruders out and me in, I thought savagely.

Well, I'd just have to break it, but with what? Quickly I searched the room, in a cupboard was a heavy directory, I flung it hard. It bounced off the glass.

Aloud I said: "It needs more than that Marion," and at the same instant realised there were other voices and someone was rattling the door handle.

In desperation I picked up the chair. In normal circumstances I probably wouldn't have been able to lift it, but now, holding the back I rushed at the window like a battering ram.

There was a shattering noise and pieces of glass flew past me. I pushed again with the legs of the chair, breaking off jagged bits of glass. Making a space to crawl through. Then I climbed on to the window ledge, threw my handbag out and squeezed through after it.

I was in the road alongside the hotel. Some distance away were a few people but they didn't seem to have noticed anything unusual, perhaps they were too muffled against the cold to see or hear.

I was outside, but which way to go. If anyone found me now Basil would certainly have no difficulty convincing them that I needed care and protection!

Then a familiar figure was beside me. Davis put his arm around my waist almost carrying me. "All right Madam," he said. "The car is just around the corner."

I don't think I have ever in my life been so relieved to see someone. I almost wept in the comfort of his arms, after all my experiences, he seemed such a refuge. So strong and reliable.

"Basil," I whimpered. "Mr. Hopper, he- - -"

"It's all right Madam," Davis said again, soothingly as one might to a distressed child.

"Marion, what have you been doing?" Betsy was sitting on the edge of her seat in the Mercedes, face flushed and her voice shrill.

Unsteadily I climbed in beside her. "I've been seeing Basil."

"But the blood, what happened?"

"Blood?" Stupidly I looked down at myself.

"Your legs, your arms. It's everywhere."

She exaggerated, of course, but blood there was, it was running down my legs into my shoes and my hands were sticky with it.

"I should have worn my long boots," I said foolishly, looking at the messy remains of my tights. There appeared to be a frightening number of cuts, quite deep ones too.

Now that I knew about them they began to hurt. How strange, I thought, that I just hadn't felt them before. In a woolly kind of way I was pondering this, remembering too that I'd been feeling ill. The last few minutes of my escape from the hotel had driven all sensations from me. The adrenaline I supposed. One was told that in an emergency it helped one to do incredible things. Now I knew that to be true.

A numbing blankness was creeping over me, I put out a hand to steady myself. Betsy edged away.

"I climbed through the window," I managed to say before I fainted.

Dora was with me when I awoke and she had what looked to me like a complete first-aid kit near her, on my bedside table. Feebly I tried to sit up: "What am I doing here? We were going, Mrs. Harland and I thought- - -"

"It was best that you came back here - until you have rested." Dora was severely practical; cleaning my various hurts, soothing and bandaging as though she was a nurse and had been doing it all her life.

"I've taken a course in first-aid," she smiled at me, answering my unspoken query, "but it's a long time since I had any practice."

I watched for several minutes. It was as if I was seeing someone else - not me. My mind was busy with a multitude of questions. Somehow I had to find out what was going on, after all there was still Basil, and at his most dangerous too. I shuddered at the memory of this morning, and at the prospect of what could happen at any time.

"Does it hurt a lot?" Dora was immediately concerned. "I don't think they are bad enough to need stitching but you do need a good, long rest."

"I was wondering," I said. "Is Mrs. Harland here?"

"She is downstairs 'keeping a low profile' I've been told." She smiled at me, again as if we were conspirators sharing the secret of Betsy being in hiding. "In fact," she went on, "I'm the only person officially in residence, Mr. Davis - and the car - are hidden away too.

I had to warn her but couldn't think how to express it without saying things which she wouldn't understand, and which perhaps Betsy wouldn't want her to know anyway.

Eventually: "Be careful," I said. "If you are alone and anyone - perhaps Mr. Hopper - comes. It could be dangerous."

She stood up, critically surveying her handiwork. "I'll be careful," she said. "And now you are going to have a warm drink and two sleeping pills. You'll be better when you wake up."

Without protest I did as she bade me, there was something about Dora which inspired confidence. Exuded it almost, I thought drowsily.

"Don't worry," she murmured giving the bedclothes a final pat before leaving me. I snuggled down into the lilac sheets and at that moment I really didn't worry.

Chapter Fifteen

It was dark when I awoke, I reached out and switched on the bedside lamp. Just gone seven o'clock. How long had I been asleep? Was it morning or evening?

In a befuddled way I tried to think: We'd had breakfast early and before nine o'clock I had been with Basil.

Then full memory flooded back and for a moment panic filled me. Where was Basil now? Was Betsy all right? And what about Jim and Dorothy, had they got safely away?

I lay back against the pillows letting my thoughts wander free, thinking of Jim and his Dorothy; wondering where they were and what chance they had of living happily together. Very little, I was afraid, with Basil on their heels. Unless, of course, Jim had, as he'd threatened, 'dealt' with him.

I sat up again, disturbed at the pictures in my mind. Had Jim really done something violent? Was Basil no longer a force to be reckoned with? Or was he still rampaging around, a threat and menace to us all? Either way there was little comfort to be had.

Determinedly I switched my thoughts. Bill, where was he, and how could I let him know what had happened to me? But perhaps the 'we' he had mentioned in his note, knew what was going on and had already told him.

Wearily I sighed, it was exhausting. There were so many questions, if I knew the answers to just one or two it would help, but in any case there didn't seem to be much I could do at the moment. Perhaps Dora was right and I just shouldn't worry.

Gingerly I moved my legs; not too bad, perhaps I'd go downstairs and see if anyone was about. Cautiously I swung my legs out over the bed, I could feel them now, a dull throbbing.

Anxiously I wondered if Dora had, after all, known what she was doing. Ought I to have gone to a doctor and had my injuries attended to? There would have been questions, of course. Wryly I visualised the scene:

Doctor: "How did you come by these cuts Mrs. Hemming?"

Me: "I broke a window in the hotel- - - and climbed out."

It would certainly have put the cat among the pigeons - and Basil hot on our trail.

No, undoubtedly it had been the right thing to come back here. Under the circumstances, the only thing to do. And no doubt my legs would be better soon. Just as Dora said.

When Betsy's head appeared around the door I was still sitting on the edge of my bed trying to decide if it would be better to stay where I was and wait for someone to come and see me, or to make my way downstairs and hope that the exercise wouldn't start the cuts bleeding again.

Betsy was brusque and unsmiling. "Ah Marion, you're awake."

"I was just wondering if I should come downstairs."

"You'd better not, Dora seems to think you should rest." Her tone said quite plainly that she did not approve of Dora taking charge of the situation.

I tried to soothe her. "She seemed to know what she was doing, I'm really most grateful to her."

Slowly I eased my painful legs back into bed and pulled the clothes over them. Betsy watched then pulled up a chair and settled herself on the edge of it.

"Now Marion" she said, "you must tell me exactly what happened this morning. I must know, we are in a dangerous situation."

I nodded. "You don't need to tell me that."

The hazel eyes looked coldly at me, obviously her concern was for the general situation - as it affected her. Well, it was understandable I thought.

"Basil threatened to keep me at the hotel. He told them to prepare a room for me because I was ill but- - -" I shivered as I pictured in my mind the events of the morning.

Betsy glared at me, "You weren't ill at breakfast time." There was disbelief in her voice.

"I wasn't feeling well but- - -" I nearly added 'but you wouldn't notice, you are too occupied with yourself.'

"What had you said to him?" Betsy's voice was getting shrill and quite plainly she was accusing me of bungling things. I took a deep breath, losing my temper with her now wouldn't help either of us - and we might need each other's help at any moment.

"I thanked him for last evening and gave him your note." I didn't add that I'd also been rude to him and that it had amused him. She couldn't have been expected to understand.

She sat up straight and her gaze was icy: "I consider you made a mess of our arrangements."

That was too much - "They weren't 'my' arrangements," I said. "You asked me to go and see Basil knowing that it would be dangerous for me." I emphasised that, rubbing it in hard.

She ignored it. "You see Marion," her tone was quieter now and somehow more frightening. "I don't think you are telling me the truth. They weren't only 'my' arrangements, I believe you also had a mission for Jim and <u>Dorothy.</u>" There was spite in her voice at mention of the name.

I stared at her in amazement, how could she know - or even suspect? I certainly hadn't given a hint and it wasn't likely that Jim had told her.

"I don't understand- - -" I faltered.

"No?" Her tone was disbelieving and the hazel eyes bored into me. "I find that difficult to credit."

Basil had said much the same thing to me earlier, I seem to have this effect on people, I thought as I lay back against the pillows and closed my eyes. Can one be punch-drunk with anxiety, I wondered. Reach a stage when fresh problems no longer register? For days worries had been piling in on me, physically as well as mentally dangerous worries and, for the moment, my mind refused to cope with any more.

Relax, I thought, sleep, blessed relief from all that is going on, and for a while I seemed to be in a sort of limbo where nothing really mattered, perhaps I even lost consciousness. I couldn't be sure.

Dimly but without interest, I was aware of Betsy's voice, then she was shaking me. I opened my eyes.

"I'm sorry," I said. "I think I fainted."

She stopped talking then and perhaps for the first time since she entered the room, really looked at, rather than through, me. "You really aren't well, are you?" She sounded surprised.

I closed my eyes again, I thought, if I start to laugh now I shall probably have hysterics. But all the same it was funny: Betsy was surprised that I was not feeling well! After all I had endured these past few days.

But when one thought about it, her concern was always for herself - and for the success of her and Jim's scheme. Inside myself I hugged the knowledge that Jim had also intended their scheme to succeed, but he hadn't been quite so single-minded about it.

"You must rest dear," now that she'd accepted my illness, Betsy fussed over me, pulling the bedclothes up and tucking them in. "I should have realised but everything has been such a worry."

That's true enough I thought, marvelling once again at her swift change of mood.

"I'll send Dora up to see you dear, perhaps your legs- - -" her voice trailed. Then, after a moment: "I'm so sorry dear," she went on. "You see you must be fit, we have to go away from here. If Basil finds us- - -"

"I know," I said.

Between visits from Betsy and Dora I had plenty of time that evening to think, to try and make sense of the day's happenings. The events of the morning were still frighteningly clear and I had to steel myself to consider them carefully.

Before he'd read Betsy's note, Basil had offered to bring me back home, it was only afterwards that he had attempted to keep me there. So I mused, he didn't want us to leave Lucerne, rather a drastic way of keeping us here, but he'd had to think quickly and I knew only too well that hastily made plans were not always the best.

No, that won't do Marion I thought. You are comparing Basil with yourself, but he is cold and clear thinking - you can't keep your mind on a subject for more than two minutes on end.

No, stick to the known facts: Basil wanted to prevent you from leaving the hotel. Whether or not he just wanted to keep Betsy nearby is immaterial. The question to answer is 'why'?

Right from the beginning the question was the same: Why had Betsy invited me here? I'd taken her letter at it's face value and half believed that she was lonely. I'd wanted to believe it because I also was lonely. Lonely for Bill.

Piqued because he was away so much, wanting to show him that I was needed and not entirely dependent on him. He hadn't bothered to let me know if he was coming home for Christmas, so: I would go away.

A lack of cooperation on both sides, I thought soberly.

Then suddenly I knew: I was here because Bill was interested in Betsy for whatever reason - and possibly Jim as well. And they both knew - or suspected it. It made a kind of sense but didn't tell me why Bill was interested in Betsy, if indeed he was. Or how my being here could possibly be of use to them.

Or, I told myself, easing my sore legs into a different position, why Betsy was coming to England with me.

Could she, I wondered, be the real villain, carrying me off to a remote hotel in Switzerland and then 'losing' me? Had Basil been trying to thwart her by keeping me in Lucerne?

Don't be absurd, this is not a fairy story, I reminded myself severely. True there were villains but even my imagination couldn't see Betsy in the role of 'bad fairy'.

Or a particularly good one either, I thought.

It was late when Betsy came to say goodnight, I glanced at my watch; a quarter to twelve. "You are on your way to bed?" I queried.

"Yes," she sat on the edge of the chair and folded her hands tightly together in her lap. The large, square topaz on her finger glinted golden in the light from my bedside lamp.

"Yes," she repeated. "It's been a very trying day. I can't look out of a window or switch on a light in case it casts a shadow - one that could be recognised from outside," she explained in response to my enquiring look.

"I've had to keep asking Dora if there is anyone about, it's such a nuisance."

Not much fun for Dora either, I thought.

She rose and moved restlessly about the room.

"It has been an eventful day," I said, "I'm sorry our plans had to be altered." Immediately I was annoyed with myself for feeling in any way responsible that we were still here.

"I haven't been comfortable either," I attempted to redress the balance, it wouldn't hurt her to be reminded that she wasn't the only person suffering.

She came back to the bed and stared unsmiling at me. "I've been thinking Marion," she said, "about this morning. I can't imagine why Basil wanted to keep you at the hotel. I would have thought- -"

I interrupted her, "He didn't want to keep me until he'd read your note. Just what did you say in it?" It was my turn to question severely.

She sat down again, "I told you, he had to know we were going away - it was only polite."

"It didn't please him," I assured her.

She was quiet for a moment then spoke slowly and deliberately, watching me closely all the while. "Perhaps he was annoyed because his wife had gone away with Jim," she said.

I gasped, how on earth could she have known? "I don't understand," I said.

"Are you sure Marion?"

Prevarication has never been my strong point, 'transparent' Bill called me. Now it was necessary at least to skirt around the truth, there were too many reasons why Betsy should not know that Jim had confided in me.

"I didn't see Dorothy this morning," I said, "Basil was going to ask her to come down but instead- - -" I couldn't go through all that again, and, in any case it would mean explaining about the German and once again this niggling warning in my mind stopped me.

Instead, "What makes you think- - -"I started.

"I don't think, I know."

Silently I waited for her to continue. If she really did know, it would certainly account for her anger and behaviour since then. Especially as she suspected my connivance.

The hazel eyes were watching me, trying to pierce through my defences, to read my mind. To confirm her suspicions of my guilt.

"This morning," she said at last. "Davis took me a devious way to the hotel - around side roads. At the time I supposed he had good reason so I didn't query it."

She sat there, quite still now, not agitated as she had been, as she often was when worried.

"We parked in a side street with a view of the rear of the hotel. Outside a café," she added absently.

The café, I thought, with its check tablecloths and pink shaded candles. And disturbing memories.

"Yes?" I prompted.

"We were there just in time to see Dorothy come from the back of the hotel, carrying a suitcase. She climbed into a waiting car and it was then I realised Jim was driving it."

"But perhaps- - -" I had to try and divert her, to prove that she was mistaken.

"I saw them embrace before they drove away," her voice was flat and expressionless. It seemed conclusive evidence.

Poor Betsy, I thought, it must have been a shock. I sank back onto the pillows and took a deep breath: "I don't know what to say."

"Did you have any knowledge of this Marion?" It was a direct question and the hazel eyes were unwavering.

"I told you, I didn't see Dorothy this morning - or Jim either. If you remember he'd already gone when I came down to breakfast."

"You saw them both yesterday."

Yesterday, Christmas Day. What a lot had happened since then. For a moment my mind drifted in a whirl of memories, visions crossing and recrossing. Then an inner voice roused me: Come on Marion, remember the best form of defence- - -

I pulled myself into a sitting position, wincing as my legs dragged across the sheets. "You were not aware that they knew each other?" I asked.

"Of course not."

"I don't see why 'of course', you know a lot of strange things about Jim - and Basil. Was that," I added in a flash of inspiration, "why you didn't want Jim to meet the Hoppers?"

It worked, her defences seemed to crumble before me.

"No," tears welled up into her eyes and she dabbed at them with a handkerchief, holding the gold-rimmed spectacles in her other hand.

"I've been foolish Marion," she said at last. "Very foolish." The short-sighted eyes were pink rimmed and misty now, not gimlet sharp or hypnotic.

"I trusted Jim," she said simply. "I had to, but one does not really know who to trust, does one?"

I could answer that honestly. "No," I said. "One certainly doesn't."

Dora came into my room early the following morning, I hadn't slept much during the night and was grateful for the cup of steaming hot tea which she brought. I sipped it and watched as she gave her undivided attention to dressing the cuts on my legs. She worked steadily and gently, head bent, and the dark curls glinted as they caught the lamplight. Just her presence gave me confidence and soothed my jagged nerves.

"It hardly hurts at all," I said when she'd finished and was wiping her hands on a towel.

"They are healing well but you'd better rest them again today," she advised. "By tomorrow you should be about again - providing you are careful."

"I'll try not to climb through any more broken windows," I assured her. "But I'm afraid it's going to be another difficult day for Mrs. Harland - and you."

She smiled then, as if, once again, we were fellow conspirators. "I'm going out shortly, while it's still dark and before Mrs. Harland is up, to see if I can find out any news - if Mr. Hopper is at the hotel - or anything which might set her mind at rest."

Immediately I was anxious for her: "You will be careful - if he were to see you- - -"

"I'll be all right, anyway I don't suppose he'd recognise me."

"He is suspicious of everyone." It seemed to be natural to be talking to her in this way, in any case, if she was to help, I supposed Betsy must have told her at least some of the problems.

"I think I understand the situation." Dora stood up and took my empty cup from me. Looking up at her I didn't doubt her ability to cope successfully with almost any situation.

I didn't hear her go out though my room was above the front entrance. She probably went the back way, I told myself. There must be a side or back door.

It was quiet in the house but it wasn't a peaceful stillness. In the dark I tried to sleep again, there was really nothing else to do. No lights must be switched on in case watching eyes had seen Dora leave and so would know there was someone else in Betsy's home.

Lying there I kept imagining I could hear someone moving stealthily about and though I told myself it was only the normal creaking and groaning of the house, I was still uneasy.

I thought, if only I could get up it would be better, as it was I felt like a trapped animal awaiting its executioner.

I wondered if Betsy was awake and hoped devoutly that she wasn't. Her patience was not reliable and she might prowl around and switch on lights - or even a torch.

And then another thought struck me, if Betsy was awake and feeling antagonistic towards me, there was no one in the house to whom I could call for help. It was a silly, unreasoning fear I knew, but very real - and a light tap on my door did nothing to help.

For an instant my voice froze in my throat, then Betsy spoke softly in the dark. "Are you awake Marion?"

"Oh, it's you Betsy." What a fatuous thing to say, I thought.

"I'm sorry to frighten you, I was trying to be quiet in case you were asleep."

I could hear her shuffling steps as she edged her way towards my bed and found myself cringing back tightly against the pillows, making as much space as possible between us.

She bumped into the bed and her hands felt their way along the edge. I could have screamed.

Then: "Oh, I've found the chair," she said and the rustle of clothes told me she had settled herself. I relaxed a little, for the moment the tension had eased.

"Marion," Betsy's voice came again in the dark, it sounded crisp and unsympathetic. 'Oh dear', I thought, she's in her authoritative mood. "I hope you will be able to travel tomorrow. Of course, now we shall have to go directly to England."

"Of course," I echoed. "You have the tickets."

That was a stupid thing to say, mentally I reminded myself, in your present position Marion, you should be trying to humour her. Not antagonise.

Thankfully she let the remark pass and her tone was a shade more gentle when next she spoke. "Have you seen Dora this morning?"

"Yes she came to dress my legs. She said they were healing well."

"Good." The reply was brief. Her only interest in my well-being is how it affects her, I thought uncharitably.

There was a pause and I strained my ears for any movement she might be making. I could hear her breathing and a slight rustling - as if she was folding and unfolding her hands.

Then she spoke again slowly, as if she was considering carefully every word before uttering it. "I told Dora that you had been attacked," she said. "But that you managed to escape."

I sucked in my breath, "Did you tell her who attacked me?"

"No, I just asked her to see if there was any information, any gossip about you in the town."

At six o'clock in the morning? I thought.

"But- - -" I started, then stopped. It wouldn't be wise to tell Betsy that I had spoken to Dora about Mr. Hopper, as good as telling her that he was the enemy. And, I reflected, Dora had seemed to know.

My eyes tried to pierce through the inky darkness, I'd have given a lot to see Betsy's face at the moment. She had to be lying, she must have told Dora quite a different story.

Because if she wasn't, it meant that Dora knew far more about what was going on, than ever Betsy suspected.

The daylight gradually crept through my tightly drawn curtains, but it wasn't enough to read by and my mind was too restive to allow sleep. I was impatient for Dora's return, to learn what she had discovered on her early morning reconnaissance.

Betsy had left me abruptly a few hours before, feeling her way across the room and closing the door sharply behind her. I'd been thankful when she had gone, but at the same time fearful of what she might be going to do. I couldn't imagine her making her own breakfast, but would she, from sheer boredom, draw back the curtains and look out of a window?

If Basil was outside and saw her it was more than likely that he would force an entry and physically assault her. And if he did I would almost certainly be next on the list.

It was a horribly unpleasant feeling, lying there immobile in my bed, scared of what might happen, unable to run away if danger really threatened.

It seemed an interminable wait before Dora came in with my breakfast tray. I was so relieved I could have hugged her.

She left the door ajar and set the tray down on my bedside table before drawing back the curtains. The brightness of the sunshine made me blink.

"It's a beautiful morning," she said. "Crisp and clear."

I struggled into a sitting position and reached for my bed-jacket. "How did you get on?" I asked eagerly.

She stood by the side of the bed and looked seriously down at me before answering: "I have already seen Mrs. Harland and reported to her," she said. "I expect she will tell you."

I felt as if she'd slapped me. "I'm sorry," I muttered. "I was interested."

"Of course. I will collect the tray later Madam." She closed the door behind her and a moment later I heard the murmur of voices receding down the passage. Betsy had been outside on the landing.

I sat there wondering: Had Dora expected me to understand that she could not talk freely to me at that moment, or was she trying to tell me as plainly as possible that her loyalty was with Betsy?

It was just another irritating mystery I thought crossly as I spread a pink linen napkin over the sheet and pulled the tray towards me.

I took my time over breakfast. For one thing I wasn't hungry, Dora's sharp rebuff had dispelled any appetite I might have had. I fidgeted restlessly in my bed and wished that Betsy would come and tell me what was going on. Even if it wasn't strictly the truth, it would at least give my mind something to work on. The fears about her which had troubled me in the dark hours seemed irrelevant now that the sunshine, reflecting from the snow outside, filled the room with a warming glow.

She came before I'd finished eating. She was carrying her cup of coffee and was obviously as anxious to tell me the latest news as I to hear it.

"We can relax a little dear," she said seating herself on the same chair she had used earlier, when her visit had seemed so sinister.

"Dora has discovered that Basil left for Geneva yesterday, but he may be back. It's such a nuisance that we can't get away now, while we are certain he isn't around."

"Yes," fervently I agreed.

"Well," Betsy got up and walked across the room. "At least it is safe to look out of the windows." She stood gazing towards the mountains, her figure silhouetted against the sunshine.

"Did Dora have any other news?" I ventured. "Has there been any gossip about me?"

She turned and came back to the bedside, she was wearing a red wool dress which glowed brightly in the sunlight. "It seems that Basil was very angry when he discovered you had escaped."

"I bet he was."

"And, of course, dear, I expect he will be liable for the damage you caused." For a moment a malicious little smile hovered around her lips.

I hadn't thought of that. "I'm afraid it won't make him feel any better disposed towards us," I said. I wanted to ask if there was any account of how he behaved when he discovered that Dorothy also had 'escaped', but that was something better not discussed with

Betsy. So far, I thought, she is telling me the truth - or the truth as Dora told her.

"I wonder," Betsy seemed to be thinking aloud, "if Davis has come, Dora said she had asked him to. I shall feel safer with him here."

That makes two of us, I thought.

She moved towards the door, "I think dear, I shall go out for a little walk, while it is safe to do so."

"Do you think it wise?" I cautioned. "Basil may be back at any time."

The anxiety returned to her face, "Do you really think so?"

"I most certainly do."

She walked to the window again and sighed, "I expect you are right but I feel as if I'm in a cage."

"I understand," there was a lot of pent up feeling in my answer.

"Do you dear?" She looked at me curiously, obviously seeing things from someone else's viewpoint didn't come easily to her.

Restlessly she moved about the room while I finished my breakfast, but as soon as I folded my napkin she paused. "I'll take my coffee cup down now," she said.

"Will you take the tray as well?" I hoped she wouldn't, I wanted Dora to come again by herself. I would know then for certain with whom her sympathies lay.

"Oh no," Betsy said. "Dora will take that."

I smiled my relief.

I was sure no one knocked, but a few minutes later the quiet closing of my door alerted me: Dora came swiftly towards the bed. She wasted no time. "Mrs. Harland is talking to Mr. Davis," she said. "So I will tell you as much as I can."

I didn't interrupt her, just watched as she spoke, a curious sensation filling me. Dora was telling me things she would not tell Betsy, for some reason she was on my side. Perhaps not really against Betsy, but at the same time not talking freely to her.

But what surprised me most was her inner knowledge of the problems. She knows more than I do, I thought, and added wryly, well that's not difficult.

"Mr. Hopper was very angry when they broke the door down and discovered you had escaped through the window."

'Hopping mad' flashed through my mind but I quelled it instantly.

"But when he went up to his room and found a note from D- - - from his wife," she corrected herself so quickly that if I hadn't been listening intently I would have missed the slip. Dora was outwardly so respectful, I was certainly seeing another side to her.

"Well," she went on. "Coldly furious was how it was described to me."

I wanted to ask who had described it thus but something in her manner prevented me. Instead: "What did he do?" I asked.

"He wanted to leave immediately for Geneva, but the manager was reluctant, you see a lot of damage had been done and he felt that Mr. Hopper was responsible for it. There was a scene and he struck the receptionist and was very rude, but in the end he was allowed to leave after he'd paid a sum of money on account, for the damage caused. So he may be back at any time - if not already, and we must be prepared. He will be extremely angry."

"Hopping mad." I couldn't resist it this time.

A brief smile crossed Dora's face then she was serious again. "He will be dangerous," she said. "It's a great pity you cannot go away today, by tomorrow- - -"

"Tomorrow?" I prompted, but she was not to be drawn.

Suddenly she picked up the tray, "I'm sorry they are so uncomfortable," and her voice was loud enough to carry beyond the room. "I will come and see to them again later on."

I took the hint, "Thank you," I said as Betsy's head appeared round the doorway.

Betsy settled herself comfortably by my bed, she looked more relaxed than she had since Christmas day. I thought, having Davis here has given her confidence.

"I'm trying to decide dear, what it will be best for us to do," she said, folding her hands in her lap.

"You mean about Basil and tomorrow?" I asked.

"Yes, but not necessarily in that order."

Gingerly I shifted my position as I waited for her to continue.

"Well dear," she went on, "we don't know for certain that Basil will be back. He may well be more interested in finding Dorothy."

And Jim, I thought. Then aloud: "I expect he will be back. I - we," I corrected myself quickly, "we have caused him a lot of expense."

She dismissed that airily, "He can afford it."

"There is also the question of Dorothy," I said. "He is sure to consider us responsible for her going."

"Why? That is nothing to do with us."

"It is really you know. Jim was staying here."

The colour left her cheeks and the arrogance was suddenly gone. "He doesn't know that - I made quite sure they never met."

"Yes but he suspected there was someone else staying with you and when he finds Dorothy he will know he was right. So," I said, "he will blame you - and me - for not telling him."

She took a moment or so to digest this, her eyes all the while searching my face.

"How do you know this Marion?"

"Basil told me."

"What exactly did he tell you?" Her voice was calm. Under the circumstances, too calm.

"That you are double-crossing him and that I am helping you."

Her mouth opened in astonishment. "But that's absurd."

"Yes, I am certainly not double-crossing anyone." I had a moment of unease about that, after all I had cooperated with Jim and Dorothy and now Dora was telling me things which Betsy did not know. And how did Bill fit in? He would certainly be on my side - and against Betsy.

Did all this add up to double-crossing her, or did it come under the heading of self-defence? Mentally I shrugged, it was a bit late in the day to be worrying about details like that.

Betsy sat forward in her chair glaring at me, her head on one side. Like a hen watching for a worm to appear, I thought.

"Just exactly what do you know about all this Marion?" Betsy asked. "About Jim and Dorothy. I didn't know they had ever met."

It was an accusation, she didn't say it but the unspoken words floated in the air between us, I could almost hear them: 'have you been double-crossing me Marion?' And in spite of myself I felt guilty.

Fleetingly I wondered, should I tell her? It would have been easy to relate all that I knew, truly there seemed no point in not doing so. Except that, if he had wanted Betsy to know, Jim would have told her himself, and loyalty to Jim, surely in this case, stupid loyalty, prevented me. Instead I tried a change of direction. "Betsy", I said. 'Why was Basil so certain that someone else was staying here? He said that if there wasn't anyone else, then I was to blame for something - and I would like to know what."

Betsy's cheeks flushed bright pink and her fingers fidgeted with her rings - rubies this morning, emphasising the red of her dress, and they gleamed as the sunshine touched them.

"I cannot imagine," she said at last. "He doesn't like to be crossed. He is a thoroughly objectionable man."

"A dangerously objectionable man," I corrected.

She disregarded the interruption, "I can understand his wife wanting to get away from him, what I cannot understand is why she married him in the first place." Then, after a pause she supplied the answer herself, "I suppose it was the money - and power," she said.

"It is surprising what people will do for them."

She looked at me sharply.

If the cap fits- - - I thought.

Through the day an air of uncertainty and danger hung over us making it impossible to relax or settle to read a book - or even hold more than a trifling, disjointed conversation.

Betsy prowled around the house, constantly coming in to see me and at one stage brought a Scrabble game. For a while we attempted to play but the effort of concentration was too much.

"It's no good dear," Betsy flung the tiles back into their box and clapped the board shut. She stood up and looked at me critically, "I suppose you really can't travel today?"

Wearily I closed my eyes, wondering how many more times she was going to ask the same question. "Believe me, I would be thankful if we could get away," I murmured.

"Hm." Obviously she wasn't impressed. "Well, you will have to go tomorrow."

Dora had said that tomorrow might be too late.

~~~~~~~~~

When, in the evening, Dora came to attend to my cut legs, Betsy hovered over her until the bandages were removed then, without comment, she went from the room.

Grinning, Dora glanced up at me, "That's the first time I've smiled today," she said.

I looked at the dark shadows under her eyes, "You must be quite worn out. I'm afraid I'm not helping either."

She shook her head, "If only Mrs. Harland would stay in one place for a while, especially now it is dark."

"Why especially now?"

She looked surprised at the question, "In the dark it is impossible to see who is around."

"Surely it is too cold for anyone to just stand outside watching?"

"Yes," she said soberly. "So it may be done in relays or- - -"

"Relays! You mean it is not only Basil we are thinking about?"

Dora looked up from her bandaging and focussed dark-rimmed eyes on me. "That's right," she said briefly.

It didn't enter my head to query if she was right - or even how she knew there might be several people, enemies out there somewhere, waiting and watching for us. For Betsy and me. In the atmosphere of the moment it all seemed too possible.

"Does Mrs. Harland know?" I asked.

Dora attempted a smile but it proved to be more of a grimace. "I expect so."

"Of course they may just leave it until the morning, or even until we are on our way home - to England, I mean."

I didn't reply. My rusty computer mind had noted that; for 'Basil' read 'they'. It was now busy coping with 'they might be leaving' - and I didn't dare to probe further. I had an uncomfortable suspicion that I already knew.

No sound came in through the double windows, there seemed to be no cars, no people walking. In any case, I thought, any noise would be muffled by the snow.

I would have given a lot to just peep out of the window to make sure the world was still there. Lying in my comfortable bed it was difficult to credit the sinister happenings, and yet, if I needed a reminder, my painful legs were enough, let alone the strange goings-on of the past six days.

It's like a novel, I thought. When it's all over will anyone believe it really happened? The answer was easy. Bill would believe because Bill was here. In a way the knowledge that he was near was comforting, but at the same time it made an additional anxiety.

Was he safe? Basil, I knew, was suspicious of 'my friend' as he had called Bill. But Basil suspected everyone. Now, if Dora was right, did the mysterious 'they' also have him in their sights? Was he too, in danger from 'them' - even as Betsy and I were?

And what part was Dora playing in this real-life drama? From being a shadowy figure, mostly hidden away in the kitchen, she had become the dominant member of the household. Guiding and advising, telling Betsy what she must and must not do.

I wondered; would the situation ever be restored? Would Betsy once again have authority over her household? Over Dora, as, until yesterday she surely had.

Or had she? Had there been an underlying trend to submission before that? Of course not Marion, I told myself. The trouble with extraordinary situations is that one begins to see strange motives and behaviour in the most innocent of actions and relationships.

When Betsy finally came in to say goodnight we neither of us felt that sleep was possible.

"If only we could take some tablets," Betsy moaned.

I agreed, at the moment there was nothing I wanted more than deep, mindless sleep.

"But, we can't dear, we've simply got to be alert in case- - -"

I didn't ask her to finish the sentence.

After a moment Betsy continued, "Dora said she would leave all the house lights on during the night, so at least we shall be able to see."

"Thank goodness!" I'd been dreading the long, dark hours. "Is Davis still here?" I asked.

"Yes," she looked as relieved about it as I felt. There was something very comforting and reliable about Davis' presence. The same as there was with Dora, I thought.

Absolutely nothing happened during the night. There were no alarms, no sounds to arouse and scare.

When she came in to me, Dora said that she and Davis had taken turns to sleep so that they both were a little refreshed. She was concerned about me travelling. "You shouldn't really," she said. "You will have to avoid all unnecessary movements. Try not to stand or walk more than is strictly necessary."

I nodded, gingerly putting my feet to the ground and easing my weight on to them. Immediately the throbbing started and seemed to 'pull' on my legs.

Anxiously Dora watched as she helped me to dress, choosing loose-fitting clothes and dark or nondescript colours that would not attract attention.

Critically she stood back to examine the completed picture. "You should melt into any background," she said with satisfaction. "Nobody will look at you twice."

"Praise indeed."

"Well it's what we are aiming for." She was busy tucking discarded garments into suitcases while I sat on the bed. "Put your feet up until we are ready," she advised. "Mr. Davis will carry you downstairs."

She switched off the lights and pulled back the curtains. Outside the sun was just peering over the tops of the distant mountains. From my bed I looked at the scene, letting the beauty of it seep right into me. It would have to last a long time, I thought. Perhaps forever.

Chapter Sixteen

I had supposed there must be a back entrance to the house, now Davis, unfamiliar in tweed instead of the uniform I was accustomed to, was carrying me out through the kitchen.

I saw that there was a high wall bounding the property, with trees showing over the top of it as well as on Betsy's side. Comforting protection from that quarter. It was a surprise to find that the driveway went right round the house and that, from the back the road was quite hidden.

How strange, I mused, that I had been staying here for almost six days and yet knew so little about it. But then they had been six very strange days.

A car was drawn up close to the back door, it was not the Mercedes, but a dark maroon station wagon. That makes sense, I thought, no point in calling attention to ourselves by using Betsy's normal car.

Inside, cases had been piled with cushions on which to rest my legs. Betsy was already ensconced in the back beside me, her face scarcely visible beneath a dark shawl which enveloped her. The hypnotic eyes hidden behind large, round sunglasses.

I was relieved when she greeted me, it was impossible otherwise to be sure who she was.

"It's a good disguise," I admired.

"Don't waste time talking dear," she wrapped a plain, dark rug over me. "Now your sunglasses," she said. "That's right, no one could recognise you now."

Most of the luggage had been stored in the car, now the final hand cases were put in with us and Dora climbed in beside Davis. She was wearing dark brown and had a scarf tied over her hair.

Davis' tweed coat and hat were in soft grey-blue shades. Nice, but the sort people would not look twice to see. I thought, what an uninteresting bunch we are!

As Davis started the engine Dora turned to Betsy and me. "Now you will both lie down please and keep the rugs right over you." It was an order we instantly obeyed.

We felt the movement and heard the crunch of snow under the wheels as the car slid round the house. Then there was a moment's hesitation and, beneath the rug, I heard Betsy whisper: "We're at the gate."

I held my breath. Were the sinister 'they' out there? I was half-prepared for the sound of gunshots and the splintering of glass. Braced for the searing pain of a bullet in my flesh.

But again there was nothing.

We drove quietly down the hill and it was probably about five minutes later when Dora said we could sit up, but to keep well back in our seats so that our faces could not be recognised by passers by.

We were a way out of the town, to all intents and purposes an ordinary family on an ordinary day's outing.

"The trouble is, dear," Betsy's voice belied her calm exterior. "We shall not know them, but they know who they are looking for."

"In which direction are we heading?" I asked.

Betsy hesitated, "Well dear, we thought it might be dangerous to go to the airport today- - -"

"But we are booked for Wednesday - tomorrow."

"Yes but we may not go then either. Not from Zurich anyway. Perhaps another airport, it just depends."

"What about the tickets? They are paid for!" Even in the present circumstances my careful nature disapproved the waste of money.

Through her large, coloured lens Betsy looked at me. "Our lives are of more value than the flight tickets Marion."

I thought, she is right of course, and how fortunate she has no need to worry about the cost of things. For me the fare represented hard-earned money. For her? Who could say what it meant.

Not happiness, of that I was certain.

We had been travelling more than an hour when I heard Dora say, "He's still there."

Davis nodded, "He's had plenty of opportunity to pass. There's a village in a few kilometers, I'll stop there and you get out. Pretend to be ill - car sick perhaps."

My heart missed a beat and Betsy's hands clenched in her lap, we had been beginning to relax. Too soon perhaps.

We drove on, Betsy and I pressed even closer to the back rest. Two dark blobs against the dark interior. The need to look out of the rear window was almost more than one could resist.

"I feel as if someone is boring into the back of my neck," I muttered.

Betsy did not turn her head when she replied. "I hope not dear."

There were a few shops in the village and Davis stopped as near as he could to the apothek. The road was narrow and the suspect car slowed almost to a halt behind us. Davis wound down the driving window and waved it on while Dora climbed unsteadily out onto the mound of unswept snow at the edge of the road and entered the shop.

Noisily the car revved and pulled out to pass us, I saw that it was a green Volkswagen with, apparently, just one man inside. He looked towards Davis and grinned.

Was it a friendly smile - or just to let us know he was keeping an eye on us? How awful, I thought, to have to be suspicious of people. The man was probably an ordinary, law abiding citizen, maybe on his way home to a wife and five bouncing children. No doubt he'd be astonished if he knew we considered him a dubious character.

But all the same the nagging anxiety about him persisted. When a few minutes later Dora reappeared clutching a packet of aspirins and we continued our journey, the green car had disappeared.

"Perhaps he lives locally," I suggested. "And the car is already tucked up in his garage."

"Perhaps," Davis sounded far from convinced. He handed Dora a scrap of paper. "The number," he said briefly.

Instantly in my mind I was back again, in the hotel on that frightening morning, a scrap of paper clutched in my hand, scribbled on it the words: 'we are with you'.

A lot had happened since those two, long days ago. I reached for my handbag, the scrap of paper was probably still there. Until now I'd not had a chance to look.

Just in time I remembered, Betsy was here, still one of the 'enemy'. She would be interested to see evidence of Bill's nearness.

Of his involvement in the business. And his scribbled message might frighten her into doing goodness alone knew what.

Forlornly I put down the handbag and reviewed my situation- - - out here miles away from Bill, on my way to somewhere. Cynically I reminded myself: 'We are with you,' Bill had written - but the only people with me now were Betsy and Dora and Davis.

I gazed in front of me at the brown, patterned scarf tied over Dora's head, at Davis' tweed hat with the shallow, down-turned brim. Glancing into the rear mirror I met intelligent, dark eyes looking back at me.

I thought: Davis and Dora? It was a new idea and one worth considering.

We had left the main road now and joined a motorway. As far as I could tell we were speeding south or east.

I racked my brains trying to remember where exactly in Switzerland the other airports were situated. Zurich had been the obvious one to use for Lucerne so I hadn't bothered about any others. Bern would be sure to have one and perhaps Basel, and certainly Geneva. All, if my memory served me correctly, in quite the wrong direction for us.

I wished I'd taken more trouble to explore the map before setting off for my visit to the country, but at the time it hadn't seemed necessary- - - There must be a moral there somewhere, I thought despondently.

Betsy was silent as we drove along. I tried to imagine what she must be thinking. Was she perhaps regretting her plan to invite me to spend Christmas with her? If she'd not done so, would it have made any difference for her as far as the Hoppers were concerned?

I didn't think so, after all Basil had not known I was in Lucerne, in fact he hadn't known me at all. He had come because he was certain Betsy had someone staying with her, so presumably there would have been trouble anyway. It was just my misfortune to have been there at that time.

But, of course, I reminded myself, my visit had been part of a plan carefully concocted by Betsy and Jim. And perhaps Davis and Dora too? Were they partners in the intrigue - possibly even the dominant members with Betsy working for them?

It seemed far-fetched, but at the moment she was certainly the one being told what to do. On the other hand they could be on Bill's side, watching and waiting, just as he presumably was.

I wanted to believe that, it would be such a relief to put my trust in Dora and Davis, knowing for certain they were reliable. With, not against me - or even neutral. But I daren't.

We had left the motorway and Davis pulled off onto a side road which wound steeply upwards. "This should do," he said to Dora. She had food prepared for us and we sat in the car and ate and drank.

It was not a cheerful meal, we were all edgy and, to put it mildly, the conversation was desultory. Betsy limited hers to 'please' and 'thank you'. I tried a bit harder.

"Where does this road lead?" I asked.

Davis answered, "Just to a mountain village, no one will come this way unless they need to."

"So we go back and join the same road again?"

He nodded.

"In which direction are we going?" I persisted. They looked from one to another, as though neither of them wanted to be the one to tell me.

Eventually Davis said, "We are heading south at the moment."

So I had been right.

"And our destination?" I asked.

"It depends."

On what, I wondered.

They packed up the remains of our lunch and we started off again. There was a lot of traffic and we had to wait before rejoining the main road. We all scanned the cars as they rushed by, looking for any occupant with more than a passing interest in us. But no one gave us more than a casual glance, and as soon as he could Davis turned out into the main stream. He drove at a moderate speed allowing vehicles to pass him, while Dora kept a sharp look out on those travelling in the opposite direction.

The winter sun was low now and shining directly into Davis' eyes; into the car, revealing, I supposed, not only the two readily visible in the front, but also the dark, shrouded figures on the back seat.

We were well camouflaged, I comforted myself, it will be a clever person who pierces our disguise. But a small voice inside me insisted: your enemies are clever people.

It was dusk when we stopped at a medium-sized hotel. Davis pulled off the road and followed signs pointing to a car park at the rear of the building. Without preamble he got out, "I'll go and see if they have accommodation for us all" he said.

In silence we waited for him to return, each of us looking cautiously around, searching for anyone familiar or suspicious. There were a lot of cars and a few people, either, like us, just arriving, or else leaving the hotel. It would be too cold, I reflected, to stand around and chat.

In the half-light it was impossible to see the figures clearly, "I suppose they are here for the winter sports," my voice sounded loud in the silence around us.

"Possibly," it was the first time Betsy had spoken since our picnic lunch.

When Davis returned he was trundling a wheelchair. "They had three rooms only," he announced, looking towards Betsy as if for guidance. No doubt expecting her to suggest that she and I share a room.

Instead suddenly she roused out of her seeming lethargy and her tone was crisp and decisive: "Very well, you Marion, will share with Dora."

I think we were all three taken aback. Secretly I was relieved, the prospect of sharing a room with Betsy did not appeal. In any case, I thought, it was a more sensible arrangement since Dora would need to tend my legs. Better that Betsy was not there.

Betsy did not wait for us or watch to see our reaction to her words, she removed her rug and stepped out on to the hard-packed snow. Then, pulling her shawl tightly around her shoulders, strode away into the hotel leaving Dora and Davis to deal with everything else. Including me.

The entrance lobby was warm, and welcoming, it seemed to abound with friendly people. With sympathetic glances they parted to let my wheelchair through.

"They imagine you've had a skiing accident," Dora surmised. "It's quite normal at this time of year."

"Good, so if they are questioned, no one will recall just another injured female."

We went straight to the lift and up to our room. I looked critically around at the pale, pine furniture and dark chestnut covers and curtains. It was a pleasant room, clean and impersonal. A room just for sleeping in.

Visions of the comfort I had left in Lucerne filled my mind. The soothing beauty of Betsy's old, well polished wood. My cyclamen bath and the delicate shades of the furnishings. At least that part of my stay had been enjoyable.

Later Dora brought me up my dinner. "The waiter would have done it," she said. "But I thought it better not to let him."

"The fewer people who remember us- - - ?"

"Yes," she locked the bedroom door and took the key with her when she returned to the dining room.

Left on my own, I wondered if Dora would talk when she came up to bed. If she would take the opportunity to explain to me how she and Davis fitted into the strange pattern of Betsy's life.

From Betsy's point of view they were obviously just servants. Good ones who were useful and satisfactory. No more. No less.

But I felt sure they were both with Betsy for some other purpose as well. Davis, I already knew, had been in some way connected with Jim, had seen him through at least one difficult period in the past, but that didn't explain what he was doing now.

Dora, I thought, was so competent she could fit easily into any puzzle. Or all of them!

Later, when she came up to our room, Dora looked so exhausted I hadn't the heart to question her. Tomorrow would do, I thought sleepily - or the next day.

I slept better that night, with Dora tucked into the adjoining bed my mind was more at ease. She had to be on my side, I thought. No one could be so kind and considerate to someone whom they wished ill.

I didn't need Dora's help in dressing next morning and she pronounced my legs to be 'a lot better'. They were too, I didn't feel them at all until I stood and even then the awful throbbing had diminished. "Thanks to your expert care," I said, and really meant it.

Dora smiled, "Don't stand about on them more than you must, we will borrow the wheelchair again to take you out to the car."

Dora brought my breakfast and a copy of the morning paper.

She looked anxious, "Mrs. Harland isn't down yet," she said. "She didn't join us for dinner last evening but we thought she probably wanted to be on her own so we didn't worry."

I watched her as she went towards the door. The strain of the past few days was beginning to tell, I thought.

She turned the handle, "I'll go and knock on her door, make sure she is all right."

It was half past eight when she came in again and as soon as I saw her I realised that something was wrong. She sat on the edge of her bed facing me, and without preamble broke the news. "Mrs. Harland has gone," she said.

"Gone?"

"Apparently she had a taxi call for her early this morning - before it was light."

"But- - -" for a moment I couldn't think what to say, so many thoughts chased through my mind. "Do we know where she's gone?" I managed at last.

Dora shook her head, "She asked the receptionist last evening - on the phone - to arrange for a taxi. Apparently she paid the bill for us all - and went."

It was wrong of me but my first feeling was of relief that she had paid the bill. I didn't know how Davis and Dora were fixed but I certainly didn't want to be faced with too many large hotel bills.

Unworthy of you Marion, I thought, for goodness' sake show a little consideration and anxiety.

"So presumably she's gone somewhere by herself," I said. "I mean, no one has taken her. She hasn't been kidnapped?"

"Presumably."

"She wouldn't go home again, back to Lucerne. Not at the moment," I mused.

As usual Dora was practical: "The immediate problem is what do we do."

I wasn't in any doubt. "I want to go home," I said.

She smiled at that, "I think we all feel the same. Thank goodness Mr. Davis has the air tickets. He has Mrs. Harland's as well," she added. "I don't suppose that bothers her."

Dora busied herself collecting our things together then wheeled me into the lift. It was full of people in bright ski clothes, chattering and laughing.

I had a moment of sheer envy. I'd been in Switzerland for a week and there hadn't been much laughter during that time, and certainly no hint of winter sports. I hadn't expected the sports, of course, but fun and happiness was different.

Davis was talking on the phone when we reached the foyer. Dora wheeled me a little distance away from him - too far to be able to hear what he was saying. She, I noticed, watched him intently, as if trying to gauge from his reactions, what the conversation was about.

Who could he be telephoning I wondered. Was he telling someone that Betsy had gone? Was he perhaps asking permission for <u>us</u> to go to England. And if so, from whom, and why? The familiar misgivings returned and with a horrible chill inside me, I couldn't avoid the suspicion that it might be Basil on the other end of the line.

There was a thoughtful air about Davis as he came towards us, he and Dora wheeled me outside the hotel, far enough from other people for us to talk without risk of being overheard. He didn't waste time: "I understand," he said, "that Mrs. Harland's home was destroyed by fire last night."

We were silent, Dora and I, while the shock hit us.

"She won't know," I said at last, thinking of Betsy out there somewhere in the hired car. Trying to imagine what she would do when she heard the news. "All her lovely things - how awful."

Dora's face looked pale and drawn. "We might have been there," she said.

For a long moment we were quiet, absorbing this new calamity. Had those responsible for the fire hoped that we were inside the house? Did they know we had gone and were they even now following us?

At length: "Do we have any idea where Mrs. Harland has gone?" I asked.

"No," again it was Davis who answered. "Not yet, but you have to trust us."

"Yes," I said. "I have to."

We set off around the building towards the car park, Dora pushing me, Davis carrying the suitcases. Neither of us spoke, I suspected that, like me, they were too anxious for words.

As we rounded the corner I located the maroon station wagon but didn't register the car next door until a sharp intake of breath from Dora alerted me.

"Do you see?" she said quietly to Davis.

Without pausing he nodded.

I looked again, there was a green Volkswagen parked next to our car.

"Is it?" I queried.

"Yes."

There was no need to comment further, even I could tell that the driver was not the ordinary, inoffensive citizen I'd suggested when we'd last seen him, yesterday, back in that village. It was all too obvious that he was keeping an eye on us and, what was more, he didn't mind us knowing.

He was standing now outside his car, stamping his feet and waving his arms about. Doing his exercises to keep the circulation moving while he waited for us. He smiled ingratiatingly as we approached. "A lovely morning," his voice was deep and guttural.

"One of Hopper's local recruits," I heard Davis murmur, and in that instant my world changed.

They were the most heartening words I'd heard for days. A weight slipped from my shoulders, the sun shone brighter and despite all my anxieties, it was a lovely morning!

Because, if a confederate of Basil's was working against us, it followed that Dora and Davis were on my side.

I felt like singing, or shouting at the top of my voice. At last here were people I could be certain of, could rely upon. And we were on our way home too.

The relief was so great I found myself beaming on the energetic man by the Volkswagen, our shadow.

Well, he'd earned a smile I thought, trying to compose my features into a more serious shape. After all if it hadn't been for him I couldn't possibly have been sure who were my real friends.

We sat in the car and Davis pulled a map from the glove pocket, ostensibly showing Dora the road we were to take, but my keyed-up mind wondered if he was merely waiting to see what the Volkswagen man would do. If we hesitated before leaving would he do the same?

As it happened, he came across and tapped on Dora's window, surprised, she wound it down and he poked his head through.

"You are wondering which direction to take?" His eyes peered around the interior of the car, while his smile embraced the three of us. He tugged at a glove and pointed a square-topped finger at the map on Dora's lap: "Not that way, it is closed. The snow," he said.

Three pairs of eyes looked suspiciously at him. He shrugged leather clad shoulders and grinned widely. "You would waste your time - and petrol."

"And yours," Davis murmured under his breath.

Dora smiled up at him. "You are kind but we haven't decided- -"

He interrupted her, a sudden anxiety raising the tone of his voice. "Your friend! You travel without her?"

We all stared at him and I suspected that my reaction was the same as theirs. He obviously didn't know about Betsy leaving early and if he was unaware of that, perhaps we could convince him that we were not the people he had been commanded to shadow.

"Our friend?" Davis' eyebrows lifted enquiringly.

"The lady."

"I think you are mistaken." It was Dora this time, her voice gentle, expression serious. "We are all three here," she waved a gloved hand vaguely in my direction. "We were wondering which road to take - for the scenery."

A frown now replaced the smile as he backed away and, without pausing, strode towards the hotel.

Dora called after him: "Thank you for your help, we will avoid that road." But it was doubtful if he heard.

Davis started the engine, "It is only a temporary respite," he said. "He will be back."

"Not a very good shadow," Dora commented as we gathered speed along the road.

"We didn't lose him yesterday-- even though we didn't see him again until this morning."

"He's not alone," Davis said. "He's getting fresh instructions from someone at this moment."

We were silent while each of us kept a sharp look out all around.

At length: "I wonder if he was right about the road being blocked." Dora sounded thoughtful.

"Could well be, we'd better not chance it. But it means we have a longer journey - and a time limit."

"We have to be somewhere on time?" I queried.

"Zurich," said Davis briefly. "We must try to catch that plane."

"But won't they be expecting us to do just that?" To me it seemed obvious that 'they' would.

"Maybe. We shall just have to chance it - and be extra careful."

We were retracing the route we had travelled yesterday, but faster this time, no looking around and enjoying the scenery. We had a plane to catch.

Thoughts tumbled through my mind as I sat there, like the other two, watching every car that passed, and even more those that followed behind us for any distance and appeared to speed when we did and slow down every time Davis eased his foot from the accelerator pedal.

I thought they all seemed harmless enough but how could one be certain? The green Volkswagen, the only one we could be sure of, was nowhere to be seen.

I wondered where Bill was at this moment, did he know we were on our way to Zurich? Was it possible he would be there to greet us?

My heart gave a lurch of excitement at the prospect, though I knew it wasn't very likely.

And Betsy, did she know about the fire? And Jim and Dorothy, were they safe? And would I ever see either of them again, ever really know why I had been invited to spend Christmas in Lucerne?

Somewhere along the road we pulled off onto a byroad which, like the one where we had eaten our lunch yesterday, wound steeply upwards. Dora fished about in our cases for a quick change of outer clothes. "They will be looking for people wearing these things," she explained, busy stowing away the discarded garments. "We might as well make it more difficult for them."

Now she was wearing a scarlet woolen hat and scarf which cheered up the dark brown coat, while white snow-boots replaced the black ones she had worn before.

"You look terrific," I said, pulling pale blue slacks over my bandaged legs and easing myself into my short black fur coat. 'Pure rabbit' was Bill's description of it, though in truth it was a good synthetic.

I thought Bill would recognise it, but then it wasn't Bill we were bothered about.

I looked out of the car window at the figure plodding through the snow a short distance up the road. "How about Davis?" I asked.

"Mr. Davis will just have to take his hat off - and wear spectacles."

"Pity it takes so long to grow a beard," I said.

She chuckled.

In ten minutes we were off again, hurrying yet watchful all the while. We ate chocolate to stave off our hunger as there wasn't time to stop for a meal. At half past one we were speeding along the motorway, nearing Zurich. "Thank goodness the airport is this side of the city," Dora breathed.

Davis paused for us to alight and we took the luggage to be processed while he parked the car. "What will happen to it?" I asked.

Dora was trundling our luggage and at the same time studying faces of the people strolling about, the way they always seem to in the limbo of a large air terminal.

"The car?" she sounded abstracted. "Oh it will be collected."

By whom, and when, I wanted to ask, but didn't.

Somewhere some people were busy organising the car and our movements. I thought: we are like puppets in a strange, manipulated world. Strange to me but not, I supposed, to Bill. Or to Dora and Davis.

We hadn't far to walk but I could feel my legs protesting at every step. I was getting slower and slower. Come on! I chivvied myself, trying vainly to keep pace with Dora. It's dangerous to lag behind. But I couldn't hurry.

The ache was becoming intolerable when I spied an empty seat and sank gratefully into it. Dora was now at a desk, busy with our suitcases and tickets, she glanced around and gave me a quick wave.

I stretched out my legs in front of me, seeking relief from the pain. Was it two days or three, I wondered, since I had last walked. Since that dreadful morning with Basil at the hotel. I sighed, no matter how many, it was obvious I wasn't going to be very active for at least several more.

I looked around, there was no one I could recognise, or who seemed at all interested in me. I thought: Bill where are you? I hadn't really expected him to be here, it was just a forlorn hope. In spite of myself Jim's words sprang into my mind, 'Bill really should take more care of you.'

A group of young folk in well-worn jeans were approaching, all swinging colourful, large plastic shoulder bags as they joked together. The youth nearest me was gyrating his bag wildly to the peril of all in his vicinity. Warily I drew in my legs, but not enough, and the bag caught them a glancing blow.

It wasn't hard and normally, I suppose the soft plastic would have caused only a slight bruise, but my sore, vulnerable limbs were not normal and I couldn't prevent the cry of pain which escaped my lips. The youth turned a surprised stare in my direction as he continued on his way.

I shut my eyes and in the closed world of my mind dealt with the pain and the fear that the blow, slight as it had been, might have opened some of the wounds, and restarted the bleeding.

A moment later Dora tapped on my shoulder, rousing me urgently. "I know it's difficult," she spoke breathlessly into my ear. "But can you hurry, I've just seen Mr. Hopper."

Sheer panic gripped me at the prospect of meeting Basil, I could feel my face becoming drawn and my eyes staring. I wanted to run somewhere, anywhere, so as not to see him. But I couldn't. I thought wildly; I can't run.

Dora fished a scarf from her handbag, "Here," she said. "Tie this over your head, cover your hair completely - he would recognise that." She pushed escaping strands of my pale hair under the scarf.

I stood up and she took my arm, hustling me along. I thought; she didn't see the boy with the bag, she doesn't know he knocked into me. And this was certainly not the time to tell her.

I had already discovered that fear can help one perform feats which normally one would not even attempt. Now for the second time, fear of Basil drove me on, forcing my legs into action they would have been better without.

We'd gone about twenty yards when I glanced down and saw the dark stain seeping through my pale blue slacks. Involuntarily I halted, pulling on Dora's supporting arm, her eyes narrowed as she followed my gaze. Then without a word she steered me towards the nearest ladies toilet. She found me a chair and placed it at the far end of the room, away from the main flow of people.

"You will be safe here," she said. "While I go and get some fresh bandages and a wheelchair."

I put my handbag on the floor beside me, a 'ladies only' room seemed to be my refuge from Basil, I reflected as I sat there, trying not to look at the spreading stain, trying to still my mind. Telling myself that somehow Dora and Davis would manage to get us safely on to the plane - and home.

Women of all ages and nationalities came and went, and then suddenly Betsy was standing before me. I hadn't seen her enter the room - or emerge from one of the cubicles, and it took me a moment or so to register her presence.

For the time being I'd forgotten her, there had been so much else on my mind. But now I remembered; she had always intended catching this plane. We had been going to travel together. She was coming home with me.

Frowning I looked up at her. "Where- - -?" I started.

"I've been waiting for you," her voice was coldly impersonal.

"Why did you go?"

"I don't care to be ordered about."

I could well believe that.

She looked around. "Where has Dora gone?"

"She is getting bandages and a wheel chair."

For the first time she really looked at me and noticed the dark stain on my slacks. "Oh dear" her hand gripped the back of my chair and I recalled her reaction to the sight of blood when I'd first been injured. When I'd got into the Mercedes she had been shocked at my state and edged away from me.

Now she looked pale and moved around to the other side of my chair, away from the ever deepening stain.

"Dora will deal with it," she murmured as her gloves dropped from her nervously shaking hands.

Automatically I leant to retrieve them for her but she gave me a none too gentle push. "No," she said gruffly. "I will get them, you sit still."

It was a small, graceless action and I turned my head away, biting back the remark it merited. Useless to expect reasonable behaviour from Betsy.

After a moment, "Are you coming on the plane?" I asked.

"Of course," her face was flushed from stooping and her fingers twitched as she smoothed her gloves over them. "I mustn't drop them again," she said, smiling at me for the first time.

It was as though now she had retrieved her gloves, the tension was somehow released and she could relax.

Chapter Seventeen

From the far end of the room Betsy waited while Dora wound fresh bandages round my open wounds, stemming the flow of blood. "You must have these cuts stitched when you get home," she advised.

I'd been thinking the same thing. "I suppose they should have been done immediately," I said ruefully.

She nodded and at once changed the subject to "Did you tell Mrs. Harland that Basil is here?"

She called him 'Basil', always before he'd been Mr. Hopper whenever she referred to him. My memory shot back to the morning a few days ago when she'd almost called Dorothy by her christian name - just correcting herself in time.

Well, I thought, what did it matter, it was part of the mystery of Davis and Dora, of the whole caboodle. Perhaps one day I'd know the answer to it all.

I shook my head in reply to her question.

"Good, if he does accost her at least she will be genuinely surprised."

"Accost her? You think he might?"

"I don't mean knock her on the head," she grinned up at me.

I said slowly, "So it is all right for Basil to know that she is travelling, but not that we are?"

Again she nodded. "It will be better if we can keep him guessing - wondering where you are." She stood up and smoothed down her coat. "Now I must try to make sure Mrs. Harland doesn't tell him."

'Mrs. Harland?" I wondered, or does she think of her as 'Betsy'.

I watched them across the room and it was obvious that Betsy was not too happy with the suggested plan. But, after all, I told myself, she had chosen to be away from us today, leaving the hotel early this morning so as to be certain of being on her own. It didn't seem too much to ask that now she should continue to ignore us. To pretend to be ignorant of our whereabouts.

She might even prefer it, but only, I guessed, if the idea came from her. It was obeying Dora that she would object to.

We set forth in convoy, Betsy leading by a few seconds, long enough to engage the attention of Basil - or whoever might be watching. Though, with the big gun around, I thought that none of his minions would be there. More likely they would be at the other end of a telephone or even cable. Waiting to be briefed, to deal with Betsy and me at some other time.

From my wheelchair with a rug covering my knees and Dora shielding me from one side while Davis propelled the chair along, the whole thing seemed unreal rather than frightening. I thought; there can't really be any danger. And then I saw the stocky, purposeful figure of Basil detach itself from the throng and move towards Betsy.

Automatically I gripped the arms of the chair tightly, as though to prevent someone physically wrenching me from it. My heart began to pound as if it would choke me.

"Take no notice of him - look away." It was an order from Dora.

Confident that he would not recognise them, she and Davis progressed steadily towards the customs point. Now Basil was confronting Betsy. He was standing, feet slightly astride, a three-quarter length, military style camel coat tightly buttoned over his dark grey suit.

I closed my eyes. Now he would be asking her where she was going. Where I was. Would she tell him? Would she be frightened into revealing my presence?

Ought we to have warned her? She was scared of Basil, in my mind I again heard her telling me 'Basil can be dangerous when he is angry'.

We deviated a little so as to pass behind Basil, I kept my head turned away, resisting a strong temptation to see the expression on Betsy's face.

We reached the barrier and Davis produced our passports, there was an agonising moment while the official examined them carefully. My ears were stretched to listen for a shout from behind us; for an arm jerking me from my chair.

I glanced up at Dora and marvelled at her composure, she was looking back, pretending to wave to someone in the crowd. Making sure that Betsy was all right.

"She's coming," she whispered as we moved forward, through to the customs and checking area - out of sight of Basil.

In the plane Davis occupied the seat next to Betsy, the one which originally had been intended for me, while Dora and I were across the gangway, me by the window, she in the outer of the three seats. In between us a swarthy, powerfully built man was busy with official looking papers. He took no notice of either of us.

Looking across at Betsy I could see that she was ignoring Davis, it was as if they had never met. I wondered: was she merely obeying orders or was she behaving that way from preference. There was time on the flight for a lot of thinking. Now we were safely away from Switzerland but it was by no means sure that we were safe from Basil.

And I still didn't know why Betsy had insisted on coming to England and with me. That, as I saw it, was the axis which supported the whole mystery of my visit to Switzerland. We were going home so presumably before long, part, at least, of the mystery would be revealed. The thought should have comforted me but it didn't. Now there were so many other problems, all of them it seemed inextricably mixed and all of them unpleasant.

I shifted my position slightly and looked through the little window down at the clouds, puffy and white, like thick layers of froth in a huge, bright blue bowl.

The clouds looked fluffy and harmless and yet flying through them could be bumpy and uncomfortable. I thought; rather like most peoples' lives, viewed from a distance they seemed smooth and uneventful, but few people escaped without bruises and scars.

I tried to fix my mind on a magazine but couldn't concentrate. Dora was lying back with her eyes closed, seemingly relaxed, and across the gangway Davis was apparently immersed in his newspaper. Betsy's head was turned towards the window so there was no clue as to how she felt.

I would have liked to ask her what Basil had said at the airport. Had he asked questions? Had he threatened her? Then suddenly I remembered about the fire. Betsy still wouldn't know about that.

Or she would have been bound to mention it - couldn't possibly have taken the knowledge calmly. All her beautiful belongings destroyed, she would be dreadfully upset.

So Basil hadn't told her that, but I felt sure there would have been searching questions, asked in the coldly ruthless manner I knew so well. Where was she going? What did she know about Jim and Dorothy? Where was I?

No, I thought dully, we'd left Switzerland but we hadn't lost him. It was just a matter of time before the menace that was Basil reappeared in my life.

It seemed no time at all before the advice to 'fasten our seat belts' came and we began the gradual descent to ground level. I thought; now the anxiety begins again, the constant alert, watching, searching for something, someone.

Our companion for the journey, the large man with his official papers was one of the first to leave the plane, he didn't even spare a glance for his fellow travellers.

Dora and I waited while the other passengers filed out, examining them one by one as they passed down the aisle. None of them looked particularly suspicious. Or else they all did, I thought wryly.

Betsy had gone, clutching her handbag and looking straight ahead of her. I wondered what she would do when we were all through customs, would she wait for us or go off on her own as she had this morning, back in Switzerland.

I found myself hoping that she would just disappear, that we would never meet again. That all would be as it had been before that fateful invitation arrived from Lucerne.

Of course, it couldn't be - ever again, I knew that. One couldn't just wipe out all that had happened, however much one wanted to.

And it was certain that Basil wouldn't want to, he presumably had too much at stake to just forget us.

We hadn't bought anything on the plane, no spirits, no perfume, we had nothing to declare so I was surprised when Dora steered me towards the customs men. "They will want to look," she said briefly.

They did. They examined my two suitcases minutely, even splitting the linings. I looked appealingly at Dora but she was concentrating on the customs officer, watching his every movement closely as though she, like him, was afraid of missing something.

"But you packed them yourself," I protested, thinking back to that morning in Lucerne when she had chosen the drabbest, least noticeable clothes for me to wear, stowing all the rest away in the cases. "You must know what is in them."

She didn't reply.

I watched helplessly as my things were tumbled on the bench, it was humiliating and quite unnecessary, why did Dora allow it? I was getting really angry, she had brought me here deliberately, she had known this was going to happen.

It seemed that once again I had chosen the wrong friends. If indeed I had any at all.

"Now your handbag Madam," the order was curt.

I passed it over to him, there was no alternative. And good luck to you! I thought. At least I knew what was in my own handbag, they wouldn't find whatever they were looking for there.

Again my things were spilled out: lipstick, comb, wallet. And then a small package which I didn't recognise. The officer pounced on it, and prodded it cautiously. Then he fixed me with a coldly impersonal gaze.

"What is in here Madam?"

I frowned at him, "That is what I'm wondering, I've never seen it before."

His look told me plainly that he was familiar with such excuses. "Will you come with me please Madam," he said.

I turned to Dora and could have sworn that she looked relieved. I glanced quickly round and was just in time to see Betsy. Presumably she had been watching the whole performance and the smile of satisfaction on her face was unmistakable.

I think I was too frightened to take in the proceedings properly, too stunned to believe I was really here, accused of bringing something undesirable into the country. Of smuggling. Of drug running. Me!

Surely the man must realise he was wrong? I'd always understood that customs people had a sixth sense about these matters, that they were able to tell at a glance if one was guilty. He just couldn't believe I was guilty.

And yet he held the evidence in his hand.

Mechanically I answered questions: I had come from Switzerland? "Yes." Who had I seen there? With whom had I been staying? How long- - -?

Dora was standing near me but I didn't look towards her; I couldn't bear to, the hurt was too deep. I had really thought she was on my side, a much needed friend and refuge. But she must have planned this, who else could have?

I put out a hand to steady myself, my legs were aching intolerably and the room seemed to be swaying.

Unsmiling the officer waved me to a chair, I think I collapsed, rather than sat on it.

Looking up I noticed that Dora was talking with the officer, she was showing him something but I couldn't see what. In any case my mind was too confused to grasp all that was happening. This experience on top of all I had been through, was almost more than I could endure.

Dora came and touched my arm, she said quietly, "The officer says you may go - for the moment."

I shrugged her hand away, "I see."

But of course, I didn't see. I didn't understand at all.

Unsteadily I got to my feet and walked away from the office without even a glance towards the customs man.

Outside, the nausea and blackness was threatening to envelop me. I declined Dora's offer of a wheelchair.

So, my legs hurt as I walked on them. What the hell did it matter. What did anything matter. Bill wasn't here and there was no one else I could trust.

Painfully I followed the signs pointing to 'taxis'. I was aware that Davis and Dora were nearby but I tried to ignore them, to forget they were there. At that moment all I wanted was to get home; to shut and bolt the door; to be on my own.

There were a lot of people around, happy people returning from their Christmas vacations. Vaguely I noticed them but without interest, I was beyond that. I was concentrating on keeping my feet moving, one in front of the other, constantly, Left - right - left - right- - -

Dimly I remembered the taxi, I was leaning against someone, and the impression of soft, blue-grey tweed penetrated my mind, there was a comforting arm around me.

Some time later I opened my eyes and focused on a face hovering near the bed. Dora, how strange, I thought. What is she doing here in my bedroom. But I wasn't really bothered. I was in my own bed, comfortable and warm, there was nothing to bother about. I drifted off to sleep again.

I dreamt. Frightening, scary dreams filled with sinister people. I was trying to escape from them but always they were there, a few paces away.

They disappeared when I awoke but were waiting and ready for me as soon as I closed my eyes again. Then one morning when I awakened it wasn't Dora who looked down at me, it was Bill.

He sat on the bed beside me and gently took my hand in his. I'd forgotten how big and strong his hands were.

Quietly he spoke: "Em, you've been a long way off. I'm so pleased you're back again."

I made an effort to pull my thoughts together, they were so muddled, so disjointed, but one thing seemed clear: "It's not me. I've not been away." The effort was great and I seemed to be shouting but Bill leant over me as if he found it difficult to hear.

"It's not me," I repeated since he probably hadn't heard the first time. "It's you. You've been a long way off - and I needed you."

His eyes looked moist and shiny. "I'm here now love, you can go to sleep again, you are quite safe with me."

I wondered how he knew about the people in my dreams, but it didn't matter, they would have gone now. Bill was here, he would keep them away.

Bill said I had been ill for 'several days', which could have meant anything, I had quite lost count of time. He said Dora had sent for him because she was worried about me. He didn't add that it had been most inconvenient for him to leave whatever he had been involved with, but I knew he must have hated doing so, and appreciated all the more that he had come home. That he had put my well-being first.

The fact that Dora was here with us troubled me, I protested to Bill, telling him how she had taken me to customs, had deliberately led me into a trap. Bill listened, nodding from time to time as though, in his mind, he was checking the things I related.

When I had finished he was quiet for a while, his expression serious as he looked down at me.

"She had to do it Em," he said gently. "It was necessary. I know you don't understand why, but you have to trust her."

Indignation sparked at that. "And you have to trust me! I've been through a lot Bill, I <u>need</u> an explanation."

He pushed a hand through his mop of brown hair in a gesture I knew so well. "Yes," he said slowly. "Well, I can't give you details," he looked appealingly at me. "You wouldn't expect me to, would you?"

We'd been this way before. "No," I said with resignation. "But I do want- - -"

He stopped me: "Dora works for - no, with me. So does Davis. Their real names are- - -"

It was my turn to break in: "Don't tell me that, I can't manage. All I want to know is why I should trust her. Because of her I've had an experience I can't forget - or easily forgive."

"It wasn't because of her, Em, she was doing her duty. We've got to catch these people and that was part of the plan."

"She could have told me."

"And risk blowing the whole thing?"

"I suppose not," I turned my head away, I felt unutterably weary. It was nice having Bill here but the problems all seemed to remain.

Bill stayed just long enough to be sure I was on the mend. "I must go Em, I really must. I shouldn't have been here at all." He looked worried and I didn't doubt that he was needed somewhere, urgently. That coming home to me might have lost him valuable time and perhaps vital information.

But when the front door closed behind him I felt horribly alone and vulnerable - in spite of Dora's presence. She had swapped Betsy's beautiful home for our flat, everything was running smoothly and her care and superb cooking was speeding my recovery.

It seemed that she was now our 'treasure' just as, apparently she had been Betsy's. But I still found it difficult to accept her as friend rather than foe.

Thanks to the enforced rest my legs were healing beautifully. I was exercising them, walking up and down the living room when Dora brought in the coffee. Her pretty green dress made me think of spring and was in direct contrast to the grey skies and steady rain outside.

We were both sipping our coffee when she spoke. "You are better now," she said quietly. "So I can say how sorry I am for what happened."

I didn't pretend to misunderstand. "So am I. I really do appreciate all you are doing now, but- - -"

She sighed. "I expect I'd feel the same."

I went on quickly: "I'm so much better now, perhaps you should be- - -"

She interrupted. "My instructions are to stay with you."

As if I was a package that had to be guarded at all costs, I thought angrily. "I don't see why."

Immediately I regretted saying it. It sounded churlish, like a spoiled child speaking. I knew that if she had her instructions I would just have to put up with her being here, whether I liked it or not.

I changed the subject, "Where is Davis now?" I asked.

She hesitated, then: "At the moment he is with Mr. Martin."

"You mean Jim," I said irritably.

She was obviously determined not to be roused. "Jim," she said, carefully emphasising the name, "is in rather a bad state."

I sat forward in my chair. "What do you mean?"

"He has had a bad shock."

I waited for her to continue, an ominous, cold chill settling inside me.

"Dorothy could not leave Switzerland with him, - you see Basil had her passport. So she waited while Jim came home to arrange something for her."

She paused and I could feel myself staring at her. My eyes riveted on her face.

"He was away for two nights but when he came back Basil had found her."

"Oh no." Suddenly I felt sick at heart. Here I was, safe and sound, being petty because Dora was here protecting me.

Inexorably Dora continued: "He made her suffer," she said. "But I'm not going to tell you how - and he made sure that Jim found her."

I could feel tears trickling down my cheeks and covered my face with my hands. "Poor Dorothy! Poor Jim" I murmured.

"So you see," said Dora gently. "Someone must be with you, you need protection, Mr. Hopper - Basil - is not a man to be trifled with."

Again Betsy's words echoed in my mind. He certainly was not a man to be trifled with.

Betsy! I thought. During my illness thoughts of her had receded into the background - and I'd been content to leave them there. Part of my nightmare stay in Lucerne from which I had thankfully awakened.

But it seemed my complacency had been premature, the torment was to continue.

Aloud, "Betsy," I said. 'Where is she? She must need protection too."

"We have managed to trace her, she is staying at a hotel in the West Country. It's a beautiful place, a lovely old house and acres of grounds."

Dora spoke wistfully and there was a faraway look in the dark eyes. I thought, she would really like to be somewhere like that, and there was no denying that she certainly deserved a rest and a holiday. That is, if one disregarded her part in the debacle of my scene with customs. And I was trying hard to disregard it.

The idea of a holiday - even just for a few days - appealed to me too. "I suppose there is no chance- - -?" I asked tentatively.

She gave a wry smile, "We've got to keep an eye on her so we might spend a few days nearby - perhaps in a cottage."

"We could pretend to be on a walking holiday."

She grimaced, "With your legs?"

"I'd forgotten my legs."

"Well that's a good sign." Dora got up and put our empty cups on the tray. "Perhaps we can go tomorrow," she looked excited at the prospect. "But I'll have to arrange it with Mr. Davis or someone - first."

"You could phone him."

"Not on your phone."

I looked at her in surprise, "You think it may be bugged?"

She said calmly. "There may well be someone listening in. I won't chance it anyway."

She went into the kitchen and I could hear her pottering about. Suspicion and caution were second nature to her, I supposed, just as they were to Bill. But the world of watching and bugging telephones was still new to me.

I glanced at the phone, I'd half a mind to ring someone and give a spurious message; like arranging to meet someone in the park to hand something over. It just might intrigue an eavesdropper - if indeed there was one - and yet not commit me at all.

But for the life of me, I couldn't think of anyone I knew who wouldn't be thoroughly mystified and need a whole long explanation about it first. Except Dora.

Excited I called to her, "If you were to phone me when you are out- - -"

She listened approvingly. "Good thinking," she said when I'd finished. "But I've tried that already - and it works."

"You mean someone did respond?"

"Yes, so at least we know one person is keeping an eye and an ear on us."

I must have looked crestfallen because she smiled and added: "You'll make a good detective yet!"

"I must go now," Dora said. "But whatever you do, don't answer the door. Not to anyone."

"Or talk to strange men," I parodied.

"I'm serious. Really I shouldn't leave you at all but there are some things I've simply got to do and I'll be as quick as possible."

The front door shut with a decisive bang. My prison door closing, I thought wryly as I crossed over to the window and looked out.

Dora was walking swiftly down the road towards the shops and railway station. Her hat and buff coloured trench coat and black boots were already streaming with rain.

I stood there for several minutes, idly watching the rain trickling down the window pane, before it occurred to me that, if someone was keeping an eye on us, it would be better not to let them see me. Not to let them know that I was here, probably alone, now that Dora had gone out.

I picked up a newspaper and tried to concentrate on the latest happenings in the world outside, but again and again my mind returned to our own problems. To Bill. To the awfulness of Basil. To the sadness of Dorothy and Jim.

I thought; if only I could help Jim. He had probably started drinking again, just as he had in Lucerne when he had been so depressed about Dorothy.

True, Davis was with him and Davis had coped with the problem before. But Jim must be at his wits end now, without Dorothy. It was so final. At least before there had been some hope to carry him through. Now there was just desolation.

I walked restlessly up and down the room, knowing the problems and not being able to do anything about them.

It was then that the front door bell rang. I stopped in my tracks and the pounding of my heart seemed to echo through the stillness of the room.

Again the bell rang, more insistently this time, whoever it was outside kept a finger on the bell-push and the noise jangled through the flat.

Then I heard a voice coming faintly through the door, calling to me.

"Marion, Marion let me in. You must, I'm desperate."

"Betsy!" I said it aloud, not certain if I should be relieved or even more anxious now that I knew who it was.

"Marion! Open the door. I know you are there, I saw you at the window."

Panic filled me. What on earth ought I to do? Dora had insisted I must not open the door to anyone, but I couldn't just leave Betsy out there, she really sounded to be in trouble. And in any case the noise she was making would soon attract attention from our neighbours.

Close against the door I shouted back to her: "Are you alone?"

"Yes, yes. Oh hurry up Marion." She practically fell in when I lifted the latch. "Thank God," she breathed. "Close it again quickly - I'm being followed."

I leaned against the door and looked at Betsy - this pseudo friend of mine. The last time I had seen her was at Heathrow, at customs. She had been watching me with a smile on her face that told of a task completed to her satisfaction.

Now she was wet and scared and vulnerable. Seeking sanctuary from me.

Dispassionately I thought: I could just turn her out, leave her to deal with whoever is following her. Money is no problem to her, she can go to a hotel.

But, of course, she had just come from a hotel and presumably she had only left it because she was afraid. She said that she was being followed, and she had led whoever it was here, to me.

"On no account open the door to anyone," Dora had said. I had let Betsy in and now a sinister someone else was close at hand. I wondered; would he - or she, also want to come in?

Until Dora returned there was nothing I could do, no use phoning, the line was tapped. In any case, who was there to call for help? Better to deal with things as they were and keep my fingers tightly crossed until Dora returned.

I didn't feel friendly towards Betsy but I couldn't just let her stand there in her wet things.

"You'd better have a hot bath," I said, leading the way along the landing. "You can borrow my dressing-gown while your clothes are drying, we will talk afterwards."

I turned on the taps and watched the steaming water gush into the bath. Our ordinary, white bath - not an exotic, cyclamen coloured one.

I looked round at Betsy, she was holding on to the towel rail, her teeth chattering. "Quickly, get undressed," I chivvied. "I don't want you laid up here with a chill."

It crossed my mind that I'd been laid up with considerably more than a chill when I was in her home, and been well cared for too. But then Betsy had been responsible for my injuries. What she was suffering now was her own fault. Her metaphoric chickens coming home to roost.

Chapter Eighteen

I prepared a hot drink and sat watching Betsy sip it, relieved to see that she was feeling better. No doubt the hot bath had helped and now the coffee and the warmth of the room was completing the cure, restoring her self-confidence.

She was ready to talk; across the rim of her cup she looked at me. "I've been staying in a hotel in the West Country," she said. "Quite near our old school."

Inconsequentially I thought: Almost full circle. The story started there where we first met. Perhaps it will finish there too. Finish! Suddenly I was scared at my own thoughts, they seemed horribly final. But, I reminded myself, it already had been final for one member of the faction. Dorothy.

Betsy wouldn't know that, and I wasn't going to be the one to tell her. Not at the moment anyway. I wanted her to talk, to tell me her side of things.

"You went there after you left Heathrow." It wasn't a question, I just wanted her to be sure I knew the part she had played in the affair.

She had the grace to look confused. "I'm sorry dear, I didn't want to- - -" her voice trailed, then, after a moment, "What happened? Did they bother you? Have you had any trouble since - I mean in court or anything?"

I thought: Of course she would want to know if her scheme had succeeded, and to find out she would have to come and see me. I should have been expecting her, but it just hadn't occurred to me.

I said: "Since then I've been very ill." No harm in telling her that. I had a sudden vision of Betsy dropping her gloves and rudely pushing me aside so that she could retrieve them herself. Obviously that was when she had planted the drugs.

"I suppose you put the package in my handbag when we were in the ladies room at Zurich airport," I said.

She stiffened in her chair, "I don't know what you mean."

"There is no point in pretending," I said brusquely, sure now that I was on the right track. "How long have you been mixed up in the drug business?"

She blustered then, putting down her empty cup and striding up and down the room, my long blue dressing-gown flapping about her legs.

"How dare you talk to me like that Marion! It's - it's treasonable."

I didn't feel like smiling. I had her on the run now and pressed home my advantage.

"Certainly drug running is punishable," I said. "I want to know why you do it - and why you wanted to involve me."

She stopped pacing up and down and I detected a crafty look in her eyes as she looked at me. "I didn't tell you who was following me," she said.

"I wasn't asking you about that," I tried to keep her to the point.

"It was that man sitting between you and Dora on the plane."

I thought quickly; there had been a man, busy with his papers and not in the least interested in us. A large man- - -

"You mean that large man?" I said. "I just don't believe you."

She shrugged, "Look out of the window, perhaps you will see him. Unless he's already waiting at your door."

I started to walk towards the window when it occurred to me that this could be another ruse. I was to look out of the window and that would be a signal for someone outside. Someone in league with Betsy, not against her.

I sat down again, "You. And tell me who you see."

A look of hopelessness came over her, she crumpled into a chair and covered her face with her hands. For several minutes I watched as her shoulders heaved with silent sobs.

"Supposing you tell me the truth," I said quietly. "I can't help you if you don't." I didn't add that in any case it was probably beyond my power to help her.

Her eyes were red-rimmed and cheeks wet when she looked up at me. "I'm frightened. I don't know what to do or where to go - there seem to be enemies everywhere." She paused but I didn't answer and after a moment she went on:

"At the hotel when I saw this man - he is that man from the plane Marion - I was so scared, I just left, leaving all my things behind. I came to you - there was nowhere else to go. And he followed me here - I saw him."

She was so obviously distressed, I went to her and put my arms around her shoulders, trying to comfort her. "You're all right here Betsy," I said. "You are safe with me."

I thought; what am I saying! This woman has done her best to incriminate you, Marion. She has schemed and plotted to hurt you, - and save herself. And now she was here, helpless and pathetic.

I moved away and looked down at her. Perhaps she may not have meant to cause me harm, she was under stress and afraid of Basil. We were all afraid of Basil.

She took a little time to recover her composure, then she stood and peered at me with a semblance of dignity. "I'm sorry Marion, thank you for being so understanding. Perhaps my clothes are dry now so I can put them on and leave you."

"What will you do?" I tried to think clearly while I waited for her reply.

Betsy couldn't just leave, she had nowhere to go and no one to turn to. As she had said, there seemed to be enemies everywhere. I didn't want her here but at least she would be safe from them - if not from Bill and her just retribution.

"I don't know. I really don't know." She sat down again abruptly. "I suppose I could go home, but Basil- - -"

I opened my mouth to say 'you can't go home, it's no longer there', but a key turned in the lock of the front door just in time to prevent me.

Instinctively we both stood, frozen to the spot. Gazing towards the door.

Then Dora's voice called, "I'm home Madam."

'Madam' I thought, surprised. She doesn't call me that now, and she'd gone straight to the kitchen - not in here to see me as she usually did.

I glanced across the room, of course, Betsy was here! And somehow Dora knew, so she had reverted to the old mistress-maid role. I grimaced, we now had a new game to play.

Betsy was sitting down again, relaxed and warm in my blue dressing-gown. "I wondered if Dora was still with you," she said.

"She looked after me while I was ill."

"What was wrong with you?" she said it with polite interest rather than concern.

I looked away from her to the window where the rain still slanted down seeming to make jagged edges to the buildings across the road.

What had been wrong with me, I mused: injuries, strain and stress beyond endurance, coping with dishonest and dangerous people. All of which was your fault Betsy.

It would have been a relief to say it aloud to her, but could serve no useful purpose and she certainly wouldn't understand.

I fixed my gaze on her again, "I'm not sure," I said. "A multitude of things, but I'm better now."

She nodded, "So presumably Dora will be leaving you."

I thought, so that's it! She thinks she can start again with Dora to take care of everything - just as she has for the past two years. Well, one couldn't blame her, it was an appealing idea, particularly in her present situation. But once again I marveled at her single-mindedness. For Betsy, it seemed other people were around purely for, and at, her convenience. To be used or jettisoned, as necessary.

Dora served a useful purpose - and I had too, but now, apart from sheltering her at this time, I was of no further use. But Dora might well be.

One way and another Betsy had a lot to learn and maybe she would soon find out that the world looked at things rather differently.

"I'm going to the kitchen a moment, Betsy," I said. "I won't be long."

She didn't reply and I thought her expression was smug now, not distressed as it had been a short time ago. Because of Dora, I supposed. Now she could see a way round her difficulties so her whole attitude had changed.

I closed the kitchen door behind me, "It's Betsy," I said irritably. "I had to let her in she was making such a noise outside."

Dora was busy preparing lunch and just nodded her understanding.

"I'm getting absolutely nowhere with her," I went on. "I think she is going to tell me things and then she sidetracks."

Dora paused a moment then, and spoke carefully in a low voice which would not carry. "While she is here, I am working for you, you understand?"

"I thought so when you came in," I said. "I suppose it's useless to ask why?"

She was putting potatoes and carrots on to boil and lamb chops under the grill. "You will know soon. I shall be in to lay the table in a moment, you had better go back to Mrs. Harland - her clothes are nearly dry."

I went into my bedroom first, I had to be by myself to think quietly for a few moments. Dora had known before she came in that Betsy was here. I felt sure of that, her whole attitude told me so. Had she by some chance also known that Betsy was coming?

I wonder if she knows how long Betsy will be staying, as well, I thought crossly. She really seemed to know everything. While I was feeling my way at a snail's pace through the problems, she was at the winning post with all the answers to hand.

I felt slow and ineffectual, "Almost unnecessary," I muttered. Even to Bill.

He'd gone away and not bothered to contact me. Anything might have happened, Basil might have done - whatever it was he wanted to do, and Bill wouldn't know. I deliberately ignored the fact that Dora was here purely to protect me and no doubt kept Bill informed about everything that went on.

In a way that made it worse. He should have been here, I told myself, taking care of me personally. And again, in my mind I could hear Jim voicing my own sentiments.

He was right too, and Jim would understand how frustrated I felt.

I took a deep breath. "This is silly Marion," I said, "And unfair too, you know that Bill has a difficult job to do. For goodness' sake stop being sorry for yourself - and go back to 'Mrs. Harland' as Dora told you to.

That rankled a bit too, however sensible I tried to be. There was Betsy, quite sure that Dora would continue to 'do' for her, and here I was meekly obeying orders from Dora. Well, perhaps not meekly, I thought as I entered the room.

I said: "Dora will be here in a moment, she says your clothes are nearly dry."

Betsy was sitting in the chair just as I'd left her, she looked up calmly. "Dora's a good worker," she remarked. "I'm glad she looked after you so well."

I turned away to hide the smile I couldn't control, Betsy was behaving as if she, from the goodness of her heart, had lent Dora especially to care for me while I was ill. Well, that was one more thing she needed to be disillusioned about.

"I've been wondering about Jim," Betsy said. "Have you seen him recently?"

Warning lights flashed in my mind; the last time Betsy had mentioned Jim's name she'd been furious with him - and Dorothy. I needed to tread very carefully, to feel my way through this delicate subject.

"No," I said cautiously.

She was looking at me with those gimlet eyes of hers. Well, I thought, it doesn't matter, I'm telling her the truth.

"I haven't forgiven him," Betsy said. "Or you either Marion, for your part in - in -"

"In what?"

"Don't be naïve Marion, it doesn't become you."

I hadn't expected that sort of reply from her and I wasn't going to let her get away with it. "I don't think you understand the situation Betsy," I said. "You are here with me to shelter from your enemies - and I'm sure you have many. You should be careful how you speak to your hostess."

How pompous, I thought. But she was completely taken aback, and I wondered how long it was since anyone had spoken to her in that way - anyone other than Basil, that is.

But Betsy didn't change her attitude or climb down, the way she sometimes did. "Really Marion," she said. "I'm not accustomed to people talking to me like that."

I stuck to my guns, "No, neither am I."

She glared at me uncertain what to do next. "You were talking about Jim," I prompted.

I could see she was mentally trying to pull herself together, to recover the initiative, and I reflected that it couldn't be easy for her. She was in a strange, and no doubt, for her, rather lowly home with someone for whom she had little respect.

She wasn't even wearing her own clothes, and furthermore, outside there were enemies - people who threatened her life - hovering close by. It would take a superwoman to be dignified under such circumstances.

But Betsy did her best, she wrapped the dressing-gown tidily across her knees and took her time before answering.

"You never explained to me Marion, just what their relationship was."

"You mean Jim and Dorothy?" I didn't pretend to misunderstand her this time.

"Yes, I had been trying to keep the Hoppers away from Jim, that is, I kept Basil away- - -"

I broke in, "You were right to, in fact you had to, didn't you?"

She disregarded the interruption. "I didn't know that Jim had ever met Dorothy. But you knew, didn't you Marion?"

"Yes," I said. "Jim did tell me."

She sat watching me while I wondered how much I should tell her - and if it really mattered anyway.

"Well," she said at last. "What did Jim say to you? I need to know Marion."

I opened my mouth to reply and at the same time there was a light tap on the door and Dora came in to lay the table.

"Good morning Mrs. Harland," she said, with just the right mixture of deference and independence.

Betsy hid her frustration. "Ah Dora," she said, as if she'd seen her only the day before. "I was wondering," she added looking at me and obviously trying to choose her words carefully. "I was wondering Marion, will you mind if I speak with Dora - on our own?"

I did mind, I would have preferred to stay, to hear what Betsy was going to say. Indeed to know what they both would say. For a moment I hesitated, feeling two pairs of eyes watching me. Then: "Of course not," I muttered. "I have a few things to do."

Outside in the hall I stood a moment, collecting my thoughts, irritated at having to leave them but at the same time offering up a silent prayer for Dora's timely interruption.

I didn't want to tell Betsy about Jim and Dorothy - or any of the other important facts that, sooner or later she had to know. That was somebody else's job, not mine.

I was just passing the front door when the bell clanged imperiously.

"I'll go," I called, completely forgetting that no one was to be admitted, and I'd already opened the door when Dora ran into the hall.

"Jim!" I exclaimed.

It was my second big surprise of the day.

"I had to come and see you," he said holding out his hands and grasping mine tightly, as if he wasn't going to release them again.

His face was pale and drawn, I knew he'd been through a dreadful experience, but even so I was shaken to see him looking so ill. He was staring down at me through eyes which seemed to peer through dark hollows and there was a break in his voice when he spoke.

"I believe you are the only sane, trustworthy person left in my life, Marion."

I had an overwhelming desire to put my arms around him, to comfort him, to let him weep on my shoulder. Then a cool voice cut across my yearning, "Shall I take your coat sir?"

Dora! For a moment I'd forgotten she was there and I don't think Jim had even noticed her. I could almost feel him striving to collect his wits and emotions together as he let go of my hands and allowed Dora to take his wet things.

She led the way to the living room, studiously avoiding my gaze. Perhaps I was hypersensitive but she seemed to exude disapproval. It was reasonable, of course, Jim was one of the 'enemy' and Dora was working with Bill.

I thought, so am I, I suppose. But at that moment I wasn't at all sure.

I would have preferred to keep Betsy and Jim apart for a while. I remembered the antagonism there was between them and it hardly seemed fair to inflict them on each other just now when they were both at low ebb.

Purposefully Dora showed us into the living room. Inwardly I smiled. Perhaps she was trying to protect Bill's interests by making sure I wasn't alone with Jim. Perhaps she was even right to do so.

"I'll bring you a drink, sir," Dora said. "Shall you be staying for lunch?"

"Yes Dora," I said firmly. "Please lay another place."

Betsy looked up startled, as we came in, then glared accusingly at me.

"You said you hadn't seen Jim, Marion. I assumed that you had no knowledge of his whereabouts."

Jim didn't wait for me to answer, for the moment his pleasure in goading Betsy returned and he looked almost his old self.

"Ah Betsy. You should never take these things for granted." He put an arm around my waist and looked fondly down at me. "You didn't think I could stay away from Marion, did you?"

I pulled away, "He's teasing you Betsy," I said. "I'd no idea where he was until now."

Betsy didn't understand teasing and certainly didn't take kindly to it now. "I should have thought one woman at a time was enough," she said scathingly. "Where have you left Dorothy?"

Jim took a step forward and for a moment I thought he was going to strike her. I put a restraining hand on his arm.

"Betsy doesn't know," I said quietly.

"Doesn't know what?" she asked sharply.

"That Basil - or his henchmen - found her." The words seemed to be wrenched from Jim.

Any colour Betsy had, drained from her face. "You mean- - -"

"Yes." There was a whole world of bitterness and suffering in the one, brief word.

I could almost feel the silence in the room as Jim subsided into a chair - and back again into his dark misery.

Betsy sat staring straight ahead and she also was probably seeing frightening things. Dangers which, until then had been unknown, were now tangible. And just that amount more horrifying.

I walked over to the window, what did it matter if any one did see me. With so many of us here no one would risk attacking, if indeed there had ever been that danger.

I thought; more likely a lonely strike when one was least expecting it, as, no doubt had happened with Dorothy.

I stared out at the grey skies and the rain, still teeming down. There were a few people about, well wrapped against the cold and wet. A woman with a bright red umbrella provided the only glimpse of cheerful colour. I watched her splash her way along the road, passing a man with his coat collar turned up, hat brim hiding his face.

With a sudden surge of interest I thought, it could be Bill! The man was just about his size and the brisk, long stride was the same.

If only it was! I tried to will the man to be Bill: "You're needed here Bill, you're needed here," I repeated silently, urgently. But it didn't work, the man paused at a door opposite and, with his key all ready to hand, quickly disappeared inside the house.

I turned back into the room, Dora was just bringing in pre-lunch drinks; a stiff whisky for Jim and sherry for Betsy and me. For a while we sat in gloomy silence, Betsy moved restlessly and her fingers tapped on the arms of the chair. I could feel that she was itching to ask questions, no doubt wanting to find out what Jim had been doing - and exactly what had happened to Dorothy.

Eventually she could wait no longer.

"Where have you been all this time Jim? I mean since- - - and when did it happen?"

Jim looked up, he'd finished the whisky in one quick gulp and it had probably helped momentarily to drown the pain of remembrance.

He said slowly, "It happened the day after we left Lucerne, and since then I've not been well- - -"

"That makes two of you, Marion has been ill too." Betsy sounded suspicious as if she believed there had been collusion, that Jim and I had decided we would both be ill at that particular time.

That we _had_ been was not so very strange, I thought. Goodness knows we had both been suffering from extremes of stress and strain. And in each case the cause was traceable to Basil.

"You've been ill Marion?" Jim sounded concerned. "I'm not surprised, you've had a hell of a time. And it was our fault," he added looking directly at Betsy.

She blustered again, "I hardly think- - -"

"Of course it was," Jim said abruptly.

"You don't know it all," I interrupted. "I was injured on that morning when we left, Basil tried to keep me at the hotel. I broke a window and cut myself badly."

He came over to me, "I didn't know Marion, are you all right now?"

"Yes, yes," I tried to brush him away. "You couldn't be expected to know, you had your own troubles to contend with."

He nodded, "All the same I wish I had known, it might have helped."

I could understand that, there is nothing like dealing with someone else's distress to make one's own seem less important. Betsy said dryly, "Marion was cared for by my maid, she didn't need you."

He looked white and drawn as he replied: "No she didn't, but I needed her."

I looked up at him, "She won't understand," I pleaded. "Please don't try to make her."

Betsy laughed mirthlessly, "Oh but I do understand Marion. More than you think and I'm wondering just what is your relationship with Jim?"

For the second time Jim made as if to strike her but this time he changed his mind, obviously preferring a different approach. His favourite one of goading her.

"You've only just realised! You're very slow sometimes Betsy."

I stood up, "This is absurd," I said. "Betsy will believe you Jim, and it just isn't true."

He looked quizzically at me then and for a brief instant the lopsided smile appeared. "Isn't it?" he asked.

Chapter Nineteen

There was no attempt at conversation while we ate, I looked at the other two, each of them apparently absorbed with their own problems, locked in the chaos which constituted their individual worlds.

I wondered if the chop Jim was eating had really been meant for the cook, but she was resourceful and had probably managed to conjure another portion from somewhere. At the moment my worries did not include what Dora had for lunch. I was busy wondering what on earth to do with Betsy and Jim.

Betsy was bad enough on her own but if Jim intended staying for long, life was going to be very difficult. I glanced across at him, he looked better already, less gaunt and drawn. I reflected that Betsy seemed to infect him with a sort of malicious enjoyment, it was worthwhile provoking her because she always responded satisfactorily.

And just now she was still attired in the blue dressing-gown and no doubt feeling vulnerable, so all the advantages were on Jim's side.

After a while he sat back with a sigh of repletion: "Delicious. It's weeks since I enjoyed a meal, thank you Marion."

Betsy spoke before I had a chance to answer. "Yes, Dora cooks very well."

Jim raised an eyebrow.

"My maid," Betsy was coolly proprietorial. "She has been looking after Marion."

"Dora," he said. "I wondered why she was here. And Davis has been looking after me."

I intervened, "Yes," I said brightly. "Wasn't it kind of Betsy to lend Dora to me?"

The irony was wasted on Betsy, she gave a self-satisfied smile but Jim looked relieved, obviously accepting my remark at its face value. And why not, I thought, he didn't know all that had happened after he left Lucerne so, under the circumstances letting Dora care for me would seem to be a natural, kindly action from Betsy.

When Dora came in to clear the table she advised me to go for my usual afternoon rest. "I'm sure that Mrs. Harland and Mr. Bellamy will understand," she said.

Betsy looked at me as if doubtful that I needed to rest but Jim immediately rose to his feet. "Yes, of course you must Marion," he said. "Betsy and I have things to discuss. We will talk later," he added softly, squeezing my hand as I passed him.

Not if I can help it, I thought. And yet- - -

I let Dora tuck me into bed, truth to tell I was relieved to be there, it had been an exhausting morning and since my illness I tired so easily and was always ready for the rest which Dora insisted on.

But, perversely, today I couldn't help wondering if I was here purely for my well-being or if perhaps Dora had an ulterior motive. Such as keeping Jim away from me. Could she be suspicious of my relationship with him? Apart from Jim's greeting this morning, she surely had no cause to be. I thought; she couldn't have any knowledge of what had happened in Lucerne. She seemed to know so much, was it possible she was also aware of that?

I felt a slow flush creep over my face and snuggled further under the bedclothes. But Dora wasn't looking at me, she was tucking my shoes tidily by the side of the bed, ready for me to put my feet into when I got up.

Inside me I marvelled at her, she was almost too good. She thought of answers to everything long before anyone else even knew there was a problem. And she was always calm and pleasant. An absolute tower of strength to Bill, I felt sure. Unlike me, I grimaced, seemingly creating problems for him all the time.

Dora smiled down at me, "What's the trouble?" she asked.

"Oh, Just thinking. Actually," I said candidly, "comparing you and me - and I didn't come off too well."

"What nonsense" she turned away dismissing it out of hand.

I changed the subject, "Seriously Dora, what are we going to do with these people? We can't just send Betsy away, not when she is so scared of whoever it is following her."

Dora had obviously worked it all out. "If need be she can have my room - I can manage on the sofa."

"And Jim?"

She looked surprised, "You are thinking of him staying too?"

"I don't know," I said. "I just don't know, but he can't go out and be - be stabbed or knocked on the head or something."

"He managed to come here safely," she said dryly.

"Yes," I nodded then a thought occurred to me. "Did I tell you who it is Betsy says is following her?"

"No," she paused on her way to the door.

"It is the man on the plane, the big man who was sitting between us."

She smiled slightly, "Interesting but not too worrying. Now," she added, "you are to sleep, we will sort the problems out later."

"You mean that <u>you</u> will," I said under my breath as she closed the door. I thought, she is never surprised about anything.

I slept for more than an hour, deep sleep which should have refreshed me, instead I awoke starkly with a feeling of unease. For a moment or two I lay there gathering my scattered thoughts, trying to understand why the disquieting sensations persisted. Then I remembered.

It had been quite a morning! Beginning ages ago with Dora and me planning a short holiday - of all things - to spy on Betsy!

I smiled ruefully to myself, there was no need for that now, Betsy was here and apparently being shadowed by someone quite different. Someone who, if I judged correctly, was acceptable to Dora.

Then Jim had come. I sat up, Jim being here was disturbing in a different way. His obvious approval of me was flattering, I would be less than human not to feel that. And he needed a friend, someone he could rely on. He had come to me.

I swung my legs out over the side of the bed, my feet feeling for the shoes Dora had placed so carefully. Of course, I told myself firmly, I would very much sooner that it was Bill who had come to discuss his problems with me. To seek solace.

But Bill wasn't here, just as over the years he so often hadn't been when I needed him. When I wanted him to need me.

In the early dusk of the winter day I sat in front of the dressing-table mirror and brushed my hair until it shone pale gold around my shoulders. You're feeling sorry for yourself again Marion, I derided myself.

All the same I couldn't help wishing that Bill did find it necessary to confide in me now and then. To come home and recharge ready to face the world again. But Bill did his recharging with other people - such as Dora. I was on the outside of his life, loved, of course, but not an everyday necessity.

I gazed at my reflection in the mirror, hating myself for comparing Bill with Jim. Feeling horribly disloyal. But the niggling thoughts persisted, and Jim was here needing me to help him through a difficult patch.

All very well for Bill and Dora to say that Jim's problems were his own fault, that my troubles were of his making - his and Betsy's. They were right, but, I thought, Jim had apologised, had even regretted his part in it. Now he was considerate of my feelings and welfare.

Unlike Bill who left it all to Dora.

I chose my soft blue wool dress and took time to look my best; now there was someone in the house who would notice and appreciate.

On my way across the room a thought momentarily halted me in my tracks; perhaps Jim had already gone and there was just Betsy waiting for me in the living room. It would certainly solve a lot of problems but the feeling of disappointment and emptiness was instantaneous - alarmingly so. I couldn't help hoping that he was still there.

Jim was there, relaxed and looking at ease in the armchair which Bill preferred. Betsy was there too, changed now to her own clothes, which obviously Dora had found time to press before returning. I supposed too, that it was Dora who had drawn the curtains, shutting off the wet gloom of the outside world and making a cosy haven for our guests.

Unlike Jim, Betsy looked anything other than relaxed, she was pacing slowly about the room and turned to me as soon as I entered.

"You didn't tell me Marion." She blurted without any preliminary, and behind the gold-framed spectacles her hazel eyes glared, boring into me.

"Tell you what?"

Jim came over and led me to a chair near his. "About the house," he said gently. "She had to know."

"Yes, of course," I looked up at Betsy, no wonder she couldn't settle, it must have been a dreadful shock. I hoped that Jim had told her sympathetically, kindly - if one can be kind about such a disaster.

"But Betsy," I said. "I've hardly seen you since - and there was no way to contact you."

She stood still a moment and looked down at us both, her expression was scathing. "You would have found a way if you'd wanted to. I can see it was not just Basil I had to fear, you two were plotting against me as well."

"That is absurd Betsy," Jim rose and put an arm around her shoulders. "You've had a frightful shock and it's understandable that you are upset. But," his tone changed, lost its warmth, "but you mustn't fall out with me you know, you are going to need me more than ever now."

She stared at him, "What do you mean?"

"I mean you will need money and I doubt if you will want to ask Basil to relinquish your account."

She sat down abruptly then, as if her legs had crumpled, but after a moment looked up again, a grim smile of triumph on her face.

"You are right, I will not want to seek Basil's help, you see for a long time I've had another account - a different bank - one which Basil knows nothing about. So I shan't need you either."

"But can you be sure Basil doesn't know?"

Again Betsy said sharply; "What do you mean?"

Jim shrugged, "Just what I say, Basil has ways of knowing most things."

I cut across their unsavoury discourse, "Have either of you heard of Basil recently, I mean where he is or- - - ?"

Two pairs of eyes directed cold, uncompromising stares at me. "It depends what you mean by recently," Jim's gaze softened as he looked down.

"No," Betsy said. "Not since I left Lucerne."

"Since we left," I corrected her. "I was there too."

Betsy turned on me, "Yes, it was because of you we were unable to leave when we wanted to. Probably Basil wouldn't have destroyed the house - or anything - if you hadn't been there!"

I bit back the obvious replies, instead, "You think he caused the fire?"

"Well, don't you?"

"I don't know," I said. "It could have been an accident."

"Don't be so childish Marion." She stamped her foot at me. "That is what most people will believe. That is what you are meant to believe."

Her face was flushed, with fear quite as much as annoyance, I thought, and it was understandable. I glanced at Jim and was astonished to see that he was grinning as he watched her.

"I don't think having one's house burned down is funny," I said crossly.

Betsy glared at him, "You have a very strange sense of humour, I really don't understand how you can find anything Basil does amusing."

"I don't," he said promptly.

"Well what were you laughing at?"

"You." The grin was even wider.

She turned away from him then and I thought there were tears glistening behind the spectacles. Her fingers felt in the pocket of her skirt but obviously there wasn't a handkerchief, and before I could fetch one Jim had handed her his.

"Here take this," he said roughly. "And pull yourself together, Woman."

Wiping her eyes, she sat down. They are behaving like silly children, I thought. Here we are faced with deadly serious problems and all they can do is squabble over next to nothing.

Betsy'd had a dreadful shock and Jim was being anything other than helpful to her. Again into my mind there flashed Bill's opinion of Jim, he was ruthless with Betsy. I wondered if he would be the same with me.

I got up and moved towards the door, "I'll go and ask Dora for some tea," I muttered, relieved to get away from them. I closed the door sharply behind me and stood for a moment, half expecting to hear sounds of fierce argument going on as soon as I'd left the room. Or secret plans being made.

But there was no sound. Of course there wouldn't be, they'd had all the afternoon, while I was asleep to discuss any schemes, to talk quietly without fear of anyone listening. It was wishful thinking to suppose I might hear something of interest now.

Dora wasn't in the kitchen but there was a tray already laid and a delicious aroma of warm scones coming from the oven.

A note written in her neat hand was propped against the tray, it was addressed formally to 'Mrs. Hemming' and just said: 'Have gone out for a little while, will be back later.'

I was reading it when Jim's voice spoke from the doorway, "Can I carry the tray?"

Quickly I looked around, my mind forming the query, 'how did Jim know Dora wasn't here and bringing in the tray herself?'

He must have sensed my thoughts because at once he added, "I came out earlier to see if Dora could make us a cup of tea and read her note then."

"I see," immediately I felt guilty of my suspicions.

He came quickly across the room behind me and put his hands on my shoulders, spinning me around to face him. "I've needed you, little Marion," he said softly, looking down into my eyes. "Have you thought about me?"

"Now and then," I made an effort at casualness but didn't try to get away. "But you see Bill- - -"

He stopped me with a kiss, gentle at first but growing fiercer and more demanding, and his arms crushed me closely to him. I didn't struggle. Insanely I'd no desire to get away, and with a shock realised that this was what I'd been wanting ever since he arrived that morning.

I must be mad, I thought as I clung to him. But at that moment it didn't seen to matter.

After an eternity his grip relaxed and, as if psychic, he answered my unspoken protest. "Bill is hardly ever here Marion. I am here now."

"We must go," I said feebly pushing him away. "Betsy will be suspicious."

The lopsided smile appeared, "Betsy is always suspicious."

"She probably has cause to be!"

I could feel my hands shaking as I filled the teapot and some of the boiling water spilled on to the table. As soon as I put the kettle down Jim clasped me tightly to him again. "We must meet soon," he said urgently. "Tomorrow Marion."

Against my will - "No," I said. "I can't."

"Yes, you can, we need each other, you and I, meet me tomorrow at the Hilton. I'll be in the foyer at midday."

He picked up the dish of warm scones, kissed me lightly on the forehead - a sort of brief farewell, I thought as I followed him into the living room.

"Does Dora often go out and leave you?" Betsy screwed her flowered, paper napkin into a tight ball and placed it carefully in her empty cup, the tenseness of her action belying the carefully casual question.

Warning signals shot through my mind. "She hardly left me at all while I was ill," I parried. "I really don't know how I'd have managed without her." Then recalling Betsy's remark to Jim earlier in the day, I added: "It was kind of you to lend her to me, Betsy."

"Yes," she said blandly. "But no doubt Bill was here too."

Betsy wanted to know both Bill and Dora's movements. I could understand her wanting to know about Bill but surely she wasn't suspicious of Dora as well?

With mild panic I thought: I mustn't allow her to be, somehow she has got to be sidetracked.

"Oh yes, Bill was here - but Dora cooks so much better!"

"I can vouch for that," said Jim with enthusiasm. "You will miss her when she goes."

"Yes, I suppose I will."

"Where is Bill now?" It was Betsy's turn again.

I shrugged, "He comes and goes, according to the job on hand." I looked at my watch. "As a matter of fact," I said, he may be home soon, I'm sure he will want to meet you both." Inwardly I murmured, 'if only it could be true'.

At once it was obvious that the prospect of meeting Bill did not appeal to either of them. Jim got to his feet immediately, "That would be nice," he said. "But I've already stayed longer than I intended. Perhaps another time."

Betsy also rose hurriedly, her face pink, hands fiddling with her clothing. "You've been very kind looking after me - I mustn't impose on your hospitality."

"You are staying Betsy," I said with as much authority as I could muster. "Remember that man who was following you, he may still be there."

She did remember, the colour drained from her face as she sat down again. It seems Bill is the lesser of two evils, I thought wryly.

I followed Jim out into the hall and helped him on with his raincoat. Seriously, he turned to face me.

"It is not because Bill may be coming that I have to go, you must believe that Marion. It will be necessary to see him sometime because- - -" his voice trailed, then went on: "I didn't tell Davis how long I'd be away or where I was going." A ghost of a smile creased his face as he added, "You see we both have gaolers, I have Davis, and Dora guards you."

He is probably right too, I thought.

There were no long, lingering farewells, just a brief peck on my cheek.

"Be careful," I called as he disappeared into the darkness.

"Don't worry, little one, I'm too valuable to lose!" came the reply as I closed the door.

I closed the door and leaned against it, trying to collect my thoughts into some sort of order. Jim seemed to hypnotise me, I didn't want to be fond of him - if fond was the right word. I knew full well that he could be ruthless and was mixed up in some kind of shady business - and that he drank too much. And that is just for starters, I told myself.

But most of all there was Bill. I wanted to be faithful to him, anything else was against all my conceptions of our union. The 'til death do us part' rule was, I supposed, bred into me. For better or worse, marriage was for keeps. And yet- - -

Reaction from the events of the day were catching up with me, I felt weary and deflated. While he was here Jim had boosted my morale, added excitement - pleasant excitement which had been sadly lacking in my life for many weeks past.

Now he had gone. "And where the hell are you Bill?" I said aloud. "If only you'd come home more often none of this would happen."

I took a deep breath and made an important decision: When Dora returned I'd break my self-imposed rule and ask her if she knew exactly where Bill was and when he would be coming to see me.

It hurt - rankled was a better word, that she should know about his movements, no doubt even saw him, while I sat at home and waited.

Slowly I walked down the passage to the living room. There was still Betsy to deal with.

Chapter Twenty

Betsy was pacing about the room, she looked worried as she turned towards me. "I really don't think I should stay, dear," she exclaimed. "Bill might not be pleased to see me. What time did you say he was coming?"

"I didn't, I only said he might be."

She stopped then and looked uncertainly at me. "So he might not," she spoke quietly, as though to herself. "Well in that case perhaps I will stay, but I don't want to- - - to be a nuisance." She finished lamely.

"I'm quite sure he wouldn't regard you being here as a nuisance." That, at any rate is the truth, I thought.

We sat opposite one another in a silence which was anything other than cosy and friendly, Betsy shifted constantly in her chair as if she found it uncomfortable. I pretended to be absorbed in a magazine but my thoughts were busy in very different directions.

Where was Dora? She had been out this morning and now again this afternoon. I thought at least she can't be too worried about leaving me and Jim; perhaps I had been wrong in assuming she was suspicious about our relationship.

But all the same it was odd that she should go out now when we had these unexpected guests, and yet normally, when we were here on our own, she was in most of the time. There had to be a good reason, I told myself, but it was puzzling and I resolved to ask her about that as well later in the evening.

And there was the problem of Jim. I wouldn't meet him, of course, though it would be fun to go out - and twelve o'clock at the Hilton probably meant lunch as well and was certainly very tempting.

"You never answered my question Marion."

Surprised, I looked up at Betsy. "I didn't hear you ask one."

"I mean earlier when I asked you about Jim and Dorothy, you didn't tell me what their relationship was."

"Didn't I? Well surely Jim did, you had plenty of time to ask him this afternoon."

The hazel eyes looked at me reproachfully. "I didn't expect that from you Marion, you know perfectly well that Jim doesn't- - -" She paused as if searching for the best way to express herself. "Doesn't like me to ask him personal questions."

"That's true," I said. Jim seemed to have two methods of dealing with Betsy, either telling her in no uncertain terms what she must do or else going out of his way to annoy her.

"Well," I said slowly. "Jim told me in confidence and I really don't feel I can break it now. In any case it is no longer relevant."

She gazed at me earnestly, unblinking, "But you see it is Marion, because of Basil, it could be most important that I should know."

"I don't see- - -" I started, and was once more interrupted by the sound of the front door opening. We stared at each other, wide-eyed with alarm and I had half risen from my chair when Dora peered into the room. "I'm home Madam," she said formally.

I sank back in my chair. Saved again I thought with a sigh of relief.

She was just closing the door behind her when an idea occurred to me. "Dora," I called. "We were expecting my husband, I suppose you have no idea when he will be home?"

I watched her reaction closely, for a moment she was taken off guard and the surprise showed in her eyes. I wondered; was it because I said I was expecting Bill, or because I had asked her, just like that, while Betsy was here.

By the time Betsy turned to look, Dora had the situation under control and she was coolly impersonal when she replied, "No Madam, do you think I should prepare a meal for him as well this evening?"

As sweetly as I could I smiled at her. "Yes please Dora, just in case."

Betsy stood up again and her expression was anxious. "I really think I should go dear, I mean it doesn't seem right for Bill to come home and find- - - that you have a guest."

"Of course you mustn't go Betsy" I was beginning to enjoy myself. To hell with all their intrigues, I'd take a tip from Jim, I thought recklessly, and goad them all into action - or reaction.

Casually I plumped a cushion and placed it comfortably behind Betsy, then I turned again to Dora, "What are we having tonight?" I asked cheerfully.

Behind Betsy's back, Dora's displeasure was obvious, she was stiff and unsmiling but her voice was controlled when she answered.

"If you care to come into the kitchen Madam, I will show you." I followed her, closing the living room door so that Betsy could not listen.

Dora spoke quietly, "I don't think that was very wise Marion."

"What do you mean?" I was deliberately unhelpful.

"Saying that Bill might be home to dinner."

"I don't see why not - unless, of course, you know that he won't be."

For the first time she looked discomfited. "He hasn't been home to dinner for a while- - -" she started.

"I had noticed!" I broke in tartly.

"I was going to say it seemed unlikely that he would be this evening - without letting you know."

"That is your opinion," I said. "And, of course, you know better than I what he is likely to do."

For a long moment she stared at me, surprise and shock mingled in her expression, then she said slowly. "Your husband is doing a difficult and dangerous job, Marion. You know that."

"Yes," I said. "But not as well as you do."

Dora pulled one of our bentwood kitchen chairs a little way from the table and sat down abruptly, elbows resting on the table, head in her hands. She looked tired and I recalled that this morning - a long, long time ago - I'd realised she was in need of a holiday.

Now, impassively I watched her. She had to be exhausted - mentally as well as physically; but it was an objective thought, at the moment I'd no intention of feeling sympathetic towards her - or Betsy. Or, if it came to that, for Bill either.

A phrase one was constantly hearing on the radio flitted through my mind: 'a hardening of attitudes'. Grimly I smiled to myself, that was just the way I felt now. I seemed to be dried up inside, there was no soft centre, no sentiment left.

Eventually Dora looked up at me. "I work with Bill," she spoke wearily. "We are part of a team trying to defeat criminals. It's not easy Marion. Surely you are on our side, on Bill's side?"

I said curtly; "If anyone bothered to tell me, to explain, I probably would be."

"Surely you trust Bill?"

I shrugged, "Sometimes I wonder. He seems to be using me - just as you are now. But no one tells me why - or what I should be doing."

Dora bit her lip reflectively, "I can understand how you must feel, but it is all part of a bigger plan - and for the very best reasons. I can't explain but you have to believe me."

'You have to believe me', she was the second person within an hour to have used those words. Two very different people but each of them in some way connected with Bill. I thought, I can't believe them both.

I felt a desperate need to be wanted, to be shielded from the subterfuge and evil goings-on. For affection.

One of these people offered me just that, but an inner sense told me he was not the one I should trust.

I moved towards the door, "Perhaps," I said bleakly, "you will let Bill know that I would like to see him - when it is convenient."

I walked down the passage then went back and peered into the kitchen again, Dora was still sitting at the table.

"I forgot to tell you," I said. "Jim left earlier."

"I didn't think you were hiding him somewhere," she replied wearily.

Betsy was hovering by the living room door. I knew she might have been listening to our conversation but felt too upset to bother about it.

"I was wondering where you had gone dear," she said. "You were a long time. What are we having for dinner?"

Dinner was one thing Dora and I had not discussed in the kitchen, I tried to bring my mind back to such mundane things. "Oh, some concoction of Dora's, you know how she is with food," I said briefly. "But it won't be for a while."

"No, dear, we have only just had tea," Betsy looked at me strangely, as if I was talking nonsense.

I thought, she doesn't trust me, no one does - even Bill. If he did I would know of his plans; after all, I was apparently very much part of them, playing an active and dangerous part too.

I had a right to know what was going on, a reason to feel aggrieved. At that moment I was fed up with everyone, everyone, that is except Jim. Compared with Bill, it seemed to me that Jim was straightforward and uncomplicated.

Betsy broke into my thoughts: "I'm not very hungry dear, could I have something simple - and easy to eat, an - an omelet perhaps?"

"I expect so," I wasn't really interested in what Betsy ate. "Why don't you see Dora yourself, she's in the kitchen."

She hesitated, then, "I'd like to go to bed early, immediately after I've eaten. It has been a trying day."

I thought, she's scared that Bill will be here, but it suited me to have her out of the way. I hadn't been looking forward to spending the evening with her.

"You can ask Dora to bring your supper on a tray if you wish," I suggested. "Then you can go straight to bed."

"Oh I should be pleased dear." There was relief in her voice and the tension visibly left her.

I went into my bedroom, "I'll find you a nightgown," I called.

I didn't see Betsy again that evening and, apart from bringing in my dinner, Dora kept out of the way. I certainly made no attempt to talk to her again but there was time on my own to think, to try and make sense of what was going on, and it wasn't easy.

I'd fallen out with Dora, Betsy was still here - and Bill was goodness alone knew where. Goodness and Dora, I thought grimly.

I wondered what Dora would do now, she probably couldn't just leave however much she wanted to, and it was going to be interesting to see if Bill suddenly reappeared on my scene. It occurred to me that I didn't feel excited or pleased at the prospect of seeing him again soon; just interested.

But, I reminded myself, my feelings were numb about everything. I thought, even if Basil walked into the room now I wouldn't feel scared - or any other sensation. I'd probably just sit still and wait for him to knock me on the head.

~~~~~~

First grey light was beginning to creep into the room when Dora brought my early morning tea. She put it down on the bedside table and, without preamble told me that Betsy had gone.

"Gone?" I repeated, trying to clear the fog of sleep from my mind. Strangely enough I had slept well and until now had not even remembered that Betsy had been here at all.

"Yes," Dora sounded impatient. "I was wondering what we should do about it."

I was fully awake then; Dora not sure what to do about something and actually seeking my advice! I sat up and reached for the cup. "There doesn't seem much we can do if she has really gone." It wasn't an earth-shattering remark and Dora ignored it.

"She shouldn't be out on her own wandering around. There are people who will harm her if they can."

"She disappeared before - in Switzerland," I recalled. "Nobody bothered about her then, I expect she can take care of herself."

"You didn't think so yesterday," Dora looked at me accusingly.

"That was yesterday - when I had feelings; sympathy for people. It seems to have gone now." I put my empty cup down on its saucer and pulled back the bed-clothes. "Thank you for the tea," I said, pointedly waiting for her to go.

I took my time dressing, there was no need to hurry. No doubt ahead of me stretched yet another day in my comfortable prison, accompanied now by a warder with whom I was scarcely on speaking terms.

And today was unlikely to be relieved by a visit from Betsy or Jim. The prospect was boring in the extreme. I thought; even a glimpse of Basil would liven it up a bit.

I was just finishing my solitary breakfast when Dora came into the room, she was wearing her dark, nondescript coat and had tied a muddy-brown scarf over her hair.

I looked at her critically, the get-up didn't do her justice, and she was really quite pretty. Of course it was camouflage, there was nothing eye-catching about her, she didn't want to be noticed.

I said, "No use to ask where you are going?"

"Afraid not, believe me Marion," she said earnestly. "I wish I could tell you. Perhaps when I come back- - -"

The implied promise slid off me like ice crystals in the sun, I would believe that when it happened.

I'd half a mind to tell her not to bother to give my love to Bill, but refrained. Instead, "Don't hurry back," I said as I followed her down the passage. "I'll try not to be overcome by too much excitement."

She opened her mouth to speak but I forestalled her. "I know, 'don't open the door to anyone'".

"That's right, and I really mean it Marion."

I turned and walked away from her, conscious of how rudely I was behaving but unable to care. Dora could go out when she chose - well almost. She certainly wasn't virtually a prisoner like me. I could have cried but one had to be able to feel sensations in order to cry.

"You are sorry for yourself again Marion," I said aloud, and the knowledge didn't help at all.

I was already in the living room when the front door slammed but, unlike yesterday, I didn't bother to watch Dora down there in the street. I'd lost interest in her and in where she was going.

For a while I sat in my friendly armchair and wondered how long the numbness would last. How long before the anxiety, the anger and the sympathy returned.

———〜〜〜———

Dora had placed our daily newspaper on the table ready for me. I picked it up and glanced idly through the pages but couldn't concentrate and after a while went across to the window and looked down into the street, dry now after all yesterday's rain.

Without any real interest I wondered where Betsy was. Obviously she had gone early this morning before anyone else was about because she was scared of meeting Bill. For all she knew he might have come home last night.

I thought; here I am sheltering, being protected from the very dangers Betsy was now facing. She was out there in the cold, doomed it seemed, to spend the rest of her life trying to escape from Basil. It would be far better if she gave herself up to Bill's tender mercies, at least that way she would stay whole, in one piece.

She had, after all, earned some sort of retribution; I, on the other hand had become involved by chance. Chance engineered by Betsy and Jim. What a muddle it all was. I didn't know what their plan had been or how much of it had succeeded, certainly part had backfired on them - as witness Betsy now on the run and scared for her life. And obviously what had happened to Dorothy was not intended.

But, and I gripped the windowsill as a grisly thought struck through my dulled senses; was it possible that Betsy had meant some evil to befall me?

Perhaps even the fate which had been Dorothy's.

Of course not Marion! I told myself. I hadn't seen or had contact with Betsy for years, what possible reason could she have for wanting to dispose of me.

And yet she and Jim had taken a lot of trouble to find me and Jim had apparently been probing about trying to discover all he could about my life.

Unseeing I gazed out of the window, remembering Christmas morning and Jim and me sitting on my bed. "I promise to do my best to see you are not hurt," Jim had said. Why should he have said that if there had not been some plan to ensure that I did come to harm.

Perhaps after all my fears had not been so far fetched. Perhaps my Christmas invitation to Lucerne had really been a sinister trap.

I wandered away from the window and flopped into my chair. Somehow Bill was involved in all this; maybe they had been trying to get at him through me, a sort of blackmail. I wouldn't be hurt if he left them alone.

I sighed, my imagination was running away with me again. In any case none of it seemed to matter now. Bill and I had drifted farther apart and that, I thought grimly, was hardly likely to have been Betsy's original intention.

I wriggled restlessly in my chair, what was I going to do with today - with any day? Everything seemed pointless. Perhaps I'd just go for a walk and see what happened, Dora wasn't here, there was no one to stop me.

I glanced at my watch, a quarter to eleven - and it was then I remembered Jim's invitation to meet him at noon in the Hilton.

A flicker of interest went through me, why not go? It would be possible if I took a taxi to the station. I ran to the phone and was about to lift the receiver when it began to ring.

Startled, I waited a moment, uneasy thoughts racing through my mind. It wouldn't be Bill, and Dora never rang, she'd be home soon anyway. I was supposed not to open the door to anyone, was there also a ban on answering the telephone?

The jangling continued, incessant, persistent, needing an answer. I thought; it just might be Jim checking to see if I was going - and in any case it couldn't possibly do any harm just talking on the phone.

I lifted the receiver and gave our number, there was no reply. I repeated it but still there was no answer - not even heavy breathing. I'll try once more, I thought, again there was silence and then I heard the receiver being replaced.

I was scared now, someone was checking on me. Not Jim, he wouldn't do that. I stared at the phone, visions of Basil, writhing like an evil genie from the instrument, filled my mind.

I had to go out now, it would be unbearable here alone waiting for someone, something to happen, caught like an animal in a trap. Better by far to be out of doors, at least there one would have a chance to run away.

I lifted the receiver again and rang for the taxi. It gave me just seven minutes to get ready.

There was no time to change, my black polo-neck pullover and slim, natural wool skirt would have to do. Hastily I pulled a gold chain and medallion over my head and glanced critically in the mirror; thank goodness my hair was all right.

Then I flung my fake leopard coat over my shoulders and grabbed my handbag.

I ran down the stairs, relieved that so far today my legs were not troubling me. Cautiously I opened the entrance door a chink and winced at the blast of cold air which greeted me. The taxi was just pulling up, I got in and sat far back on the seat.

All being well the drive to the station should only take a few minutes, but that was long enough if anyone wanted to intercept us. I kept peering around, the traffic seemed to be moving normally and as far as I could tell no one was trailing us.

I wondered what on earth I should do if I suspected we were being followed. Ask the driver to 'lose that car' as they do in films? He would probably think I was mad and drive me to the nearest police station - or mental institution. Thankfully I didn't have to put it to the test.

There were a lot of people milling around at the station, all apparently intent on their own affairs. I had to keep reminding myself to be cautious, to keep a sharp eye out for possible danger. This wasn't a game, it was for real: Betsy was in fear for her life, mine was probably at stake too. Dorothy's had already ended.

I needed to watch all the while and at the same time to appear casual so as not to draw attention to myself. On the escalator I looked ruefully down at my coat, if there'd been time to consider, it might have been wiser to wear something less eye-catching. A mental vision of Dora in her somber clothes came to me. Dora knew only too well what she was up against and dressed accordingly.

Well I thought, she'd had practice, I was new to it and still couldn't quite believe it was really happening to me.

I waited until just before the doors closed before getting on the train, figuring that anyone following me then, might be suspect. I thought I'd do the same when I left the train - always supposing I got that far!

Inside I studied my fellow passengers and decided they all looked suspicious. Two men opposite had their faces hidden behind newspapers so they went to the top of the list.

Betsy had insisted that the large man from the plane had followed her about so I took special note of the tall men but none looked at all familiar - or in the least interested in me.

Of course, the offender - if indeed there was one - might be female. I gave up then; why worry? Whatever had to be- - -

Jiggling along in the underground I wondered if Dora was home yet, and had a moment of compunction about not warning her of the phone call. I should have left her a note, perhaps by now she had come face to face with some uninvited visitor. Perhaps she was struggling- - - I pushed the uncomfortable thought to the back of my mind. Dora was well able to take care of herself, and in any case Bill would probably protect her.

And at that moment I couldn't have cared less.

At Green Park I put the reverse plan into action and as it happened, a young lad who'd had his head in a comic, suddenly realised where we were and made a bolt for the door. I smiled to myself as he raced ahead of me down the platform and was lost in the crowd. So much for my home-made alarm tactics!

There wasn't a cruising taxi in sight when I emerged from the depths. I thought, better not to stand around and wait for one - it was too cold, and anyway I'd be an easy target. So I walked towards the hotel, leaning against the strong, cold wind.

Twice I stopped on the pretext of smoothing my hair, but really to have a quick look around. There were a lot of people, all, it seemed, like me with heads down battling against the chilling wind. It was impossible to recognise anyone or to know if they were trailing me.

The hotel was only a short distance and normally I would have found the brisk walk invigorating. Now it was frightening with the constant feeling of unseen, cruel eyes watching my every movement. Perhaps I shouldn't have come. Perhaps in spite of the phone call it would have been safer to stay at home.

Again Jim's words came unbidden into my mind: 'Bill should take more care of you.' Be reasonable Marion, I told myself crossly. Bill doesn't even know you are here - and certainly wouldn't approve if he did know. All the same, I thought perversely, Jim was right; I wouldn't be here at all if Bill came home to see me more often.

At the entrance to the hotel I avoided the revolving door, they always seem to catapult me, willy-nilly out of them, and now I wanted to look around with my way of retreat ready and immediate.

Jim was standing behind the seats in the centre of the foyer, he came at once to greet me taking my hands in his. "We will go up to the roof restaurant," he said leading me quickly into a lift. "It will be quieter there."

For 'quieter' read 'safer' I wondered? Aloud: "I've never been here before," I said.

"That sounds like dialogue from some old film," the lopsided smile was in evidence. "Do you come here often?" Then seriously he added. "Neither do I little Marion, but I'm going to enjoy it this time."

I felt my spirits revive in keeping with the speeding lift. It was going to be a happy adventure.

Chapter Twenty One

We sat at a table looking out over Hyde Park with much of London spread before us and toy cars and busses creeping silently along narrow, ribbon roads.

Jim ordered aperitifs from the attentively hovering waiter and as we sipped them we tried to identify buildings, familiar from street level but looking strange now, seen from above. It was fascinating and for a while I forgot the troubles and anxieties which had led to my being here. Jim, too, appeared to relax.

"What are you going to eat Marion?" he asked as we studied the menu. "It has to be something special, this is a celebration you know."

"Your birthday?"

"How did you guess?" It was the mocking smile this time, the one I'd seen him use on Betsy, but softened now by tenderness and affection.

I forced myself to disregard the message his eyes told me. "Let me see," I peered at him over the rim of my glass. "You must be sixty-five and are on your way to collect your first pension."

He laughed aloud then. "Very good Marion." Then seriously, "I don't have to prove to you how youthful and virile I am do I?"

The implication was unmistakable and I felt myself colouring. I thought, if we were fencing that would have drawn first blood.

It was necessary to reply quickly. "How were you so sure I would come today?" I asked. "I mean, what would you have done if- - -"

He interrupted, "Gone home, of course, to the tender ministrations of my gaoler. How did you get away from yours Marion?" His hand reached across the table and closed over mine. I didn't resist.

"Dora went out for a while," I hesitated as the coldness of remembered fear came back to me. "The phone rang and I was too frightened to stay there alone."

I felt the muscles in his hand stiffen, "What was the call about?"

"I don't know, that was what made it so frightening. No one spoke - it just seemed that someone was checking on me."

He was silent for a moment, then: "Did anyone follow you?"

I shook my head, "I don't think so, I was as careful as possible and looked- - -"

He nodded understandingly, "You can't be sure, can you?" He was watching me closely and after a moment added: "We do seem to have let you in for some trouble my love."

"We?" I queried.

"Betsy and me."

The waiter brought our starters, paté for me and whitebait for Jim and then went to fetch the red pepper which Jim requested.

"I shouldn't have accepted Betsy's invitation in the beginning," I said when we were alone again. "But it was Christmas and Bill- - -"

He nodded again, "I know it all my dear. I made it my business to find out."

"You said Bill should take more care of me," I murmured to myself, but Jim heard.

"I meant it, still do. But Bill has a difficult job, you mustn't blame him too much. There are - people - he has to keep an eye on."

I looked at him in amazement, whose side was he on, for goodness' sake? But before I could answer he pulled himself up straight in his chair and grinned at me. "This is a happy occasion Marion? Why are we wasting our emotions on such unpleasant topics?" He raised his glass, "To us little Marion, but not to the future."

1 drank the toast but couldn't shake off depression so easily. The future, if there was to be one, did matter. And so did his attitude to Bill. I wanted to hit low, to draw his blood too.

"Dorothy," I said tentatively. "You were very fond of her."

He was immediately serious. "No one can replace her - not even you Marion."

I opened my mouth to deny that I had any wish - or intention - of doing so, at the same time ashamed of the sensation deep inside me. Against my will I wanted to be important to him. If need be even to supersede the memory of Dorothy.

Jim put up a hand to stop me, "No Marion, don't say anything you might regret. You must understand that Dorothy and I were very alike, she was used to living dangerously - she enjoyed it." He smiled reminiscently, "She was bored when nothing exciting happened."

I couldn't think of anything to say and after a moment Jim went on: "My life wouldn't suit you. There is no certainty, no routine, only danger and suspense, you would hate it."

I thought; it sounds familiar, Bill's is like that too. Aloud: 'I haven't said I want to share it - but you make me sound very dull."

"Far from it, I'm just being sensible. I'm sure Bill needs you - he ought to anyway, but," and again he reached across for my hand. "I need you too and I think you want me."

I looked away from him out across the park to the comparatively simple life in the city of London where, it seemed to me at that moment, life was a nice, steady grey, not a dangerous complex of black and white checks, like an enormous game of chess. The Jim and Betsy life that I was now so involved in.

What Jim said was true. I did find him attractive, exciting. You are a traitor Marion, I thought. But the desire for him was there.

Jim had another quick change of mood. "Cheer up! I'm not suggesting you commit your life to me here and now, just that we enjoy each other's company, have a refuge - someone to turn to when no one else will do, or understand."

I tipped my glass back and emptied it, "I'll have a refill please," I said.

The wine helped to push Jim's proposition to the back of my mind where it belonged, I told myself firmly. I concentrated on enjoying his company now - and the delicious food. This, I determined, was to be an oasis of pleasure in the midst of a seemingly endless desert. And I reckoned I'd earned some pleasure.

Soon enough the world outside would close in on me again and all the problems would fight for supremacy, for the right to be solved first. And now Jim's proposition had to be added to the list.

We were half way through our thick, juicy steaks, Jim's rare, mine well done just the way I like it, when I became aware that Jim had stopped eating and the knuckles of his hands were clenched and white as he gripped his knife and fork.

I looked up at his face, it was pale and drawn and his eyes cold and hard.

"What- - -" I began, alarmed.

"Marion," his smile was a travesty but he was obviously making a great effort to appear natural, to speak lightly. He fished in his pocket then leant across the table and pushed a flat object into my hand. "Listen carefully," he said quietly. "This is the key to room number eleven on the eleventh floor, I want you to go there now - at once." Then, as I demurred, "No, don't speak Marion, you see Basil has just come in and is sitting with one of his cronies just behind you."

I think my heart stopped beating for an instant and then rushed on so madly I could hardly hear what Jim was saying for the throbbing in my ears.

"I'll ask a waiter to take you to the lift and to make certain you are alone in it." Jim was obviously thinking quickly, trying to decide what was the best thing to do.

"When you are in the room Marion, phone Bill immediately- - -"

I interrupted him, "I can't- - -"

But he went on as if I hadn't spoken. "Tell him where you are - and where I am. And that Basil is here."

I hesitated, unable and unwilling to accept that this was happening. How could Basil be here? And how could he possibly harm us up here, high above London with people all around us?

Again I tried: "I can't phone- - -"

"Go now Marion!" It was a whispered command. "Our lives may depend on it."

Somehow I got to my feet and clutching my handbag, followed the waiter to the lift. As we passed by, out of the corner of my eye I could see the man Jim said was Basil, but from such a quick sideways glimpse I couldn't be sure and didn't dare to look more closely.

No one tried to follow me into the lift - did that mean Basil was content to stay and deal with Jim - now up there on his own with seemingly no defence to offer? The thought flashed through my mind as I sped down to the eleventh floor.

It was like a gangster film with me playing the leading role, the heroine escaping from a wicked villain. But who was the hero? And heroine didn't seem an appropriate role for me.

I peered cautiously out as the lift came smoothly to a halt, there was no one in sight. At least Basil doesn't know where I am at the moment, I thought. Thanks to the triangular plan of the building it took only a few seconds to find No. 11, my shaking hands fumbled with the key.

Inside I ran to the phone then paused, who to ask for? It was easy for Jim to say 'phone Bill', not so simple to put into practice. I had no idea where Bill was, the only thing I could do was to phone Dora. I thought grimly, she would know Bill's whereabouts.

I gave the operator our home number and prayed that Dora would be home and answer quickly.

It seemed an age while the call clicked its way along the lines; I drummed my fingers on the table, "Come on Dora, Come on!" I said with rising panic. Supposing she wasn't there- - -

And then she answered: I didn't announce myself, my words tumbled out, where I was, Basil in the restaurant- - -

"I see," she said briefly. "You are in room eleven on the eleventh floor - wait there."

"Jim!" I shrieked down the phone. "Jim is up there too, in danger."

Dora didn't answer and I heard the receiver click into place.

I seemed to have been sitting by the phone indefinitely, the numbness in my mind fostered by the soulless, soundless room, but it could have been only a few minutes before I stood up and, for the first time looked around me.

The room was as comfortable and welcoming as an impersonal hotel room can be, it was all prepared and waiting for its new inmates, for the individuals who would briefly inhabit it and give it some character.

I looked down at the key, still in my hand, and with a start remembered it must be Jim's room.

I glanced quickly around again, there was nothing of Jim's here, nothing to show that he was staying in it. And yet he'd had the key - had handed it to me - so he must have meant to stay.

I went across to the window, and then, like a flash the answer came to me. It was a double room, Jim had intended to use it, he must have meant us both to do so. Maybe just for a few hours after lunch.

In the stillness of the room I could feel the hot colour suffusing my face. Was Jim so sure of me? Had I given him cause to be?

Probably, was the answer.

There were all sorts of mitigating circumstances, but the fact remained, I had encouraged him, had wanted to.

I sat down heavily on the edge of the bed and covered my face with my hands. Dear God, what a mess!

It would be possible to explain away my lunch date with Jim - even Bill must be able to understand the strain I had been through, the need for some pleasant happening which he certainly wasn't providing.

But being in this room which Jim had reserved was a different matter altogether. And Dora knew I was here, there could be no way of bluffing my way out of that.

It seemed dreadful to be considering my own reputation when upstairs Jim was threatened with far worse: perhaps with murder. And I knew that if I attempted to escape from this room something equally horrible could befall me.

Basil was seeking me, there was plenty of proof for that, and this time, I thought ruefully, it wouldn't be possible to break a window to escape. Not from eleven stories up.

I was striding about the room now. "Think Marion" I told myself. "Think constructively, there must be something you can do."

I sat down again and tried to concentrate my mind, to stop it leaping about like a March hare. I couldn't possibly help Jim - or myself - if I didn't think clearly and constructively.

Quickly I ticked the main points off on my fingers.

Jim is upstairs - so is Basil.

You are in this room.

Basil's henchmen are probably manning the hotel exits.

Very elementary Marion, I thought, but where on earth do you go from here?

And there is also this: Dora is on her way - and maybe Bill as well. It was the only comforting fact available, but it didn't tell me what exactly I should do right now.

I could open the door of the room and go out, it was as simple as that, there was no one to stop me. But would it do any good, and could I possibly help Jim by doing so?

Act as a decoy perhaps, but that was hardly sensible.

So, I could just stay here in reasonable safety and wait for Dora - or whoever - to arrive.

The 'whoever' stopped me in my tracks. Supposing it was Basil who came, not Dora? With alarm my feverish brain considered the possibility.

It couldn't have been chance which brought Basil to the Hilton today, he must have known we were here. And if he knew that, he might also know of room eleven on the eleventh floor.

To my shame, for an instant my mind conjured with the thought that Jim could be secretly working with Basil, have told him I was coming to the Hilton, and that I would be alone now, an easy target.

But of course not! Jim had his own score to settle, a grim and grisly one too.

For no reason at all my scatterbrain suddenly fixed on Betsy. How strange that Jim had not mentioned her, he'd seen her yesterday installed in my flat and yet, when I told him about the phone call he'd not even asked where she was.

Could they have discussed it yesterday while I was resting? Did Betsy tell him she was going to leave and, more important, where she was going? Did it matter anyway? I answered myself: if Jim was working with Basil it mattered a lot, he could tell Basil where to find Betsy as well as me. Tidy us both up in one smooth operation.

I shuddered, for goodness' sake Marion, things are bad enough without imagining them even more complicated and sinister.

I glanced at my watch, I'd been here for about ten minutes, time enough for Basil to have dealt with Jim, time enough for him to be now concentrating on me. Was it also long enough for Dora and Bill or whoever was coming to the rescue?

I was pacing the room again, thinking feverishly. Someone must have followed me this morning, must have watched and waited for just such an opportunity. The phone call had been a check - but could whoever it was have known it would have spurred me into action? Or was it to make quite sure I was still at home, that he, or she, hadn't missed me on my way to the Hilton?

If Jim wasn't involved with Basil then he also must have been trailed this morning. It seemed odd that someone - that Basil - should be watching both Jim and me so closely, unless he was sure that one of us would inevitably lead to the other.

Now panic was rising to stifling point. What was happening up there on top of London? Was Jim safe? Was he- - - I didn't dare to think. One thing was certain, I couldn't stay in this room any longer - whatever Dora, or Jim said, I had to go out and see for myself.

I picked up my handbag and ran to the door, at the same time there was a gentle rap on the other side. "Dora!" I breathed as I opened it. "Thank God- - -"

But it wasn't Dora, it was Basil.

He was in before I'd recovered my senses, before my instinct told me to push hard on the door. But, of course, he was prepared, even if I had shoved hard it wouldn't have worked, he had a foot already inside the room.

He was in full command of the situation. He motioned me to one of the chairs then drew the other one up exactly opposite, and close so that he could stare into my eyes.

I sat down. Under the circumstances it didn't seem worth arguing with him, making a big issue of whether I stood or sat. It was probably immaterial anyway.

For what might have been a full minute Basil sat and glared, the cold, grey eyes expressionless. In my mind I could picture him looking in just such a way, quite unmoved while some poor wretch was tortured. While Dorothy, his faithless wife was murdered. While I - - -

At last he spoke quietly, conversationally almost. "So you are expecting Dora."

I made no attempt to confirm the statement.

"Please do not trouble to reply Mrs. Hemming - Marion, there is no need, but there are a few things I must say to you before- - -" He left the sentence unfinished, hanging in the air like the proverbial sword, poised and unsheathed, over my head.

"It will not take long, but in any case Dora is not likely to trouble us, someone will take care of her."

I decided he had a hypnotic effect on me up here in room eleven. It was an unreal room - a stage setting. An unreal situation and Basil certainly wasn't real, he was an evil genie conjured from my imagination, who, if only I could find the right word or switch, would disappear in a puff of unholy smoke.

The trouble was I didn't seem able to think properly, my senses were numb and frozen. It did just occur to me to hope they remained that way while Basil carved me up - or whatever he intended doing.

"I don't care to be trifled with Marion."

He was speaking again. I tried to steer my eyes away from his steely gaze, if only I could manage that, I felt the spell might be broken; I'd wake up and find this was just a nightmare, that Basil wasn't really here.

Suddenly I heard myself speak. It surprised me, I hadn't meant to, hadn't realised I could. And what I said surprised me too. "Where is Jim?" I said.

"Ah, Jim," what passed for a smile crossed his face. "I was going to talk to you about him."

He paused and there was no vestige of a smile when he resumed. "I now know that Jim Martin was also staying with Betsy at

Christmas, you should have told me Marion because I thought it was you working with Betsy. But you didn't cooperate when I gave you the opportunity and I find that difficult to excuse."

"So," I said. "Do I go the same way as Dorothy - and anyone else who offends you?"

He laughed then and put out a hand and touched mine where it rested on the arm of the chair. His hand felt warm and dry and hard. "I told you before that you should be working with me," he said. "We would do famously together."

I remembered now; he liked it when I was rude to him, when I gave as good as I received. I thought, I might as well carry on now, it could hardly make matters worse - and at least it would give more time for the rescue forces to arrive; for Dora, and whoever else to get here.

I drew my hand away sharply, "What Betsy and Jim do is not my business, neither is- - -" I was going to add 'your connection with them' which was, of course, not strictly true, but he interrupted.

"It is your business Marion, you were meant to be involved."

"Perhaps - - -" I started.

He looked at me coldly, cynically, "You don't need me to tell you that, so please don't pretend."

"You haven't answered my question," I hoped the coldness in my voice matched his.

"About Jim Martin? It is not important any more." He dismissed Jim with an airy wave of his hand.

"You mean that he is being 'taken care of'?" I tried to sound flippant while inside me the fact registered that each time Basil referred to Jim, he called him Martin. Could it be he didn't know about Jim Bellamy? That his sources of knowledge were not infallible, that his henchmen did not always come up with the right answer?

In a small way it was encouraging, there may be other weaknesses I could probe. Why not? Presumably I had nothing to lose.

"About Dorothy," I said tentatively.

"Dorothy was unfaithful, I found that quite unforgivable." His steady gaze did not shift from my face. I tried to ignore it.

"Was it necessary to be quite so - drastic?"

He interrupted: "I came here Marion to deal with you and Martin, not to discuss - other matters."

I said dryly: "The other matters are connected, Dorothy and Jim certainly were. In my opinion you must have felt very insecure to have dealt with her in that way."

"With them," he said calmly.

So Jim had been 'dealt with'. I could feel the colour draining from my face and it must have been reflex action which made me grip the arms of my chair. Reflex action and cold fear.

Basil was looking more relaxed now, the bait had been taken, I was scared and wriggling on the end of his line and this was obviously what he had come for; what he enjoyed most: seeing his victims writhe.

I looked at him with revulsion, this loathsome being who found his pleasure in filling others with fear. "How did Betsy ever come to be involved with you," I said and didn't bother that my disgust was obvious.

He answered calmly: "She had to after her husband was sent to prison."

"Prison?"

"You are very innocent Marion, or should I call you ignorant. William Harland was apprehended with a large supply of drugs when he was in the Middle East. He is still in custody - uncomfortably so, I understand."

For a brief moment his gaze wandered across to the window where the grey, winter sky showed gloomily, then the gimlet eyes were back on me again.

"Drug carrying is a dangerous business," he said.

In the almost tangible silence which filled the room my mind was busy coping with this information. I could see why Betsy had refused to talk about her husband but it still didn't answer why she was now personally involved with Basil.

"Betsy," I said at last. "What do you mean by 'she had to'?"

"It was necessary for her to continue the business."

"You mean that you insisted."

He nodded briefly. "If you choose to put it that way. She will always do so because she will be too frightened to do otherwise."

I took a deep breath, "And you will punish her if she doesn't. Burn her house down - or something equally horrible."

"Your imagination is too vivid Marion." His expression was of self-satisfaction.

Basil glanced at his watch; do we have a time limit, I wondered and didn't dare to look at my own watch for fear that he would interpret - rightly - that I was expecting someone to come. Because despite what Basil said, help must be here soon; Dora was wily, she wouldn't allow herself to be trapped.

Strange, I thought, the confidence I had in Dora's ability to rescue me. Particularly strange when one considered how unpleasant I had been to her recently. Feverishly I searched my mind for something to say which would delay him for a few more moments. But it wasn't easy with his cold, hawk-like eyes watching me so closely.

At length it was he who provided the subject, "I hope you enjoyed Betsy's visit yesterday."

I looked at him with distaste. "Do you have to trail her all the time?"

"Yes," he said evenly.

"In that case you can tell me where she is now."

I saw a flicker of uncertainty cross his face. He doesn't know I thought exultantly and felt as if I'd beaten him myself, managed to put one over on him, and it was quite absurd the satisfaction the knowledge gave me.

"No." The reply was sharp.

"You don't know" foolishly I taunted.

Immediately he stood: "It is time we were going, get up Marion."

It wasn't a tone of voice one disobeyed. I got up but I wasn't defeated yet. "Aren't you going to deal with me now, in here?" I asked. Might as well put my head right in the lion's mouth while I was about it. Though anyone less like a majestic lion would be difficult to imagine. A hyena perhaps, I thought critically, or a rattlesnake.

He disregarded the remark, instead gave me instructions in a clipped, Sergeant Major voice: "You will go out of this room ahead of me and straight into a lift, ignore anyone you might see. I shall be following closely so do not attempt to escape."

"And if I do?"

His right hand felt in a pocket and brought out an object on which even the dim winter light reflected. As if hypnotised I watched as he held it out for my inspection.

He would choose a knife, I thought. For a moment faintness and nausea swept over me but I forced myself to take a deep breath and stand my ground, determined he shouldn't see how scared I was.

"One more question," my voice sounded strained and tense. "How did you know I was here in this room?"

"How do you think Marion?" He was smiling unpleasantly again.

"I can't imagine." But the implication was that Jim had told him. I'll never believe that, I told myself fiercely.

I gave a final glance around the room, imprinting on my mind the soft rose colour of the curtains and bed cover. The comfortable chairs which had proved to be so unwelcoming to me. The television set with the programme of events beside it. This room eleven which had been intended to witness a very different scene.

Then I obeyed and walked towards the door.

A woman was just stepping into the first lift we reached, I nipped in beside her before Basil could insist we go to another.

"You are going down to the lobby?" She had a strong American accent and bright, friendly eyes.

"Please," I said without looking at Basil, and offered up a silent prayer of thanks as I edged to the far side of the woman, away from danger - though surely Basil couldn't threaten me while this lady was present.

She was the talkative sort too, and after she had pressed the button, turned her attention to us. "You're on vacation?" It was a deep southern drawl.

"Well," I started, Basil glared but she wasn't put off.

"Mine is really a business trip - my husband you know. We always stay at the Hilton, it's so comfortable, don't you think?"

"It's my first visit," I said, and nearly added 'and probably my last'.

"Oh." She obviously found this difficult to understand, then enlightenment appeared to dawn: "You're British!" she laughed as if that explained a great many things - presumably even Basil's ill humour.

"Yes," I smiled back, trying to show how truly thankful I was to talk with her.

"Well," she persevered. "I'm Emily Shapmaker," she put out a hand and grasped mine, pressing it hard and long, and her finger seemed to be tracing a pattern. I concentrated on it and could have sworn that she wrote the letters 'OK' on the back of my hand.

Imagination again Marion, or wishful thinking, I asked myself looking at her anxiously, but Emily Shapmaker had turned her attention to Basil and was offering to shake his hand too. Basil kept his firmly at his sides and his look was anything other than friendly.

She grimaced as she turned back to me. "Your husband isn't feeling well?"

In the split seconds before we reached ground level I dismissed the impulse to tell her Basil was not my husband, that he was evil and I was being kidnapped. Almost certainly it would embarrass her; she wouldn't want to be mixed up with any unpleasantness or danger. To begin with it would be bad for Mr. Shapmaker's business - whatever that was.

No, the best thing was to make a friend of her, to hang on to her like grim death. The hollow feeling inside me increased at the knowledge of such near truth.

"We come from room eleven," I said quickly. "Is your room nearby? I mean perhaps we can get together." The words were falling over one another in my haste to make friends but she seemed not to mind.

"Oh yes. That would be just great."

We had reached our destination and as the door opened she grabbed my arm. "You must meet my husband, he's waiting for me in the entrance here."

I was propelled out of the lift and Basil had to follow. There wasn't time to look around - to see if Bill was nearby, or Dora. Or if there were any suspicious characters who might be working for Basil.

I was hustled along by Mrs. Shapmaker and she was chattering all the time.

Behind me Basil pounded across the carpet and suddenly I felt a sharp stab in my back. Involuntarily I cried out and immediately Basil caught hold of my other arm and pulled me in the opposite direction, halting our progress.

Mrs. Shapmaker turned and let go of me so that I slumped against Basil, he gripped my arm so tightly it felt as if I was in a vise. "Madam," I heard him say. "You do not understand, my wife is ill. You will kindly leave us alone."

"No!" I tried to shout and reached out a hand to my new friend but everything was growing hazy; the foyer with its dark red seats were waving gently as if reflected in rippling water. And then it seemed that Basil was pulling me down and falling heavily on top of me.

There were people running and talking anxiously all around but I couldn't understand what it was all about.

Chapter Twenty Two

I felt heavy, leaden when I regained consciousness. Cautiously I tried to open my eyes, the throbbing in my head making the effort superhuman.

Dora was standing beside my bed.

At first I thought I was reliving a nightmare; that my legs had been injured; that she was looking after me at home. My home.

Carefully I tried to move my legs to see how they felt but my body was numb and didn't respond or even seem to belong to me at all.

I tried to speak: "Dora," I said but she was looking away and took no notice.

"Dora!" I shouted this time, using all my strength, the banging in my head intolerable, but she didn't hear.

Some time later I prised my eyes open again, this time Dora was standing looking down at me, she had a tissue with eau-de-cologne on it and was dabbing my forehead. I was aware of the fragrance and the soothing effect.

"Dora- - -" I started.

"Don't try to talk, just sleep, you'll feel better soon." Her voice was gentle, quiet, but even so it reverberated around inside my head, the inflections banging about as if trying to get out again.

In a muddled way, as I drifted into blessed unconsciousness again, I thought she looked relieved but couldn't be bothered to wonder why.

Another time when I opened my eyes Bill was there, his face pale and strained. I tried to smile. "Now I know I'm dreaming," I murmured.

He leaned down, his unruly hair brushing my cheek. "Oh Em," I heard him whisper. I tried to raise my hand to touch him but it wouldn't move.

Dora said it was three days before I took any interest in my surroundings, I only knew that the unbearable throbbing in my head had lessened to a dull, bearable ache and that some feeling had returned to my limbs.

Then came the day when Dora brought me a cup of tea and I reached out and picked it up myself. I drained the cup before looking up at her. "You saw?" I said, the sense of achievement filling me.

She laughed aloud, then soberly: "Marion I can't tell you how pleased I am, we've been so worried."

"Expect I would have been if I'd known," I said. "Dora there is such a lot I want to know, will you- - -"

"Yes, when you are stronger, I think you should be told, you've been through so much."

She rose to take my cup but I put out a hand to stop her: "You've been so good," I could feel tears of weakness welling up in my eyes. I don't know why when I was so horrid to you."

Her eyes were wet too when she replied, "I understand, we will sort it all out when you are fit. What you mustn't do now is worry."

I didn't worry, the world seemed to glide by with Dora once again in charge. The difference now was having Bill around, not all the time, but often. Concerned, helping, sometimes just chatting.

It was what for so long I had been wanting. Companionship, caring, the feeling of being needed. Such simple things, so difficult to hold on to.

Dora told me my illness had been due to shock - triggered by the hefty dose of drugs which Basil had injected that day in the Hilton. "Not surprising, you were so ill," she said, and added, "after the strain of so many weeks."

But now I was better, had passed the frustrating period when I wanted to do something and tired of it as soon as I started. Bill and I were sitting cosily together one evening, Dora was away 'on a job' Bill said without enlarging on it.

"Is it a dangerous one?" I asked.

He looked at me, his brown eyes serious, one hand ruffling his already untidy hair. "Em, you know I can't tell you - it has to be that way."

I could feel the old irritation returning and bit back a hasty reply. Instead: "I thought I'd served my apprenticeship," I said.

"You've done more than that love, you've been marvellous and you are certainly going to know all about that business, - but not the ones on hand at the moment. You do understand, don't you?"

He looked anxious, like a small boy pleading for something. For affection. I went and sat on the floor, leaning back against his knees. "Yes, I understand, I just thought now that I've been thrown in at the deep end it might be possible to share some of the other problems."

"I wouldn't let you do that again love."

"I didn't mean in quite such a physical way! Just that you could tell me - explain- - -" my voice trailed away, I knew it was useless and there was no point in making things more difficult for Bill.

"What happened to Betsy?" I asked. "And Basil and- - -" I wanted to say Jim but stopped in time. It might be better to ask Dora what happened to him, not Bill.

He sighed deeply and after a moment leaned down and put his arm around my shoulders. "There is a lot of explaining to do Em, I think we will leave it until Dora is here to help, we have better things to be doing." His fingers weaved gently through my hair. "I thought I was going to lose you," he whispered close to my ear.

I had thought so too, but now I tucked those thoughts away into the deep recesses of my mind.

It was lovely having Bill around every day on a normal, nine to five job, like it used to be when we were first married. The traumas of the past weeks were receding into the background and I was feeling relaxed and sufficiently recovered to think seriously of finding a job. We were having a leisurely, weekend breakfast when I discussed this with Bill.

"Good idea Em."

He said it with such enthusiasm that I was immediately suspicious, an awful foreboding filling me.

"You're not going away again?"

"I've loved being at home with you Em but - there is this job. It's a sticky one again and - I must do it, be there on the spot."

"Wherever that is."

He put his hand over mine and squeezed it hard. "I wanted to tell you before but didn't know how to." He wore his helpless, little boy look again. "You know Em, I don't want to leave you it's just that I have to."

It took a moment for this information to sink in.

Suddenly my appetite disappeared and the remains of my toast and marmalade lay uneaten on my plate. I looked away from Bill, out of the window to where a watery sun was casting shadows on the houses opposite. A dull, sinking feeling inside me foretelling the loneliness and anxiety to which I must again resign myself.

"Well," I said eventually. "That decides it, I do get a job." I got up and started to clear the table when the thought occurred to me: "Don't forget before you go you promised me an explanation. That I'd be told about - everything."

"Yes, of course." He sat upright and the hand which had held mine riffled through his hair in the familiar gesture. "As a matter-of-fact I asked Dora to come here this evening."

"This evening - to a meal?"

He had the grace to look guilty, "Well yes, it will be all right won't it, Em?"

I could have thrown the plates at him. "You're impossible. Dora's such a wonderful cook, we can't give her just anything. If I'd known- - -"

"Oh, she won't mind some fish and chips."

"That is probably just what she'll get," I said tartly, heading for the kitchen.

"When are you going then?"

"Tomorrow - Dora is too."

Bill was leaving tomorrow. Tomorrow my world was going to return to its pre-Christmas routine. To being alone again, this time with no Dora to cook and watch over me. Long working days and lonely evenings of worry. Anxiety, wondering where he was. Worse now that I had for a while been a part of the danger and had an inkling of how hazardous his days were.

We didn't have fish and chips, we had takeaway Chinese, followed by a tin of lychees and cream.

Bill had insisted, he said it was his last day at home for a while and he was blowed if I was going to spend it all preparing food.

Instead we had driven down into the country-side and ate ploughman's lunch beside a blazing pub fire, and afterwards tramped along lanes and across crisply frozen fields. And finally we sat in the car holding hands and watching the late winter sunset glowing through the skeleton trees.

"I'll remember this day," Bill said quietly as he started the engine.

I snuggled close to him. "Me too." I nearly added 'must you go?' but stopped myself in time, it would have ended our beautiful day on a jarring note.

We ate by candle light and it was a cheerful meal. Dora claimed that Foo Yong and Sweet and Sour Pork were quite her most favourite foods. We drank a bottle of Côtes du Rhone which Bill had been hoarding for a special occasion. Then, relaxed in our armchairs, we sipped Grand Marnier with our coffee.

It seemed a pity to spoil the cosy atmosphere with mundane questions but there was a lot I needed to know and it was now or not at all.

"About Betsy- - -" I started.

Bill groaned loudly and turned to Dora: "She hasn't forgotten, you know."

"I should think not," Dora said firmly. "Betsy is in safe keeping."

"Meaning?"

"Just that really. She is being kept somewhere - for her own safety."

"Then Basil is still at large?" In spite of the warm, snug surroundings, a chill crept down my spine at the thought of Basil - and the prospect that he might still be in a position to hurt. To destroy.

"No," Dora assured me quickly. "He is also in safe keeping - awaiting trial. But we didn't get all the wretches and they are a wily lot. One never knows what they might do - just to try and get even."

We were silent for what seemed a long moment while I tried feverishly in my mind to sort out which of the many questions needing answers, was of prime importance.

Eventually: "Is Betsy- - - repentant, I mean- - - "

Bill's laugh broke through my stumbling words. "Betsy repentant? Well I suppose she is sorry - sorry she was caught, that is."

Dora spoke gently, explaining the situation to me. "Betsy had been led along by her husband. To begin with she didn't know what was going on - and then it was too late. She gained a lot of money but lost in peace of mind."

"And it was dangerous," I said quickly. "She was in fear for her life - and she lost her home." What am I doing, I thought, defending this woman who had caused - deliberately caused - me so much trouble.

"It was a lovely home," there was a hint of wistfulness in Dora's tone.

"What will happen to her, will she be charged too?"

"Yes," it was Bill again. "But there will be mitigating circumstances."

"Such as?"

"We shall know when the time comes," Bill said abruptly, and I intercepted his warning glance, aimed at Dora.

End of that subject I thought and tried another tack. "Why was I invited to Switzerland, we had never been friends, not even at school."

Bill rearranged himself in his chair, "That's easy, Betsy planned to use you as a sort of ransom. She knew we were on to her and hoped that by involving you we would leave her alone."

My mind travelled back over the weeks and settled at Heathrow with Dora and me and the customs official. And Betsy's smile of satisfaction as she hovered near enough to witness my discomfiture.

"So, she put the drugs in my bag believing you would not let anything happen to me." It was as I'd suspected. "But Dora, why - - -?"

"It was part of our plan," she broke in. "For the time being she had to believe she was successful. I didn't like doing it."

"Why didn't you tell me?" Suddenly I was fed up with them all - in spite of our happy evening. Fed up with Bill, Dora, Betsy, the lot of them, all conniving - and me in the middle being pulled all ways.

I sat upright and held out my glass, "I need some more brandy," I said.

Bill smiled as he reached for the bottle. "She has this terrible weakness," he told Dora.

I was glad the lights were subdued and hid the blush which memories of another occasion caused. I took a sip and felt the warmth tingling down inside. I wanted to ask about Jim but wasn't sure how to without arousing suspicions which must surely be in Bill's mind, as well as Dora's.

Then from the silence Dora spoke. "It was lucky you found that room at the Hilton with the open door." She said it quietly, conversationally.

For a second I hesitated: Dora was offering me a way out, was trying to save me embarrassment, perhaps even to save my marriage.

"Yes," I said, and hoped the relief in my voice wasn't too noticeable. I plucked up courage. "You never told me what happened to Jim."

Bill's eyes were fixed on my face, I could feel them boring into me, perhaps searching for what he was afraid to find.

"You never told me why you were there with him." He spoke quietly, a personal question for me alone.

"I was having lunch. It had been a long time since anyone invited me out - to enjoy myself."

He looked away then. Slightly ashamed? I wondered.

I pushed my advantage, speaking now to Dora: "How did you know I was there?"

"We knew a lot, you see your flat was bugged."

Bill jumped to his feet, his face flushed and angry, obviously he hadn't wanted me to know. "That wasn't necessary," he said sharply to Dora.

"I think you owe Marion that," she replied calmly. "It was a rotten thing to do."

"But necessary - and helpful."

"May I ask what you hoped to discover, and," I looked around me, "is there still someone listening in?"

Bill sat down again, "No, of course not, it was removed while you were ill. You see Em," he put out a hand, pleading now for me to understand, "we had to get these people and it was probable that all of them would come to you at some time or other."

"That was why I was there guarding you and why you were not to open the door to anyone when you were alone," Dora explained.

"The bugging was only in the living room" she added. As an afterthought, to set my mind to rest? I wondered.

Bill got up, "We'll all have another drink," he said gruffly.

After a while: "You still haven't answered my question," I said.

"Can't remember what it was," Bill was feeling mellow again.

"I can," Dora was still quite sober. "You see Davis had been looking after Jim - he'd been drinking again - and had followed him to the Hilton so was there to protect him when the thugs attacked."

"So he's all right?"

She nodded.

"Good," I said and tried not to let it sound too pleased or relieved.

"I didn't know you were going to Switzerland - to stay with Betsy." Bill spoke accusingly. "I wouldn't have let you if I'd known."

"I wouldn't have gone if you'd been here," I pointed out.

He ignored that: "But with Dora and Davis there - and Jim as well - I knew you couldn't come to much harm. It was a bonus," he added with satisfaction, "when the Hoppers arrived."

"Was it?" I watched him. He had a faraway look in his eyes, as if he was there now, in Switzerland, on the job. And it seemed to me that the job, catching the offenders, meant a lot more to him than I did.

"We had been waiting a long time to find the brain behind it all," Dora explained quietly. "But it was worrying," she added, "because of the risk involving you."

"I can see you must have been worried," I deliberately emphasised 'you'. "Did you know Basil was involved - that he was 'the big chief'?"

"We suspected but there had to be proof. Betsy supplied that herself - with assistance from Dorothy and Jim."

"I don't understand," I said.

"That package which Betsy put in your handbag. Dorothy had persuaded Basil to wrap it up himself so his fingerprints were on it. Betsy's were as well, she didn't wear her gloves - do you remember?"

"And I didn't even know it was in my bag." I shivered, reliving that awful time at the airport.

Dora looked at me sympathetically. "You've had a dreadful time Marion," she said. "Bill is a lucky man."

I looked across at him and he smiled sheepishly.

"I don't understand," I said again, "what part Jim had in all this, I thought he was on Betsy's side."

"Sort of double-agent. Not all that reliable, but useful," Bill admitted grudgingly.

"He played an important part - and he's a good actor." Dora was looking away when she spoke so it was impossible to tell how she really felt about him.

Chapter Twenty Three

Bill and Dora left early the next morning leaving behind them a cold, empty Monday.

I washed up the breakfast things and the clatter of the plates and cups was the only sound. I switched on the radio, welcoming the impersonal voices, the ethereal company they provided. I had to break myself in gradually to the loneliness and anxiety which, once again, stretched ahead of me. For however long.

I joined a secretarial agency, it meant an immediate job with which I was well able to cope, new interests and challenges. New people to know - but never to know really well. Each evening my colleagues decamped into their own suburbs, their own small worlds, to emerge again at nine the next morning.

Acquaintances, pleasant people but unwilling - or unable - to be more than shadowy, daytime companions.

I tried evening classes but the same things applied: As soon as our shared interests had finished we all scurried to our respective nests.

A city can be a very lonely place and I longed for Bill to be with me in the endless, dark evenings.

Then my world suddenly came alive: A letter from Bill told me he would be home the next day.

It was Saturday. I shopped and cleaned and cooked. Bill was coming home! It was a special occasion and I was determined that everything should be perfect, a sort of second honeymoon.

Because I couldn't know for certain what time he would be home the meal had to be something which wouldn't spoil if kept waiting.

By seven o'clock on Sunday the table was laid and a bottle of white wine cooling in the fridge. In the centre of the table a small posy of lilies-of-the-valley, their scent filling the room, nestled under pale green candles.

I was wearing a new dress - blue, Bill's favourite colour - and my freshly washed hair gleamed. I smiled to myself in anticipation of Bill's welcome homecoming.

At eight o'clock I turned the oven down to very low, even the best tempered casserole can be overcooked.

It was difficult to settle, I moved restlessly around the flat. If only it was possible to telephone somewhere, to find out where he was, if he'd been delayed. If he was all right.

It was half past nine when the phone rang and Dora's voice told me Bill wasn't coming after all. "I'm desperately sorry Marion," she said. "I know how you must be feeling."

"Couldn't he tell me himself?" I asked.

There was a pause, then: "He is very involved, I'm sure he will be in touch with you."

"I see. Have you any idea when he will be home?"

"Not really Marion. Could be next week."

"Thank you Dora," I said and replaced the receiver. I was too disappointed to cry - or to be hungry. I fetched a glass and poured myself a stiff drink.

~~~~~~~~

I was leaving work the next evening when Jim appeared. It had been a wretched day. A new firm dealing with products of which I had absolutely no knowledge, unhelpful people to guide me and, worst of all I was still feeling miserable from the previous evening.

It was an enormous relief to see a friendly, cheerful face.

"So Bill didn't come home after all," he greeted me.

I stared at him, "You knew?"

He smiled, "I know a lot little Marion."

"Wish I did," I sighed.

"Come on, let's go and eat," he took my arm and led me out of the building. "Not the Hilton this time. But somewhere you can tell me all your troubles in comfort."

"There is a perfectly good meal at home." I was thinking aloud.

He stopped, "You really mean that?"

"Why not," I said.

It seemed that Jim was a man for whom empty taxis appeared like magic. He had only to look round and one was cruising along the street towards us. He directed it to the garage where his car was parked.

We didn't talk a lot on the journey home; there didn't seem to be much to say - or else there was far too much. Everything. My whole world.

Jim made himself at home immediately, pouring the sherry while I switched on the oven to warm yesterday's abandoned casserole. The rest of the food was already prepared. The table laid just as it had been last evening. I'd not had the heart to touch anything.

We sat in separate arm chairs and sipped our sherry. Jim hadn't attempted to kiss me and I was grateful for that. I was feeling horribly guilty about him being here at all, as if I was being disloyal to Bill.

"There are things you want to know Marion?" Jim was serious, his voice gentle. As though, without being told, he understood how hurt and rejected I felt.

There was so much I wanted to know, the difficulty was where to start. At length: "A lot," I said. "For instance what did you and Betsy talk about that afternoon when you were alone in this room?"

"It was all monitored Marion."

"You knew the room was bugged?"

"Of course, you mustn't blame Bill too much," he added hastily, seeing my expression. "He has a job to do, a difficult job."

"I understand, but that doesn't make it any easier to live with."

"Bugging your home was going a bit far, I agree."

"Where was Bill at the time, while he was listening to you?"

"He hasn't told you?" The eyebrow was raised but he was still serious. "Not far away, but I think he should tell you himself."

"So do I." Suddenly, in my mind I was back in those miserable, imprisoned days; looking out of the window in this room. Seeing a man walking down the street, a man who looked like Bill, but had a key and let himself into the house opposite.

"So do I," I said again.

Jim got up and refilled our glasses. "So far I'm not being very helpful," he smiled - the lopsided one. "Think of something I can answer properly."

"Betsy," I said. "How did she know you were Jim Martin as well as Bellamy?"

"Oh that's easy, we decided on 'Bellamy' to try and foil Hopper. If he knew she was associating with Jim Martin he - er - wouldn't have liked it."

I smiled at the understatement. "So simple, I should have thought of that."

"You had other things to bother about. What else?"

"I don't know." I was tired and it was all beginning to be unimportant, to recede into the background, just something which had happened and was best dismissed from my mind.

"Right," said Jim taking control. "Food. Come on Woman, I'm starving."

"That sounds more like you," I laughed.

The dinner wasn't as good as it would have been the previous evening but we enjoyed it. Jim was in good form, a cheerful companion, and for a while I was able to forget the disappointment and dejection of yesterday.

Jim drained the bottle of wine into our glasses and remarked casually, "I hope you realise I shall not be able to drive home tonight. Not after all this debauchery."

It didn't seem to matter if he stayed. In fact I didn't want him to go, to leave me alone with my thoughts.

"I'll get the coffee," Jim said. "Up to now you've done all the work. Relax Woman." He sat me down on the sofa, "Put your feet up," he said, and did it for me and his hands resting on my legs for longer than was necessary, were warm and exciting.

"Tall and graceful," he said, thoughtfully looking down at me.

"Why did you say that?"

"Oh, it's just what I told Davis - how he would recognise you."

"I wondered - - but why not Bill?"

"Husbands don't know how to describe their wives, I've often noticed it." He leant and kissed me lightly on my forehead, "I'll be back in a moment," he said as he disappeared into the kitchen.

It was wonderful to be taken care of. Bill I thought, why don't you- - - and then I put him out of my mind.

Jim was back with hot, black coffee and a bottle of brandy. "You will have some Marion?" The lopsided smile was there and the raised eyebrow.

I took the glass. "I do have this weakness," I said.

Printed in the United Kingdom
by Lightning Source UK Ltd.
132167UK00001B/46-51/P